RANDOM TARGETS

A sniper launches a series of deadly attacks on Britain's motorways, striking during rush hour and causing total carnage. No one knows who he is, or why he's doing it — and as the death toll rises, fear grips the nation. It's up to DCI Jeff Temple of the Major Investigations department to bring the killing spree to an end — but, as he closes in on the sniper, Temple makes a shocking discovery about the motive behind the attacks. A ghastly precedent has been set, and Temple realizes that any motorway driver risks becoming a random target . . .

Books by James Raven
Published by Ulverscroft:

ROLLOVER

SPECIAL MESSAGE TO READERS

THE ULVERSCROFT FOUNDATION
(registered UK charity number 264873)
was established in 1972 to provide funds for
research, diagnosis and treatment of eye diseases.
Examples of major projects funded by
the Ulverscroft Foundation are:-

- The Children's Eye Unit at Moorfields Eye
  Hospital, London
- The Ulverscroft Children's Eye Unit at Great
  Ormond Street Hospital for Sick Children
- Funding research into eye diseases and
  treatment at the Department of Ophthalmology,
  University of Leicester
- The Ulverscroft Vision Research Group,
  Institute of Child Health
- Twin operating theatres at the Western
  Ophthalmic Hospital, London
- The Chair of Ophthalmology at the Royal
  Australian College of Ophthalmologists

You can help further the work of the Foundation
by making a donation or leaving a legacy.
Every contribution is gratefully received. If you
would like to help support the Foundation or
require further information, please contact:

THE ULVERSCROFT FOUNDATION
The Green, Bradgate Road, Anstey
Leicester LE7 7FU, England
Tel: (0116) 236 4325

website www.foundation.ulverscroft.com

For most of his working life, James Raven was a journalist on local, regional and national newspapers. In 1982 he moved into television as a news scriptwriter with TVS, where he then worked his way up to become Director of News across Meridian, Anglia and HTV. When Granada took over most of ITV he became Managing Director of Granada Sport, before setting up his own production company. James spends much of his time writing and travelling, and also performs magic at various venues across the country.

You can find out more about the author at: www.james-raven.com

JAMES RAVEN

RANDOM TARGETS

Complete and Unabridged

ULVERSCROFT
Leicester

First published in Great Britain in 2014 by
Robert Hale Limited
London

First Large Print Edition
published 2015
by arrangement with
Robert Hale Limited
London

A catalogue record for this book is available
from the British Library.

ISBN 978–1–4448–2581–7

Published by
F. A. Thorpe (Publishing)
Anstey, Leicestershire

Set by Words & Graphics Ltd.
Anstey, Leicestershire
Printed and bound in Great Britain by
T. J. International Ltd., Padstow, Cornwall

This book is printed on acid-free paper

This one is for Sally-Ann for
being such an avid reader of my books.

Prologue

No one saw it coming.

In the minutes leading up to it, the motorway network was running smoothly. There were a few rush-hour incidents, but only what you'd expect on a frosty evening in January.

A lorry jack-knifed on the M1 near Luton, causing a three-mile tailback. A stray dog was slowing traffic to a crawl on the M25 in Kent. And on the M6 near Birmingham a five-car shunt meant misery for motorists heading north.

But on the M27 in Hampshire there were no problems. At 5.45 p.m. the usual heavy flow of vehicles was thundering along the carriageways in both directions. It seemed that most drivers were sticking to the 70 mph speed limit.

Many of them were tuned in to a local radio station and its live traffic updates. They came from an 'eye in the sky' reporter named Owen Jay, who was in a helicopter above the motorway. Jay was telling his listeners that it had so far been a pretty uneventful evening on the county's roads.

'For a change there've been no hold-ups or accidents,' he said. 'With any luck it'll stay that way.'

But it didn't.

As Jay was speaking a car on the westbound carriageway suddenly went into a dramatic spin for no apparent reason. It veered across two lanes and crashed with bone-shuddering force into the central reservation.

The car, a grey Honda Civic, was then hit side-on by a white transit van that was unable to avoid it. The crunch of impacting vehicles was like a series of bombs going off.

A second later a ten-ton tipper lorry ploughed into the van, crushing it beyond recognition. The lorry then rolled on its side, spilling its load of wet gravel across the road.

A Vauxhall Astra hit the gravel at 60mph and flew into the air before flipping over and crashing down on its roof.

And that was just the beginning.

Vehicles continued to pile into each other for another ninety seconds. The noise was deafening and survivors would later describe it as 'terrifying'.

The shriek of burning rubber and the thump, thump, thump of vehicles colliding was followed by several small explosions.

Then a huge fireball engulfed the Astra and

shards of hot metal were flung in every direction. The flames shed light on a scene of utter devastation that spread far back along the westbound carriageway — burnt and broken vehicles; black smoke; mangled steel; shattered glass and hissing radiators.

Suddenly the noise ceased and a heavy, unnatural silence descended on the motorway.

Then came the cries of anguish.

1

Detective Chief Inspector Jeff Temple was told about the pile-up on the nearby M27 ten minutes after it happened.

The news spread like lightning through police headquarters in Southampton city centre. By the time it reached Temple's office in the Major Investigations department, it had already created a buzz of excitement throughout the building.

Most of his team had been about to leave for the day and for some the way home lay along the M27. They were now discussing alternative routes and alerting friends and relatives to the chaos that was about to spread to other roads in the area.

Temple was glad he lived in the city and he pitied all those luckless drivers who were stuck in the jams. The tailbacks along the motorway were already stretching for miles apparently.

It sounded pretty bad, but it was too soon to know if there were many casualties. Emergency units were scrambling to get to the scene and the true picture had yet to emerge.

All the commotion made it hard for Temple

to concentrate on the report in front of him. It involved a three-week-old murder in Winchester that was proving to be one of those cases where nothing comes together.

A 19-year-old student had been stabbed to death in an alley as he walked home from a pub late at night. No witnesses. No CCTV footage. The killer left no clues and robbery did not appear to be the motive. The victim had no known enemies and was by all accounts a well-liked, decent individual.

The team had reached a dead end with the case and Temple was going over all the statements from friends and relatives and trying to see if they had missed something. He was too distracted now to do a thorough job so he decided to leave it until the morning.

He stood up and was slipping on his suit jacket when DS Dave Vaughan appeared at the door to his office. Vaughan was an earnest looking 40-year-old with black-framed glasses and a thin face. His skin was rough with a day's stubble.

'A few of us are going for a drink, guv,' Vaughan said. 'We wondered if you'd care to join us? No point trying to get home with all that's going on. It'll be mayhem on the roads for a while.'

Temple looked at his watch.

'Well, it's tempting,' he said. 'But DI Metcalfe is expecting me at her flat with a takeaway. It's her day off and she's been studying.'

'Well, give her a call and tell her to meet us at the pub,' Vaughan said. 'If I know Angel she'll jump at the chance to get out for a bit and have a couple of gin and tonics.'

It struck Temple as a good idea and he was sure Angel would be up for it, especially as she was a big fan of the pub's steak and ale pie.

'I'll call her then,' he said. 'I'm sure she won't need much persuading.'

'That's great,' Vaughan said. 'We'll be leaving in about fifteen minutes.'

Temple went back to his desk to use the phone. He got no reply on Angel's home number so he tried her mobile. That too went to voicemail. He left a message for her to call him ASAP. It had been a month since the pair of them had gone out after work with the team. In fact it was just before Angel let slip that she was having an affair with her boss. The rumours had been circulating for some time, but Temple had thought it best not to confirm them.

Now that it was out in the open he felt awkward about it and had been steering clear of social gatherings. He sensed that the rest of the team disapproved of the relationship, partly because Angel would almost certainly have to be transferred to another department once they were living together.

That wasn't actually a big issue with her because she didn't plan to spend her entire career in major crime. She was keen to broaden her experience and explore other opportunities within the force. She was even contemplating a move to the Scientific Services department, which was why she was taking a course in forensic science.

Temple was at one with the rest of the team in not wanting to lose her. She was a first-rate detective and an asset to MIT, but he accepted that living together and working together could make things difficult for both of them in the long term.

The current situation was bad enough. He had to be careful not to show favouritism towards her, or to appear unduly concerned when she came into contact with dangerous felons.

But it was never easy.

He glanced at his watch again and decided to send her a text message in case she'd popped out and was in a location where she didn't have a signal. But just as he was about to, DS Vaughan appeared again.

'I think you might want to come and listen

to this, guv,' the detective said. 'The news on this motorway accident is getting worse by the minute.'

★ ★ ★

Out in the large open-plan office the team were glued to various TV screens. There were nine detectives and five admin staff. Phones were ringing, but they were mostly being ignored.

All their attention was focused on a conversation between a news presenter and the well-known traffic reporter, Owen Jay, who was speaking live from a helicopter above the M27.

There was a photograph of Jay next to a map showing the 25-mile long motorway that runs through southern England from the New Forest to Portsmouth. The scene of the accident was marked with a red cross and Temple had to move nearer to see that it was just east of junction five, which was a couple of miles from the centre of Southampton.

'The scene below me is hard to describe,' Jay was saying above the roar of the chopper's rotor blades. 'Scores of vehicles have collided. I can see flames and smoke and I can see people moving around in the dark amongst the wreckage.'

Temple felt a shudder run through him. He could imagine what it must be like for the people involved. Multiple crashes on Britain's motorways were thankfully rare, but when they happened there were almost always a high number of casualties.

'The pile-up is on the westbound carriageway,' Jay continued. 'The tailback stretches into the distance. The eastbound carriageway is also at a standstill now.'

Temple wondered what had caused the accident. Had a lorry driver fallen asleep at the wheel? Had one car rammed into the back of another — perhaps while the driver was speaking into his mobile phone? Or had someone suffered a puncture that caused his or her vehicle to swerve?

It would be up to the Collision Investigation Unit to determine the cause and Temple didn't envy them that task. Just as he didn't envy the paramedics and fire officers who would soon be dealing with the bloody aftermath.

From experience Temple knew that serious road accidents were frequently more gruesome than a typical murder scene. The victims usually suffered multiple injuries and they often had to be cut from the wreckages of their vehicles. During his time as a PC he'd attended crashes where heads had been severed and bodies flattened.

On the TV screens the shot changed to show the news presenter at a desk with an image of Jay over her shoulder.

'Did you actually see what caused the accident?' she asked him.

Jay gave his answer through a blizzard of static.

'No, I didn't,' he said. 'One second I was looking down on a fast-flowing river of tiny bright lights and the next everything was grinding to a halt. I thought at first it was a tailback caused by sheer weight of traffic, but I quickly realized it was far more serious.'

Temple was familiar with the M27. He drove on it at least once a week. It was always busy and during rush hours it was usually a nightmare. But then the same could be said for all of Britain's motorways. There was just too much traffic, too many lorries, too many tired and inconsiderate drivers, too many speed merchants.

'I feel like I've had a bleeding lucky escape,' someone said behind him.

Temple turned around. The speaker was Fiona Marsh, a 28-year-old detective with flaming red hair and sharp, intelligent eyes. She was the newest recruit to the team, a brash, ambitious Londoner with a broad, cockney accent.

10

'I was going to leave here about forty minutes ago,' she said. 'Looks like I would have been caught up in it if I had.'

She was clearly shaken and her normally healthy complexion had taken on a grey, sickly pallor.

'Seems to me you could do with a drink,' Temple told her.

She nodded. 'I think we all could.'

Temple came to a decision. 'Then why don't we retreat to the pub? We can monitor developments from there and drink to your near miss.'

There was a collective murmur of agreement and those whose shifts had finished started heading towards the doors. As Temple returned to his office to collect his things he tried again to reach Angel. But she didn't answer her mobile or house phone. He left a message on both to either call him or drop in at the pub.

'Try to make it, sweetheart,' he said. 'There's a steaming steak and ale pie with your name on it.'

★　★　★

The pub was busier than usual and all the talk was of the accident on the motorway. Temple and his entourage claimed their usual table in a cosy alcove next to the fireplace.

The TV above the bar was tuned to Sky News and a screen caption read: *Serious pile-up on the M27 in Hampshire. Casualties reported.*

'Do me a favour and make mine a double, guv,' DC Marsh said when Temple offered to get the first round. 'I really think I need it.'

He gave her a sympathetic smile. She smiled back and raked a hand through her hair.

'I know I must be coming across as pathetic,' she said. 'But my heart is still going like the clappers.'

He could tell she was anxious about what might have been. But that was entirely understandable. If she'd left the office earlier she might now be seriously injured or even dead.

'Why don't I make it a treble?' he said.

She chuckled. 'I think that's a very good idea.'

At the bar he ordered the drinks. As he plucked a twenty pound note from his wallet his eyes were drawn to the photograph he kept next to his warrant card. It had been taken three months previously and showed Angel and him at a local restaurant on her thirty-sixth birthday. Her short brown hair was combed back and pinned behind her ears and her pretty, angular face held a beaming smile: she looked terrific.

By contrast he looked every one of his forty-eight years. A tired, sagging face and receding hairline. Eyes that were dull and sunken. In fact in the harsh glare of the camera flash he looked old enough to be her father. Was it any wonder then that he pinched himself every morning? He still could barely believe his good fortune.

Eleven months ago — almost five years to the day since the death of his wife Erin — Angelica Metcalfe had entered his life. She'd moved from London to Southampton after breaking up with her boyfriend and had joined the team as a detective sergeant. She'd spent the previous few years working for the Met and had a solid reputation.

What began as an office fling turned into a passionate affair that had been going on for six months. Now she was set to move in with him and he couldn't wait.

'So where the hell is she?' he murmured to himself as he glanced yet again at his watch.

He was becoming a little concerned because it wasn't like Angel not to respond to calls or messages. He'd spoken to her at lunchtime and she'd told him she had no plans to go out. So maybe she'd grown tired of studying and had decided to have a nap. Or maybe she'd popped out to the shop without her phone.

While he waited for the drinks he tried again to contact her, only to be disappointed. He left another message and decided that if he didn't hear from her soon he'd head home after one beer.

Back at the table, DS Vaughan said, 'So is Angel on her way over?'

Temple shrugged. 'I can't reach her. For some reason she's not answering her phones.'

'Then she'll probably turn up at any minute,' Vaughan said.

They drank to DC Marsh's lucky escape and then had a brief chat about the various cases they were working on. It wasn't long, though, before their attention returned to the TV which began showing aerial footage of the motorway carnage.

There was enough light on the ground to illuminate the appalling scene. Temple was horrified by the extent of the damage. He saw at least one car on fire and two overturned lorries. Scores of other vehicles had smashed into each other. The emergency services had arrived at the scene, but it was clear that they were overwhelmed.

Temple and the others watched the story unfold on the screen. Reporters gave updates to camera from a bridge above the motorway. They used words like 'horrific' and 'distressing' to describe what they could see. Then a senior fire officer gave a brief interview in which he revealed that at least five people were known to have died, but that the toll was likely to rise.

An air ambulance helicopter was filmed landing on a clear section of the westbound carriageway. Minutes later casualties on stretchers were shown arriving at Southampton General Hospital's emergency unit.

When Temple next looked at his watch he was shocked to see that a whole hour had passed since they'd arrived in the pub. He felt a rush of guilt because he'd completely lost track of time. He quickly checked his phone to see if he'd had a message from Angel. He hadn't.

So where in God's name is she?

He was about to call her mobile when his phone rang. He checked the ID, hoping to see her name. Instead he saw that the caller was his boss, Chief Superintendent Mike Beresford.

'Where are you, Jeff?' Beresford said without preamble when Temple answered.

'The Red Lion, sir. What's up?'

'I assume you're aware of this crash on the M27.'

'Of course. We're watching it on the TV. Looks really bad.'

'It is. And you need to get out there right away.'

'What for?' Temple said, confused.

'I've just had a call from the scene,' Beresford said. 'A paramedic has made a rather startling discovery and you need to check it out.'

'What do you mean?'

Beresford took a breath and said, 'At least five people have been found dead in the wreckage so far. One of them has apparently been shot.'

'Shot! Are you serious?'

'That was my reaction too,' Beresford said. 'I insisted on speaking to the paramedic in question. He's adamant that a male driver has a bullet wound to the head.'

'Jesus.'

'I've notified the pathologist and the scene of crime officers. They're on their way. I've also briefed the Chief Constable who wants a full report as soon as possible. So you need to get moving. And take a couple of the team with you. It'll be chaos out there.'

2

The Chief Super said he'd arranged for three squad cars to pick them up from the pub. While they waited for them to arrive, Temple briefed the others on what he'd been told and said he wanted them to go with him.

Ten minutes later they were racing towards the motorway in three fast-response BMWs with sirens blaring and lights flashing. But the roads were clogged and it was slow going. They eventually reached junction five where a police patrolman directed them onto the motorway via the slip road. The three cars then travelled the wrong way along the westbound carriageway towards the scene of the crash.

Temple knew that what he was about to encounter would be ugly and upsetting. He also knew that if a driver had indeed been shot then the investigation would be anything but straightforward. He was still half expecting to discover that the paramedic had made a mistake and had wrongly identified a bullet wound. After all, it seemed inconceivable that a motorist would be shot in the head whilst driving along a busy motorway in the rush hour.

But what if the paramedic was right and someone had been shot at the wheel of his car? How might it have happened? Temple could come up with only three possible scenarios.

The man had shot himself.

He was shot by a passenger.

He was shot from a distance by a person firing indiscriminately at the traffic.

The last scenario was the scariest. It suggested a random killing with no link between the shooter and the victim. It also suggested that the shooter was unconcerned about collateral damage. He or she wouldn't care if other people were killed or injured in the ensuing crash. This prospect filled Temple with dread. Random murders were the most difficult to solve, especially those committed out in the open where any evidence would most likely have been contaminated instantly.

As the BMW sped along the motorway Temple's stomach twisted with grim apprehension. He could feel his muscles getting tight. And when they finally reached the crash scene and he saw how bad it was, the air locked in his lungs and it felt as though the blood had stopped moving through his veins.

★ ★ ★

Temple wasn't prepared for the sight that greeted him. He got a shock as the BMW screeched to a halt between an ambulance and a fire tender.

What he saw astounded him. Ahead of them was a wall of charred and twisted metal. Dozens of vehicles had piled into each other. Some had rolled onto the hard shoulder. Others had crashed into the central barrier.

He saw a tipper lorry on its side, a pile of gravel on the tarmac beside it. Then he spotted the mangled mess of a white transit van. Fire officers were using cutting equipment to try to get to whoever was inside. Wrecked vehicles littered the carriageway across all three lanes. Some were covered in white foam. Some had been crushed into unrecognizable heaps. Others were upturned with wheels buckled or missing.

Temple had never seen anything like it. This was destruction on an appalling scale. His palms started to leak hot sweat and his temples throbbed. As he climbed out of the BMW his senses were assailed by a blinding array of flashing lights and a strong smell of petrol. He felt his mouth dry up and suddenly found it difficult to swallow.

All around him there was frenzied activity. The air crackled with radio static. Police and paramedics in fluorescent jackets were shouting at each other. Some were guiding shocked and injured motorists towards the ambulances. A helicopter hovered overhead, sweeping the scene with a bright cone of light.

People draped in foil blankets were standing around in a daze. Some were sobbing, others being sick. Temple saw a small child being comforted by a police officer. Then he watched as a paramedic tried to revive a man lying face-up on the ground next to a half-crushed car.

'This is horrendous,' DC Marsh said as she stepped up beside him. 'Much worse than I imagined.'

He threw her a glance. Her jaw was clenched and her eyes were popping. He suddenly felt protective towards her.

'Are you going to be OK?' he asked, concerned.

She nodded and blinked rapidly a few times. 'Don't worry about me, guv. I'm just thankful that I'm not among the casualties.'

They were handed fluorescent jackets and Temple told his team to stay together until they got a fix on what they were going to have to do. Then he slipped on the jacket and returned his attention to the scene in front of him. Almost immediately he caught sight of a traffic officer waving him over.

Temple responded with alacrity and the others followed. The closer he got to the wrecked vehicles the faster his heart thumped in his chest. The smell of burning oil and smoke became more intense and he had to force down a sudden urge to vomit.

The traffic cop who had signalled to them was a middle-aged sergeant with a sweat-soaked face.

'Follow me,' he shouted above the din. 'But tread carefully. There's stuff everywhere. It's like a scrapyard.'

The tarmac was littered with broken glass and dark oily puddles. Temple stepped on someone's coat and then had to step over a dislodged wheel. His eyes began to water and he felt a stinging sensation at the back of his throat.

They were led through a narrow gap between smouldering wrecks to where four people in yellow had gathered. Temple immediately recognised the tall, grey-haired figure of Dr Frank Matherson, the Hampshire pathologist. The others were police officers from the traffic division. They were standing next to a badly damaged car that looked like a Honda Civic. As Temple got closer he saw that the front driver's-side door was missing and a man's upper body was hanging out. It appeared that his legs were trapped beneath the distorted steering column.

There was hardly any space around the Honda. The front end had crashed into the central barrier and the passenger side of the vehicle had been crushed. Steam was boiling from its ruptured radiator. Temple coughed to clear his throat. The air was thick with the stench of vomit and hot metal. And he was acutely aware of the sour, coppery odour of blood.

The four men, including Matherson, turned towards the detectives as they approached.

'You got here quickly,' Temple said to the pathologist.

Matherson gave a curt nod. 'I was at the hospital when the call came through. Got a lift on the air ambulance.'

Temple gestured towards the body which now became the focus of his attention.

'Is this the driver I was told about?'

Matherson nodded.

The man was on his back and wearing a grey suit that was drenched in blood. Part of his face and head were missing and it looked as though his right arm was hanging on by a thread.

'Have you examined him yet?' Temple asked.

Matherson drew in a ragged breath. 'Only briefly.'

'And was the paramedic right? Has he been shot?'

'I'm afraid so,' Matherson said and at the same time the muscles in his neck tightened. 'A bullet entered his forehead just above the left eye. It passed through the skull and the exit wound is clear to see. There's massive internal damage. The bullet appears to be lodged in the seat head-rest.'

'Bloody Hell,' Temple said, alarmed. 'Are you sure?'

Matherson nodded. 'Positive. The bullet must have come through the windscreen. It seems he was alone in the car and there's no sign of a gun.'

Temple shuddered and leaned forward to peer inside the car. The driver's seat was inclined forward, but he could clearly see a hole in the leather head-rest.

As he straightened up he felt the unease twist tighter in his gut.

'We need to spread the word that this is a crime scene,' he said aloud so all of those around him could hear. 'I know it won't be easy but we need to keep it clear for the forensic technicians who'll be here shortly.'

He turned to DC Marsh who was wearing an expression of outraged disbelief. It looked as though she had stopped breathing.

'Get with it, Fiona,' he snapped. 'I need you to do something.'

His raised voice jolted her out of her trance and she gave a sharp nod.

'What is it, guv?'

He instructed her to get on the phone to headquarters and tell them to send out as many armed officers as they could to search the surrounding area.

'There's a bridge about a hundred yards along the carriageway,' he said. 'Someone could have taken pot shots at the traffic from there or from one of the embankments. Maybe the shooter is still out there watching the show. Let's get word to the police chopper. The crew can use thermal imaging to check for unusual movement in the woods and fields around here.'

DC Marsh turned abruptly to go to where it would be safe to use her mobile phone. But her path was blocked by a uniformed PC, square in his luminous jacket, who suddenly appeared looking breathless and anxious.

'You won't believe this, sir,' he said, addressing himself to Temple, 'but we've got another one.'

'Another what?' Temple said.

'Gunshot victim, sir. This time it's a woman and she's been shot in the chest.'

3

Temple's scalp prickled as he stared down at the woman. She was in her thirties and dressed in jeans and a leather coat. She'd died at the wheel of a red Ford Focus that had left the road before crashing headlong into a signpost on the embankment.

There was extensive damage to the front of the car including a shattered windscreen, but the woman had only one visible injury: Matherson quickly confirmed that it was a bullet wound high up in her chest. When her body was moved forward they saw an exit wound in her back and realized that the shell had gone through the chair into the rear seat.

Blood covered her coat and was splattered about the car's interior. She was still sitting behind the wheel and strapped to her seat. The airbag had been deflated by the paramedics who had wanted to find out if she was alive. It seemed obvious to Temple that she must have lost control of the car after being shot. Even so he found it hard to take it in.

What could possibly possess someone to

kill indiscriminately in this way? he wondered. There was no doubt in his mind that they were random killings — no way could the shooter have known the identity of the people in the vehicles he was shooting at. It was dark and they would have been travelling at high speed. Plus, the shooter must have fired from a distance, possibly with a sniper rifle.

He turned to DS Vaughan and said, 'I want you to act as crime-scene manager. We have to work quickly because we'll be under a lot of pressure to get things done so the motorway can be reopened.'

'I'm on it, guv.'

'And tell the techies that I need a ballistics report on the bullets as soon as possible.'

Temple then asked Matherson if he could determine the trajectory of the bullet from the wound in the woman's chest.

'Well, we know it came through the windscreen,' Matherson said. 'And there doesn't seem to be a marked angle of entry, so I'd say that whoever fired the shot was ahead of the car up on the embankment to the left. How far away, though, would depend on the type of weapon used. The wounds on both victims would suggest a high-powered rifle so the killer could have been positioned hundreds of yards along the motorway facing into the westbound traffic.'

The scale of the task facing them was immediately apparent to Temple: two murders; a motorway pile-up and a psycho killer with a rifle. It couldn't get any more high profile.

Turning to the police sergeant who had brought them there, he said, 'What's the situation with the other casualties? Has everyone been accounted for as far as you know?'

The officer nodded. 'So far we have three other fatalities. All suffered multiple injuries consistent with collision damage. The paramedics who attended them assure me they were not shot. Five other people are seriously hurt, but their injuries are also crash-related. No bullet wounds. Two of them are still trapped in their vehicles. The others are on their way to hospital. A further fifteen or so people have sustained minor injuries.'

Temple's heart was like lead and for a few moments he felt disoriented. The scene around him was still chaotic with the emergency personnel struggling to cope. He could hear people shouting and sobbing. Sirens wailed and the drone of helicopters throbbed constantly.

He turned towards the embankment which rose steeply beyond the Honda. There were people on the grass in front of clumps of bushes, among them shocked and injured motorists who were being tended to by paramedics. At the top of the embankment there were woods and every now and then the light from one of the choppers would wash over the trees.

Was that where the bastard had fired from? Was he still up there getting a perverted kick out of what he'd done? Or was he long gone by now, having left not a single clue in his wake?

Temple reckoned it was safe to assume that the shooter was male. This wasn't a woman's crime. Rifles were almost always the weapon of choice for men.

He was told that officers with the armed support team were already up there searching the woods, but he doubted that they would find anything. He decided to hang around on the motorway and talk to those motorists who had not been injured and were still here because their cars were either damaged or stuck in the jam. There was a faint chance that someone had spotted something — maybe a muzzle flash — as the shots were fired.

He also wanted to pick the brains of the traffic cops and the collision investigation officers. Perhaps they could shed light on exactly how the drama had unfolded.

The questions were already mounting up in his head.

Which lanes were the gunshot victims in when the bullets struck?

Was this stretch of the motorway covered by traffic cameras?

How far away was the nearest road or country lane?

Answers to these kind of questions would help them build up a picture of what had happened.

Temple was also keen to brief the scene of crime team when they finally arrived. This was probably going to be the most difficult job they'd ever undertaken. They'd be working in extreme conditions; forensic evidence would be limited to the bullets — unless they managed to find out where the shots were fired from. And that was a big *if*.

He stepped away from the Honda onto the hard shoulder, leaving Matherson to examine the woman's body in detail. He walked about halfway up the embankment to get a look at the scene from an elevated position. The destruction stretched for about three hundred yards along the westbound carriageway. Beyond that, there was a queue of stationary vehicles reaching into the distance.

Scores of cars, lorries and vans had collided. Smoke was still rising from some of the wrecks. Temple counted five lorries. Two of them had overturned and one had been gutted by a fire. He also saw a coach which had come to rest across two lanes and three cars had ploughed into it. He tried to imagine what it would have been like for the drivers. Most of them would have been on their way home from work. The majority would have been driving at around 70mph and it was likely that some had been tailgating.

The cars driven by the gunshot victims would have slewed out of control in an instant, causing the drivers behind them to stamp on their brakes. Multiple collisions would have been unavoidable. In the blink of an eye dozens of cars had concertinaed into each other with devastating consequences.

Temple took out his mobile and called Mike Beresford. The Chief Super had already been given the news that two drivers had been shot dead.

'It's unbelievable,' he said. 'This is going to put the fear of God into anyone who uses the motorways.'

'Have the media got wind of it yet?' Temple asked.

'No, but they soon will. The pile-up itself is topping all the news bulletins. This is not something we can hold back.'

'We need to shut down the areas either side

of the motorway along this section,' Temple said. 'Set up road blocks and draft in the specialist search unit.'

'I'll organize it,' Beresford said. 'But what's your gut feeling? Could this be a terrorist attack?'

'I'm not sure,' Temple said. 'It's not your typical terrorist MO. If I were you I'd alert the Anti-Terrorism Command in London anyway just in case they feel the need to muscle in.'

'The Chief Constable has already done that. They're sending a man down tonight to monitor developments.'

Temple said he would keep Beresford up to date and cancelled the call. As he walked back down the embankment, he struggled to order his thoughts. In all his years as a detective he had never felt so overwhelmed by a case — never had to attend a crime scene quite like this one.

It was going to take many hours to clear the backed-up traffic and to examine the gunshot victims and their cars thoroughly. Then the Highways Agency would have to arrange for the wreckages to be removed and the road surface to be repaired.

Temple pushed his fingers through his hair and drew in a heavy breath, bracing himself for a long and difficult night. He stepped back onto the hard shoulder and paused to look around. Two fire officers rushed past him. He watched as they joined several others who were struggling to put out a fire that had reared up suddenly in the engine compartment of an overturned van.

His attention was then drawn to a car a few yards away which was a real mess. There was no one inside and he wondered whether the driver was one of those who'd been killed or seriously injured. The back end of the car was compressed by a couple of feet and the front offside wing was crushed, exposing the engine. The windscreen had gone and one of the rear wheels was missing. Then he noticed the front number plate which was hanging loose.

HYO4 XGA.

His breath caught in his throat as a memory snapped into place. *No, it couldn't be*, he told himself. *It's not possible.*

He rushed forward for a closer look. The car was a red Peugeot 307 with grey leather upholstery.

Oh God.

Panic swirled through his head as he realized that he knew this car as well as he knew his own.

It was Angel's car.

And it was probably her blood that he could see splattered over the front seat.

4

Temple couldn't move. It was as though his muscles had seized up. But his thoughts spun wildly and a rush of adrenaline made his body tingle. He told himself that the wrecked Peugeot did not belong to Angel. Surely he'd made a mistake about the number plate; easily done in all the confusion.

Angel was at home studying. She had told him earlier that she had no intention of going out. She was safe, unharmed.

So why hadn't she been answering her phones?

He fumbled for his phone and speed-dialled Angel's mobile. It rang three times before Angel's voicemail kicked in.

Shit.

He stared down at the car, refusing to believe the evidence in front of his eyes. The blood on the front seat made his heart leap in his chest.

After a few more seconds of paralysis, he leaned inside the Peugeot and flicked open the glove compartment. The first thing he saw confirmed his worst fear. It was the Rod Stewart CD he had bought Angel for her last birthday. He held on to the Peugeot's roof to steady himself. Then he drew in a couple of long breaths and tried to focus.

He needed to find out where Angel was and how badly she was injured. He had no religious convictions, but that didn't stop him praying now that she wasn't among those who had been killed.

He rushed over to where the fire officers were tackling the engine blaze. None of them knew who had been in the Peugeot. They suggested he talk to the paramedics or the traffic officer who was keeping a record of all those who were injured and required treatment. As he dashed around Temple felt somehow detached, as if out of his body and watching himself. It was a chilling sensation.

Eventually he found the officer who was keeping a written record of the casualties. And sure enough the name Angelica Metcalfe was on the list.

And she was alive!

'She was in a red Peugeot,' the officer said. 'I'm afraid she suffered severe injuries and was taken to hospital by air ambulance about an hour ago. We recovered her handbag and were able to identify her.'

A wave of relief washed over the detective. He asked the officer if he knew how badly hurt Angel was but the guy said he didn't know.

'I got the information from a paramedic,' he said. 'I didn't actually see her myself.'

Temple decided to go straight to the hospital even though he was the investigating officer in charge of the crime scene. Too bad if the move drew criticism from higher up the chain of command. But first he sought out DS Vaughan who was shocked to hear about Angel. He and she were good friends and usually worked as a team.

'You just go, guv,' Vaughan said. 'Don't worry about what's going on here. We've got it covered. Call me when you know how she is.'

Temple commandeered one of the fast-response BMWs and told the driver to take him to Southampton General Hospital.

'Get me there as quickly as you can,' he said.

*   *   *

The police driver dropped him outside the emergency entrance and he hurried in.

Not surprisingly it was full to capacity. He walked past the queue at the admittance desk and stopped a male orderly who was carrying a clipboard.

He showed the orderly his warrant card and said, 'I need your help. A police officer named Angelica Metcalfe was brought here by air ambulance from the M27. I want to know where she is and how she is.'

The orderly must have sensed from his tone that he wasn't about to be fobbed off. He told Temple to wait while he went to find out. Temple stood there feeling dread pour through him. The scene around him appeared chaotic and the staff were extremely busy. All the seats in the waiting area were taken and several people were nursing physical injuries. He saw two uniformed police officers enter through swing doors and was about to approach them when the orderly appeared at his side.

'Miss Metcalfe is in resuscitation, sir,' he said. 'I've been asked to take you there.'

At the entrance to the resuscitation area Temple was met by a chunky nurse with bottle-blonde hair and a husky voice. She introduced herself as Nurse Fisher and asked to see his credentials.

'Angel is not just one of my officers,' he explained as he flashed his ID. 'She's also my girlfriend.'

The nurse's features softened slightly and she reached out to take his elbow.

'Oh, I see. I didn't realize.'

'So how is she?' Temple asked, his voice cracking with emotion.

The nurse clenched her bottom lip between her teeth, as though wondering how much to tell him, then said, 'The good news is she's alive and receiving the best possible treatment, Mr Temple. We're in the process of carrying out various tests. However, she has suffered significant injuries, but her condition is stable. The doctor will explain things to you in more detail.'

The nurse tightened her grip on his arm and steered him into a busy room with cubicles along both walls. Some had curtains across them. Others were open to reveal patients lying on beds.

The nurse gestured towards an open cubicle on the left. Two men stood next to it — one in a white coat and the other in green medical scrubs. They both looked up as the nurse led him towards them. But Temple's eyes were fixed on the bed and the person in it. He recognized Angel immediately despite the bandages across her forehead and shoulder and the oxygen mask covering her mouth and nose. The sight of her sent a bolt of ice down his spine.

He stepped up to the bed and swallowed back the lump that rose in his throat. A collection of electrode pads was attached to

Angel's chest, relaying a flow of information into a computer. A raised monitor bleeped and hummed and told the doctors what was going on inside her body. What Temple could see of her face was the colour of alabaster and there were dark bruises on her neck and right cheek. She was unconscious, but it was impossible to gauge the extent of her injuries beneath the light sheet that covered most of her body and was stained in places with blood. Her left arm was resting at her side and an IV tube was inserted into it. Temple reached out and grasped her hand. It was soft and warm and he was disheartened when her fingers did not respond to his touch.

He suddenly became aware that someone was talking to him. He turned and saw that it was the man in the white coat. The other man had disappeared.

'I'm Doctor Bellamy,' the man was saying. 'The nurse tells me you're Miss Metcalfe's boss — and her boyfriend.'

Temple nodded as he pulled the doctor's face into focus. The man was about fifty with grey hair and wrinkles bunched around the edges of his mouth.

'How badly hurt is she?' Temple asked, his voice pitched high with concern.

The doctor twisted his lower jaw as he

considered his response and Temple felt his stomach roll.

'Her injuries include two broken ribs and a punctured lung, plus various contusions,' the doctor said. 'The damage to the lung should heal by itself in time. As you can see we've managed to stabilize her and, although she's wearing an oxygen mask, she is able to breathe by herself, which is very encouraging.'

Temple turned to look at Angel and felt the heat of tears rise in his eyes.

The doctor continued speaking and every word jabbed at his mind like a sharp object.

'She has also suffered a concussion, I'm afraid. In the collision she was thrown against the windscreen quite forcefully. We're about to take her down for CT and MRI scans to see if there's any brain damage. However, she did regain consciousness briefly when she came in and that's certainly a good sign. She's out to the world now because we've given her a strong sedative.'

Temple's head was full of words he couldn't say. He stared down at Angel, the woman who had given him his life back after his wife's death. He would have done anything to be able to trade places with her. But he knew he was completely powerless. All he could do was wait and worry and pray that she pulled through.

'She's in safe hands, Mr Temple,' the doctor assured him. 'Given the circumstances her condition could have been much worse.'

Nurse Fisher took Temple by the arm and eased him away from the bed. He was reluctant to go.

'It's best if you wait outside for now, Mr Temple,' she said. 'We're taking her for the scans.'

As she led him towards the door he found it hard to control his thoughts. She guided him to a small empty waiting room. On the way she handed him Angel's handbag which had been retrieved by the paramedics at the scene.

'Her phone and purse are inside,' she said. 'I checked.'

The waiting room was bathed in a harsh light and contained two armchairs and a sofa. There was a strong hospital smell of disinfectant and floor polish.

Temple sat down clutching Angel's handbag and the nurse went away to fetch him a cup of tea. It was then that it really hit him and, despite his best efforts, he started to cry. As the tears flowed, he made a promise to himself. He swore that he would find the bastard who had done this to his beloved Angel.

No matter how long it took.

5

Temple had hated hospitals ever since the long, drawn-out death of his wife from cancer. Waiting around and watching Erin suffer had served only to compound his sense of hopelessness.

Now he was reminded of those long, dark days and nights. He was back in the same hospital trying to come to terms with another tragic event. And the same feelings of dread and despair were surging through him. By the time the nurse came back with his tea the tears had dried to salty tracks on his cheeks and he had regained his composure.

'You should go home and get some rest,' she said. 'If there's a change in her condition we'll call you.'

'I want to be here when she comes back from the scans,' he said.

'Well, as soon as we have the results I'll let you know.'

The nurse left him alone and for several minutes he just sat there sipping at something brown and tepid that masqueraded as tea. A restless energy burned through him and the headache that had started at the base of his skull spread quickly. In need of a distraction he took out his phone and called the Chief Super.

'DS Vaughan told me what happened,' Beresford said. 'How is Angel?'

'She's not well,' Temple said. 'Broken ribs, punctured lung and concussion. They're doing an MRI scan now.'

'Well, I'm about to head out to the motorway to have a look for myself,' Beresford said. 'I'll stop by the hospital on the way. So hang in there, Jeff. I'm sure she'll be fine.'

Temple hung up and opened Angel's handbag. He rummaged inside and found her purse, her notebook and her mobile phone. The phone was still on and the first thing he noticed was that she'd had several missed calls. The last couple were from him and there was one at 2 p.m. that afternoon from a number he didn't recognize. The caller had left a voice message and when he opened it up a woman said, 'Hi Miss Metcalfe. It's Kate here from Regency Fashions. Just to let you know that your dress is in and ready for collection.'

Temple recalled that Regency Fashions was the name of a shop they had visited the previous Saturday at Gun Wharf Quays in Portsmouth. Angel had bought a dress that had required alterations. He quickly phoned the shop to ask whether she'd been along that afternoon to pick up the dress. The shop was closed but a member of staff who introduced herself as Julie was still there to answer the phone.

'Yes, Miss Metcalfe was here,' she said. 'She tried on the dress and left with it just after five.'

Temple felt his heart freeze over. Jesus, he thought. How could Angel have been so unlucky? A simple trip to pick up a dress had almost got her killed.

He got up and started pacing the room, his breath suddenly so laboured that he was almost wheezing. He was still alone in the room half an hour later when Beresford turned up. The Chief Super was a broad-shouldered Welshman with a misshapen nose that gave him a rugged appearance. He was out of uniform and chewing nicotine gum — a habit he'd acquired whilst trying to give up cigarettes. Temple had a lot of respect for the guy. He was a decent, no-bullshit boss who was pegged as a rising star in the constabulary. He'd been running Major Investigations for a year and had made a big impression on the team and the hierarchy.

'Is there any more news?' he asked.

Temple shook his head. 'She's still having

tests. I should get an update any minute.'

They both sat down and Temple told Beresford about Angel's injuries. His voice came out shaking and he fought to control it.

'Then you need to stay with her,' Beresford said, his Welsh accent suddenly more pronounced. 'That's why I dropped by. I wanted to tell you not to worry about the case. I'll put someone else in charge.'

Temple shook his head. 'I want to stay on this one, guv. I want to find the maniac who did this to her.'

'But I don't think you'll be able to concentrate.'

'I will if I know she's going to be OK. It'll be my way of coping. If I have to sit around all day worrying about her I'll go insane.'

Beresford started to speak, but stopped himself when the door opened and Dr Bellamy walked in.

The doctor told Temple that the scans showed no significant injury inside Angel's head.

'But we'll need to monitor her closely,' he said. 'She suffered quite a blow and we can't be sure there isn't microscopic damage to brain cells which wouldn't show on the CT scan. Also, concussion can be unpredictable and cause other problems to develop.'

'Such as?'

'Well, physical symptoms can include seizures, blurred vision, chronic headaches and a reduced sense of smell. It can also cause depression, memory loss and personality changes.'

'My God.'

'I'm not saying she'll develop any of those symptoms,' the doctor added quickly. 'At the moment she's responding well to treatment and she'll be out for the count until morning. You're welcome to stay here with her, but I don't think it's necessary. She won't wake until morning and we've got everything under control.'

'I'd like to see her,' Temple said.

'Of course.'

Angel looked worse than she had before and Temple felt a sudden jolt of alarm. The colour had been sucked out of her face and there were deep hollows under her eyes. He leaned over the bed and kissed her forehead.

'I love you, sweetheart,' he whispered.

He wanted to wrap her up in his arms and comfort her, but she looked too fragile even to touch.

Dr Bellamy, who was standing beside him, said, 'Give the nurse your contact details and go and get some rest. We'll take good care of her. I promise.'

The nurse walked with him back to the

waiting room and he asked her to put Angel's handbag in a safe place.

'I've taken out her purse and mobile,' he said. 'But it's got her make-up and stuff in it and she doesn't like to be without it.'

The nurse smiled and took the bag. He also gave her one of his cards.

'I'll be back in a little while,' he said. 'But don't hesitate to call me in the meantime.'

Beresford was standing with his back to the window and his phone to his ear. He ended his call abruptly when Temple entered the room.

'She looks rough,' Temple said.

Beresford nodded. 'She's bound to, Jeff. Are you going to stay?'

Temple shook his head. 'My being here won't speed up her recovery. If anything I'll only be in the way. They'll call me if there's any change in her condition. So let's get going. We've got a killer to catch.'

6

Temple experienced a spasm of guilt as he left the hospital. Maybe I should have stayed, he thought, leaving probably made him seem like a heartless bastard to Beresford.

But the doctor had told him there was no need to remain at Angel's bedside because she was sedated and would be asleep until morning. At the same time he'd make sure he would get regular updates from the hospital. So there seemed little point in hanging around when he could be putting his talents to good use tracking down the psycho responsible.

Nevertheless, he had to force himself to stop thinking about Angel and focus on what had happened on the motorway.

He hadn't yet had time to construct any theories. All he knew was that Angel and the other motorists had been the victims of a gunman. To his knowledge it was the first time someone had shot at drivers on a motorway in the UK with a highpowered rifle. He'd heard of it happening some years ago in the Netherlands, but the details were vague so he made a mental note to check it out.

As Beresford's chauffeur-driven car sped towards the motorway with the siren on, he concentrated on things that needed to be done and questions that needed to be asked.

What kind of weapon was used by the shooter? Which car was targeted first? What exactly would the killer have seen from where he was positioned? Were they sure that no other cars had been fired on?

They also needed to determine whether a terrorist was responsible. If so, then someone higher up the foodchain would probably assume control of the investigation; it'd change from being a local murder case to a full-blown national inquiry.

* * *

They made good time despite the heavy traffic on all roads close to the motorway. Their driver took them down the same slip road that Temple had taken earlier in the evening.

Hundreds of cars were still backed up along the carriageways where their occupants would be stranded for many hours to come. The crash scene was revealed in all its gory details beneath a collection of floodlights that had been placed around it. It reminded Temple of a scene from a Mad Max movie.

There was a riot of high visibility jackets and pulsating blue lights. The area was teeming with police officers and forensic technicians in white suits.

When they got out of the car the air felt cold and sharp in Temple's lungs and he experienced a shiver of trepidation.

Beresford used his mobile to let Vaughan know they'd arrived and the DS appeared within minutes. Vaughan looked exhausted and his face was smeared with grime, but he was clearly surprised to see Temple and the first thing he did was ask about Angel. Temple quickly filled him in. Vaughan was visibly relieved and gave a half smile.

'Thank God she's not more seriously injured,' he said. 'I've been worried.' Then, after a pause, he added, 'We've found something you should both see.'

They followed Vaughan as he walked along the westbound carriageway away from the crash scene. The road was packed with emergency vehicles that were parked at all angles with their lights blazing. There were other cars and vans from the Collision Investigation Department and the Highways Agency. Several recovery trucks were stacked up waiting for clearance to haul away the wrecks.

The frigid air was filled with the crackle of

police radios and the stench of burning metal. From above came the constant stutter of helicopters.

The muscles around Temple's eyes tightened as he took it all in. It struck him yet again that the scale of the task facing them was a formidable one. This crime was going to be compared with the atrocities committed in America by crazy men with assault weapons who slaughter innocent people. It was bound to freak out motorists and maybe even deter some from using motorways in the short term.

They were approaching a road bridge over the carriageways when Vaughan stopped and pointed towards the embankment.

'We're pretty sure the gunman was positioned behind those bushes in front of the bridge,' he said. 'From there he would have had a good view of the oncoming traffic.'

A floodlight had been placed about half way up the embankment and Temple could see forensic officers searching the area.

'There are fresh shoe prints in the grass,' Vaughan said. 'And some of the branches have been snapped off.'

'You did well to home in on the spot so quickly,' Beresford said. 'With any luck the shooter will have left some trace evidence behind.'

'But that's not the best of it,' Vaughan said. 'Follow me.'

He walked under the bridge and the other two followed. Then he stopped walking and Temple frowned.

In front of them were two huge pre-cast concrete blocks that supported this side of the bridge. Between the vertical blocks the embankment beneath the bridge had been completely paved with grey slabs.

Vaughan took a torch from his pocket and turned it on. He shone the light on the slabs and said, 'So what do you make of that?'

At first Temple didn't see it. His eyes were slow to adjust to the light. But then he saw the words and numbers that had been spray-painted in bright red across the concrete slabs. As he read them a cold sensation gripped his chest.

5.45 P.M. JAN 15
THIS IS JUST THE START.
MANY MORE WILL DIE.

7

There are some anonymous threats that you don't take seriously. Temple knew that. But this wasn't one of them. The guy who had left the message on the paving slabs was the same guy who had carried out the senseless slaying of two motorists. And he wanted everyone to know it — hence the time and the date.

How sick was that? How unbelievably insane? They were dealing with a crackpot with a gun. It was the worst kind of nightmare.

'Whoever wrote it would have been shielded from the road by those blocks,' Vaughan said.

Temple knew that it was unlikely anyone had seen him. The traffic would have been blasting by at high speed and it would have been pitch dark beneath the bridge.

'Is the paint still wet?' Temple asked.

Vaughan nodded. 'It is in places where it's been sprayed on thick. I reckon it was put there a few hours ago — just before the shootings.'

Temple took a step back and looked up at the embankment. Scenes of Crime Officers were carrying out a meticulous search of the grass and the bushes. A couple were crawling around on their hands and knees.

'When we came across the words we started searching this area in front of the bridge,' Vaughan said. 'That's when someone spotted the shoe prints and the broken branches.'

'Let's have a look up there,' Temple said.

A crime scene van was parked under the bridge and from it they helped themselves to forensic suits and paper boot covers. Then they scrambled up the embankment. They were shown the broken branches and three shoe prints — two in the grass and one in a patch of bare earth at the top of the embankment where it joined the road. They couldn't be certain they belonged to the shooter, but there was a pretty good chance.

'We should be able to get a plaster cast of the one in the dirt,' Vaughan said.

Temple stood just outside the floodlight's beam and looked back along the carriageway to the pile of tangled metal that was the crash scene. It was about fifty yards away. He figured the two drivers had been about thirty or forty yards further back along the road when they were shot.

He held his arms aloft as though holding a rifle and pretended to pull an invisible trigger.

'It's the perfect position,' he said. 'He would have been shielded by the bushes and yet have a clear view of the oncoming traffic.'

The vehicles would have been like ducks in a shooting gallery. From a range of eighty or ninety yards the shooter would have had no trouble finding his targets.

'He probably used a night vision scope,' Vaughan said. 'It's the only way he could have been so deadly accurate. Otherwise he would have had to fire at the windscreens and hope for the best.'

'Maybe he fired more than two shots,' Vaughan said. 'We won't know for certain until we've examined all the wrecks and that's going to take time.'

Temple clambered up to the top of the embankment and stepped onto the road bridge. It had been sealed off at both ends by police cars. A fingertip search was underway along the nearside pavement. Vaughan told him the road was called Allington Lane. It was in the north part of Southampton, close to the airport. On either side of the bridge the road was lined with thick clumps of trees. It was poorly lit and he couldn't see any houses in either direction.

'There's a small estate about a quarter of a mile along the road to the left,' he said. 'To the right you have to travel a lot further

54

before you come to any buildings. And I'm told there are no traffic cameras along this stretch.'

'It's quite narrow,' Temple said. 'So I don't reckon our shooter would have parked his car up here. It would have caused a problem for passing traffic and stuck out like a sore thumb.'

'Maybe he gets around on a motorbike,' Beresford said. 'Or even a push bike, which he could have hidden in those bushes.'

They could only speculate at this stage because they really had no idea how the gunman had got there or what mode of transport he'd used. For all they knew he could have walked for miles with his rifle concealed in a bag of some kind.

A police helicopter swept across the sky above them, so low Temple felt he could almost touch it. For a few moments its engine drowned out the constant moan of sirens.

Temple made the point that things needed to be controlled and organized. As with any serious motorway crash, each group had its own objectives and responsibilities, but this time everyone had to feed information into the murder investigation as soon as they had it. They decided to go back down onto the motorway and convene a meeting of all the team leaders, including the traffic officers, fire chiefs, Highways Agency staff and scene-of-crime technicians. They were half way down the embankment when one of the forensic guys called them over. He was holding up a clear plastic bag.

'We're definitely at the right spot,' he said. 'This is a shell casing from a high-calibre bullet.'

'Can you be more specific?' Temple asked.

The forensic guy nodded. 'It's a .338 Lapua Magnum. They were specially developed for top notch sniper rifles — the kind that can kill at a range of hundreds of yards.'

Temple felt his blood pressure plummet. He was familiar with those particular shells. They had a fierce reputation and were among the deadliest ever manufactured. In fact they were a favourite with the military and had been used for years by British troops in Afghanistan.

8

What kind of nut opens fire on motorists with military grade ammo? And what possible motive could he have?

These questions and more were bunching up and Temple knew that once the facts were made public everyone would be demanding answers. Speculation would be rife. Half-assed theories would be put forward. The government would pray that it wasn't the start of a major terrorist campaign. And that couldn't be ruled out, of course. Terrorists try to instil fear in the public. And this would be a low-risk way to do just that. A pull of the trigger and, hey presto — death and destruction on a vast scale.

For some reason Temple knew that there were 2,000 miles of motorways in the UK; essential arteries that drove the economy by transporting people and freight between towns and cities. These would make perfect targets for religious fanatics. On the other hand he knew it was just as likely that this was the work of a lone psychopath; someone who was doing it for fun or to fulfil some warped fantasy; someone who'd watched too many violent video games. Or someone with a mental illness who saw it as a chance to draw attention to himself.

Temple did not allude to this stuff when he got the various team leaders together on the hard shoulder of the westbound carriageway. He asked them to be mindful of the murder investigation. He said that anything that might be relevant to the inquiry should be passed to DS Vaughan or one of the other detectives.

It was no secret by this time that two motorists had been shot. The news had spread like wildfire. The two had been named as Ross Priest, a carpet salesman from Bournemouth, and Veronica Chester, a music teacher who lived in the New Forest. There was a press embargo on the identities until the relatives had been informed.

Only a few people knew about the warning that had been sprayed in paint under the bridge. Temple had instructed the forensic technicians not to draw attention to it. And he'd told his officers to put a tent over it.

After the meeting Beresford made a call to update the Chief Constable who would in turn pass on the information to the Anti-Terrorism Command in London. Temple wasn't sure what those guys would make of the painted message. After all, it wasn't the kind of thing terrorists usually did. Their modus operandi was to make threats via the internet.

Temple then had a separate meeting with his detectives. They'd spoken to dozens of the drivers who hadn't been injured, but none of them had seen anything in the moments before the vehicles started to crash into each other.

DS Vaughan confirmed that a bullet fragment had been taken out of the head-rest of the car which Mr Priest had been driving. It had been taken away by forensics and an attempt would be made to match it with the shell casing found near the bridge.

'I want a couple of you to go to the hospital and talk to the walking wounded,' Temple said. 'One of you should stay here with Dave to gather the evidence. The rest of you team up with uniform and start checking out nearby houses. Someone may have seen our shooter.'

Temple looked at his watch. 11:15 p.m. So much had happened in such a short period of time — Five people dead; his girlfriend in hospital with serious injuries and one of the country's busiest motorways still closed off.

But what swam through his mind — and caused his heart to pound like a jack hammer — was the crude threat scribbled in red paint under the bridge: *This is just the start. Many more will die.*

9

Three miles away from the crash scene the man who left the message under the bridge sat in front of his TV watching the rolling news on Sky.

The central heating in his tiny flat was on full blast, but he was still wearing his polo sweater and khaki coat. He hadn't bothered to change after getting home. He was too cold and in too much of a hurry to see what they were saying about the carnage on the M27.

The details were only just beginning to emerge: five people dead, two of them shot as they drove along the motorway in the rush hour. At least fifteen people injured. The motorway was still closed along a 15-mile stretch and would probably remain closed until well into tomorrow.

A senior police officer was interviewed. He said they believed that just one gunman was responsible and that he fired shots from the embankment or from a nearby bridge. Probably using a high-powered rifle. A massive search was underway and extra police had been drafted in from neighbouring forces.

As he listened he couldn't resist a self-satisfied grin. It had, after all, been a resounding success and it had imbued him with a sense of power and fulfilment. He'd managed to kill five people with two shots. And it could not have been easier. Now the cops were running around like headless chickens wondering what the hell was going on.

He felt elated. There's something deliciously impersonal about murdering total strangers at random. It heightened the thrill of the kill because there was no emotional attachment. No inner voice telling him that maybe this person didn't deserve to die.

When he targeted the two cars he couldn't even discern the faces of the drivers beyond the windscreens. Despite ten times magnification through a night-vision scope their heads and shoulders were still little more than blobs in the dark. But it was enough. After adjusting his aim to take account of the speed of the cars he'd let them have it.

Faceless people he didn't know and couldn't even see properly. The perfect victims.

He decided he'd had enough of the news and switched off the TV using the remote. By morning there would be a lot more of it. The victims would be named and people would be queuing up to condemn what had happened. He wondered if the cops would reveal what they'd found under the bridge. Maybe not since it might cause some panic.

He got up from his chair and threw off his jacket. He was hot now and could feel sweat trickling down his back. He went to the fridge and helped himself to a beer. German-made and cold as ice. Just how he liked it.

Then he picked up his custom-made canvas rucksack and put it on the table that stood between the kitchenette and living area.

It was time to clean the rifle. He felt duty-bound to take care of it, especially after the outstanding way it had performed that evening. He unzipped the bag and took it out.

He had always been in awe of this particular weapon. The Arctic Warfare Super Magnum — better known as the L115A3 long-range sniper rifle. It was considered so deadly that the British army had dubbed it 'The Silent Assassin'. It had a range of over a mile and had been used to kill scores of insurgents in Afghanistan.

The man ran his fingers over the folding walnut stock, then across the stainless steel barrel and finally over the state-of-the-art telescopic sight. In his humble opinion it was a work of art and he was proud of the fact that it was British made. In fact the manufacturers, Accuracy International, were based along the coast in Portsmouth — just a few miles from where he decided to launch his first attack. How gloriously ironic was that?

He kept the cleaning equipment in a kitchen drawer. He took it out and got to work. Fifteen minutes later the rifle was in pristine condition. Clear of prints and greasy smudges and looking as though it was brand new.

He loaded two more shells into the detachable magazine and put the rifle back in the bag.

It would stay there until tomorrow.

10

It took all night to clear the traffic that had built up behind the crash scene. For the hundreds of people trapped in their vehicles it was a ghastly ordeal.

They had to wait for some of the wrecks to be moved so that a single lane could be opened up. But that didn't happen until the SOC officers gave the go-ahead. They had to be sure that the area had been properly processed and that all potential evidence had been removed and catalogued. Then the road surface had to be cleared of debris and ash.

Temple stayed at the scene until 3 a.m., by which time his eyes burned and his muscles ached. He was tired and hungry and worried about Angel.

Before getting a lift home he sent out a message to his team that there'd be a full briefing in the office at 8 a.m. and he wanted everyone there.

His small house on the outskirts of the city was cold and lifeless. It was a typical bachelor pad which lacked character and felt sterile. Angel had been planning to improve things.

When she moved in she was going to make the place warm and homely with new curtains, bright cushions and more pictures. He was looking forward to it.

The first thing he did was blast a ready meal in the microwave. Then he picked at it as he read through his notes. At one point he closed his eyes while he thought about what questions to raise at the briefing.

The next thing he knew he was coming awake with a start. He checked his watch and saw that he'd slept for two hours. He showered and shaved and put on fresh clothes. White shirt, blue suit, red tie. Smarter than usual because he knew he'd be expected to front a press conference at some point during the day. Then he called a taxi, as his own car was still at the station. It arrived just as dawn was breaking. It looked like it was going to be another gloomy day. Dark clouds were gathered like gargoyles above the city.

On the way to the hospital he got the driver to stop outside a newsagents so he could buy some newspapers.

The headlines screamed at him.

Carnage on the M27.

Rush Hour Murder.

Two drivers shot by motorway sniper.

It was pretty alarming stuff even without

the line about the scribbled warning under the bridge. All the reports went into graphic detail with vivid descriptions of what had happened. There were quotes from motorists who had seen the pile-up and from emergency personnel who had to deal with the immediate aftermath.

Temple read through all the stories and there was nothing in them he didn't already know. Except for a short paragraph that appeared on page two of the *Daily Mail*.

One woman told our reporter she saw a man acting suspiciously close to where the shootings happened. He was apparently standing on a bridge looking down on the traffic when she drove past.

Temple immediately called the office and asked the detective who answered if he knew about the woman. He didn't, but he said that was probably because most of the team hadn't yet got back with their reports.

'Chase it up then,' Temple said. 'If she hasn't already given us a statement then contact the newspaper. We need to talk to her right away.'

★   ★   ★

At the hospital Temple was greeted by a different nurse. Her name was Pritchard.

Thirtyish, with tied-back dark hair and a small, oval face.

She told him that Angel had had a comfortable night and had spent it in a private room. She'd woken earlier and had responded to questions. A doctor had spoken to her briefly and told her about her injuries.

'She remembers some of what happened,' the nurse said. 'And that's a good sign. With head trauma cases memories often get lost or fractured.'

'Is she awake now?' he said.

'She is, but maybe not for long. We've had to give her another sedative.'

He entered the room nervously. As soon as he saw Angel his heart leapt into his mouth. She was still on her back, rigged up to an array of cables and computers. But her pillows were raised and the oxygen mask had been removed.

The nurse accompanied him to her bedside and then retreated. He looked down at Angel, his body trembling. She seemed to be sleeping peacefully. Her breathing was shallow but wheezy and sounded painful. The skin beneath her eyes was tinged purple. Her hands were resting on her chest and one was still attached to a slim white continuous pulse monitor. He grasped the other and squeezed it gently.

To his surprise her eyes flickered open. She moved her head slightly to look up at him and a smile touched her lips. He felt the emotion well up inside him and for several moments he couldn't speak.

'Where's my kiss?' she murmured.

He was overcome by a wave of joy and relief. This was something he hadn't expected and he could barely believe it. He leaned over and gave her a soft kiss on the mouth. He tasted the bitter tang of medicine.

'How are you feeling?' His throat was dry and the words rasped out.

She swallowed and it seemed to cause her some difficulty.

'My head hurts,' she said, her voice low and scratchy.

'Have you told the nurse?'

'She gave me something, but it still hurts.'

'You need to give it time to work,' he said.

He brushed his fingers across her cheek. Her skin felt smooth and supple.

'How much do you remember?' he asked.

She blinked a couple of times and swallowed again.

'I was driving home,' she said. 'Suddenly everything came to a stop and I hit the car in front. Then I remember waking up in the ambulance. That's all.'

'Did the doctor tell you about the crash?'

'No. But I imagine it was a bad one.'

'You were very lucky.'

'So what happened?' she asked.

The question hung in the air for several seconds and she obviously picked up on his hesitation.

'I'll find out soon enough,' she said.

So he told her, holding nothing back. And he watched as her face registered shock and disbelief.

'I'm in charge of the case for the time being,' he said. 'That's why I wasn't here most of the night. I knew I'd only be in the way. So I went back to the scene.'

He realized he sounded sheepish and it compounded his sense of guilt.

Angel must have picked up on it because she said, 'There's no need to explain. I know how much you hate hanging around hospitals. And I know you'll be taking this case personally. So have you got any theories yet? Why would anyone do such a thing?'

'It's anybody's guess at this stage,' he said. 'There's a lot of speculation, but nothing definite.'

'The motorway was busy,' she said. 'Busier than usual.'

'That's almost certainly why the killer chose to strike at that time,' Temple said.

'Rush hour. People driving fast because they were eager to get home. And in the dark it would have been virtually impossible to see anything on the embankment.'

Angel started to cough and the pain contorted her features. Temple swallowed and felt his heart flutter.

'Are you all right?' he said. 'Do you want some water?'

She shook her head and clenched her teeth.

'I'm just really tired.'

'I'm not surprised,' he said. 'You need plenty of rest.'

She took a breath and closed her eyes.

'I know I'm lucky to be alive,' she said. 'But what if I can't do my job anymore? What happens then?'

'Don't be silly. You'll get better. Injuries to the lungs and ribs are pretty common and easily treated.'

'But the doctor said they don't know for certain if the blow to the head has caused any permanent damage.'

'I'm sure that if it had it would have shown up on the scan. So don't worry.'

'I can't help it,' she said. 'I've got my heart set on a new career in forensics. If my head's fucked up then so is my future.'

Temple told her she was worrying unnecessarily and he was confident she would make a full recovery. Then he went on to say that he would take time off work to be with her after she was discharged.

But after a while he realized that he was speaking to himself. Angel was fast asleep.

11

The open-plan office of the Major Investigations Team was now being referred to as the incident room. Overnight more phones and computer equipment had been moved in along with TV monitors, fax machines and printers.

It was also packed to the rafters for the morning briefing. Every available detective had been summoned and all leave cancelled.

A smartly dressed DI named Kev Slater introduced himself to Temple. He was the officer dispatched from London by the Anti-Terrorism Command to find out first-hand what was going on. He explained that Hampshire police were still in charge of the investigation, but his team were on standby to take over if necessary.

'There'll be no need for us to get involved if this is a one-off crime committed by some lone psychopath,' he said. 'But if the evidence starts pointing towards a terrorist, or if there are more attacks, then we'll have to take over.'

'Well, let's hope it doesn't come to that,' Temple said.

At 8 a.m. Temple stood at one end of the

room next to Chief Superintendent Beresford. The atmosphere was electric despite the fact that everyone was tired. There was also an air of fearful apprehension. Very few officers had got any sleep and some had only just returned from the motorway. They'd all seen the dramatic images and heard the interviews with tearful survivors. Everyone knew that this case was going to dominate their lives for the foreseeable future.

Temple kicked off with an update on Angel. There was spontaneous applause when he said she was conscious and talking. The open display of affection towards her touched him and he felt a lump rise in his throat. He had to cough to clear it before carrying on.

Then it was down to business. He started by introducing DI Slater and explaining why he had travelled down from London.

'If and when his lot take over I'll let you all know,' he said. 'In the meantime we're running the investigation from here and everyone continues to report to me.'

He then referred to the video footage they'd just obtained from the motorway traffic centre. One of its cameras had actually recorded the pile-up. Some of the team had already viewed the sequence, but most hadn't. The tape rolled and there was silence as a grainy image of the busy motorway appeared on the various TV monitors around the room. But all it showed was a string of tiny lights moving at speed in the dark. Then after a few seconds one of the vehicles lost control and veered across the lanes. Another vehicle then appeared to jack-knife and in the blink of an eye all the lights were bunching up. It was both chilling and surreal.

But there were no helpful details on the tape. The embankments either side of the road were blacked out and the camera was too far away to show up something as small as a muzzle flash.

Temple then went through the headline points. The post-mortems would be carried out on all the victims later that day. Their relatives had been informed. So far no connection had emerged between the man and woman who had been shot.

Three of the fifteen people injured were still in a serious but stable condition, including Angel. One man had yet to regain consciousness, but the hospital was hopeful that he would pull through. A section of the motorway was still closed but the traffic from last night had been cleared. Forensic technicians from the Scientific Services Department were still at the scene looking for evidence. So far there was no evidence to suggest any more than two shots had been fired.

Temple mentioned the warning that was spray-painted under the bridge and said he did not want to go public with it just yet.

'But we have to take it seriously,' he said. 'There's no question it was put there by the sniper and we have to assume it's not an idle threat.'

He then invited DS Vaughan to provide a report on the evidence gathered at the scene. The detective had been home to put on a new suit and scrub himself up. But he still looked tired and dishevelled.

'Let's start with the bullets,' Vaughan said. 'We found two shell casings close to the bridge. We also managed to retrieve the shells that killed the two victims. They're clean of prints, unfortunately. According to ballistics they were fired from the same weapon and they're .338 Lapua Magnums, which are made for long-range rifles.'

'Does that mean we're looking for a professional shooter?' someone asked.

Vaughan nodded. 'Most probably. Those shells are used mainly by big game hunters and military snipers, including those serving in the British army.'

'Our man is no amateur,' Temple said. 'I don't think for one second he just fired into the traffic hoping to hit someone. He got those two drivers in his sight before squeezing the trigger. It would have required a high degree of skill considering they were moving targets and it was dark.'

'We've only found two shells and so far no other bullet holes have turned up on any of the damaged vehicles,' Vaughan said.

'Which tells us the guy showed some restraint,' Temple pointed out. 'He did just enough to cause a major collision. He didn't keep shooting just for the sake of it. And he probably took to his heels even before the vehicles came to a stop.'

Vaughan then stepped up to a large whiteboard on which he had prepared a diagram of the crime scene; it showed the motorway and the sniper's position in front of the bridge. It also reflected their understanding that he'd shot at the cars when they were about a hundred yards from him.

'He must have picked the cars at random,' Vaughan said. 'Two shots in quick succession. He was shielded from the traffic by the bushes.'

'We need to check gun clubs and the military,' Temple said. 'If our guy is a professional marksman then he might be on someone's radar.'

Vaughan then referred to the paucity of

solid evidence. There'd be none of the killer's DNA on the victims. And there was almost certainly no connection between them and the killer. All they had were a few broken branches and a couple of shoe prints.

'The shoe prints are a size ten and suggest a guy of average height and weight,' Vaughan said. 'We'll be getting a plaster mould of at least one of them.'

He referred to the message under the bridge. It had been freshly painted using the kind used to spray cars which was widely available across the UK. No cans had been found at the scene.

'It's obvious he took his time with the message,' Vaughan said. 'It doesn't look as though he rushed it. The letters and numbers have been carefully sprayed on and each one is about eight inches high and five inches across. We have to assume that he chose to launch his attack from where he did partly because he was able to leave a message like that under the bridge.'

DC Marsh then reported on the wider search and the house to house inquiries.

'The search teams haven't found anything of interest,' she said. 'Nobody living nearby heard shots or saw anyone running away, but there is one glimmer of hope — a woman who drove across the bridge shortly before the shootings did come forward to report a possible sighting.'

Temple had already been briefed on the woman who'd been mentioned in the newspaper. In fact they'd already been in contact with her by phone and Temple wanted to see her himself later in the morning when he returned to the scene.

The briefing lasted another half-hour and a whole range of issues was discussed. Beresford then said he would liaise with the Chief Constable and the Anti-Terrorism Command to find out how they wanted to play it. He would also talk to the traffic police and Highways Agency to see if anything could be done to improve security along the county's motorways. Everyone knew, though, that they barely had the resources to monitor what was happening on the roads let alone what was going on either side of them.

Detectives were assigned various tasks from checking out CCTV footage on nearby roads to collating more information on the type of rifle that had been used. Those who'd been up all night were told to go home and get some sleep.

Before the meeting wrapped up, Temple said, 'What little evidence we have suggests we're looking for a guy who's proficient in the use of a high-calibre rifle. We don't know at this stage if he's a terrorist working with a group or a lone psychopath who's decided to embark on a killing spree. What we do know is that he's caused a lot of damage with very little effort. And he's told us that he intends to do it again.

'If he carries out his threat then God help us. I can envisage a situation where people are afraid to use the motorways, leading to major disruption. This may be his objective.

'So it's our job to find this bastard before he carries out another shooting. Next time he might decide to fire more than two shots and the death toll could be much higher.'

On that grim note Temple ended the meeting and headed downstairs.

It was time to face the media.

12

The press conference was by far the largest ever held at the police headquarters in Southampton. There were dozens of reporters, photographers and TV crews.

Temple recognized a couple of the local hacks and a woman who often presented the news on the BBC. He saw from the various microphone hoods that there were representatives from Sky, CNN, AP and ITN.

He sat behind a table alongside Beresford and the constabulary's media director, a pasty-faced guy named Ron Williams. Beresford dealt with the introductions and announced that DCI Temple would be leading the investigation into what they were treating as five cases of murder. Two of the victims had been shot and three others — a woman and two men — had been killed in the ensuing multi-vehicle collision.

'This was a premeditated and despicable attack on innocent motorists,' Beresford said. 'Whoever fired those shots chose to do so at the peak of the rush hour on the motorway. Therefore, his objective must have been to harm as many people as possible. As yet we have no idea what his motive is.'

Beresford handed over to Temple who read out a prepared statement containing the basic facts. It included the time the first shot had been fired, based on the traffic camera footage; the names of those who had been killed; the number of vehicles involved in the pile-up and the type of bullets used. He also said they believed the killer to be male. He went on to praise the emergency services for the way they'd responded to the tragedy and said that forty detectives were already involved in the investigation.

He then opened the floor to questions and they came thick and fast.

'Do you believe this was a terrorist attack?' asked a fair-haired woman from *The Guardian*.

'We don't know at this early stage,' Temple said. 'But I can tell you that no terrorist organization has yet claimed responsibility for it.'

'But I understand the Anti-Terrorism Command is now involved,' the *Guardian* reporter persisted.

Temple nodded. 'They're working with us on this. And it should be seen as evidence that we're taking what's happened very seriously.'

'Is it likely that the Command will take

over the investigation from Hampshire police?' she pressed.

'It depends how things develop,' Temple said. 'But that is a possibility. For the time being Southampton MIT will be taking the lead.'

'Did the sniper fire more than two shots?' This from a guy holding a CNN microphone.

Temple shook his head. 'The evidence suggests that only two shots were fired and that the two drivers were picked at random. Their cars were close to each other when they were hit.'

'There are reports that a witness saw a man on the bridge just before the shootings,' someone asked. 'Can you confirm that?'

'That's one of many lines of inquiry we're following,' Temple said. 'And I'd like to say now that if anyone watching believes he or she might have information that will help us they should come forward without delay.'

'When will the motorway re-open?' asked an ITN reporter.

'Later today we hope,' Temple said. 'It's still a crime scene and there's a lot of debris that needs to be cleared before it's safe to use.'

Temple was then asked if the police thought the killer was a trained marksman. He said it was highly likely. Next he was asked if they were going to release the traffic camera footage. He said that this was still being considered.

The questions continued for another fifteen minutes and Temple and Beresford took turns to answer them, but just as they were about to draw the conference to a close the woman from the BBC raised her arm and said, 'Can you tell us about the warning the sniper left under the bridge?'

The room suddenly went quiet and Temple's jaw dropped.

'Where did you hear that?' he asked.

'Our newsroom has just received an anonymous phone call,' she said. 'A man told us the sniper wrote that the attack was just the start and that he intended to kill more people. Is that true?'

Temple swore under his breath. He should have known it'd get out. Too many people at the scene had been made aware of it.

He drew a long breath and suppressed the urge to tell the woman that she was an irresponsible moron.

'We did find a message,' he said. 'It was scrawled in paint and is now undergoing forensic analysis. As soon as we're satisfied it was left by the killer we'll release the details.'

'We already have the details, Inspector,' the woman said, with a smug grin.

She then proceeded to read aloud exactly what had been written in paint on the paving stones under the bridge.

There was pandemonium. Cameras flashed and reporters started waving their arms and leaping to their feet to attract attention.

Temple suddenly faced a barrage of new questions.

Are you taking the message seriously?

Where exactly was it left?

What could be his motive?

Have you got a suspect?

The press conference suddenly descended into a raucous free-for-all. Beresford and Ron Williams appealed for everyone to calm down, but it was a couple of minutes before order was restored. Then Temple started to answer each new question as best he could.

There was one question he struggled with and it was asked several times.

'What are the authorities doing to protect those people who use the motorways?'

He didn't know the answer and instead of saying so he waffled on about traffic police being put on high alert and more patrols being sent out. But his response was vague and unconvincing and it was obvious that no one swallowed it.

He didn't blame them. The truth was there was very little they could do to protect motorway drivers from a madman with a rifle.

13

Temple was immensely relieved when the press conference finally ended and he was able to get away. He felt bleary-eyed and dyspeptic from the experience. And he knew it wasn't going to get any easier. The pressure was going to build on this investigation unless they were able to bring it to a speedy conclusion. And right now that seemed highly unlikely.

He decided to go by himself to interview the woman who'd reported seeing a man on the bridge. She lived near the motorway and he wanted to return there anyway to have a look at the scene in daylight.

DC Marsh approached him on the way out. She looked knackered. Curtains of red hair were drawn back from her forehead and the strain showed in her young, pretty face.

'I plan to visit Angel in the hospital on my way home,' she said. 'Is that OK with you, guv?'

'Of course it is. Give her my love and tell her I'll pop by again this afternoon.'

Marsh and Angel were good friends and he

knew that Angel would be pleased to see her. The pair occasionally went for drinks together or to see a girlie movie. He was glad Marsh was going to the hospital, partly because it made him feel less guilty about not being there himself.

As he drove across the city his eyes ached with tiredness. Outside the sky was the colour of dirty chalk and the air thick with invisible rain. The weather just about matched his mood. He knew that the pressure would really be on him now that the sniper's message was in the public domain. The powers-that-be would want a quick result. Beresford would be leaned on by the Chief Constable. The Chief Constable would be leaned on by the Home Secretary. And the Home Secretary would be leaned on by the Prime Minister.

It was that big a deal now for sure. A media firestorm was underway and it would gather momentum in the days ahead. Temple had a sneaking suspicion that it was the sniper himself who'd tipped off the BBC about the scrawled message. He wanted to spread fear and panic. It was a classic terrorist tactic, but that didn't mean he was a terrorist in the accepted sense of the word.

Temple's intuition told him the guy was a loner who'd flipped. Maybe he'd decided to vent some pent-up rage by going on a killing spree.

Or maybe he woke up one morning and simply decided to join the ranks of the world's most notorious mass murderers.

★ ★ ★

Penny Larkin lived in a modern semi a few hundred yards from the M27. To get to it Temple drove over the Allington Lane bridge, which had been opened again to traffic.

Flowers had been laid along the east-facing pavement as a shrine to those who'd been killed on the motorway below. Temple planned to stop and have a look around on the way back.

But first he wanted a first-hand account from Mrs Larkin of what she saw the previous evening. So far she'd only spoken to a PC whose notes on the conversation were lacking in detail.

Temple had phoned ahead so Mrs Larkin was expecting him. She appeared the moment he parked his Mazda at the kerb outside her front door. Middle-aged, plump, with a bun of auburn hair curled tight on her head. Her eyes were blue, almost turquoise.

'Thank you for seeing me,' he said. 'I'm sorry I couldn't give you more notice.'

She smiled, revealing mint-white teeth. 'That's all right. My husband and I run a shop close by. He can manage without me for a few hours.'

She waved him in and closed the door. It was a clean, bright house with tasteful furniture and a warm feel. He followed her through to the kitchen where she invited him to sit down and asked if he wanted a tea or coffee.

'I won't, thanks,' he said. 'I've had more than enough already this morning.'

She sat opposite him at the table and said, 'I saw you on the news just now. This is such a terrible business. Is it true that whoever did it is threatening to do it again?'

'There has been a threat,' Temple said. 'But he might just be trying to scare people.'

'Well, he's scared me. I don't plan on using the motorway until he's caught.'

Temple's instinct was to tell her there was no need to overreact, that the chances of her becoming a target were infinitesimal. But he held back because he knew he'd be wasting his time. He took out his notebook and pen and placed them on the table in front of him.

'As discussed on the phone, Mrs Larkin, I'd like you to tell me what you told the officer. About the man you saw on the bridge.

88

And take your time. Try to remember every detail.'

'Do you think he was the sniper, Inspector?'

Temple shrugged. 'It's possible, but we won't know for sure until we trace him.'

She sat back and cleared her throat.

'It was just after five,' she said. 'As my husband started preparing to close up the shop I took the car to fill it with petrol ready for the morning. The petrol station is on the other side of the bridge.'

'Was there much traffic around?'

'A fair bit, but no more than usual. That road doesn't get busy until around half five.'

'So where did you see this man?'

'He was crossing the road. When he saw me driving towards him he stopped in the middle. I slowed down so he could get all the way across.'

'Did you get a good look at his face?'

'I'm afraid not. It was dark and when my headlights were on him he turned away and raised his arm to acknowledge me. He was also wearing a hood.'

'What kind of coat did he have on?'

'It was a parka, I think. Green or khaki. I can't be sure.'

'You told the officer that the man was carrying some kind of bag.'

She nodded. 'That's right. It was on his back, like a big rucksack.'

'What do you mean by big? Aren't rucksacks all about the same size?'

She shrugged. 'They usually are, but this one seemed to be bigger. Not bulky but long. I remember thinking that maybe he was carrying a musical instrument or a snooker cue.'

Or maybe it was a rifle, Temple thought.

'So what happened then?' he asked.

She gave a lopsided grin. 'Well, I drove on after letting him cross, but when I got to the station I realized I'd forgotten my purse. So I had to turn around and head back to the shop.'

'And that's when you saw him again?'

'Yes. I noticed him because he was standing on the bridge looking down at the motorway. I didn't really think anything of it at the time.'

'Was he still there when you went back to the petrol station?'

'I didn't go back straight away. I decided to help close up the shop first. But then we heard the sirens and everything went crazy. The road outside was suddenly blocked with traffic and it wasn't long before we learned about what had happened. Then a few hours later a policeman came to the house and asked us if we'd seen anything suspicious, so I

90

told him about the man. Not long after that a reporter phoned here. God knows how he got my number.'

Temple made some notes and then asked her if she could draw a diagram showing exactly where the man crossed the road.

'I can do better than that,' she said. 'I can show you if you like.'

★ ★ ★

Five minutes later they were approaching the bridge over the motorway.

'It was about here.' Mrs Larkin said suddenly and Temple pulled over to the kerb. 'He was standing in the middle of the road having got half way across.'

Both sides of the road were lined with deep foliage all the way to the bridge about thirty yards ahead. The pavements were narrow and deserted. There were no walkers, joggers or people with dogs.

He twisted round in his seat to look back the way they'd come. Mrs Larkin's small housing estate was about a quarter of a mile away and there was nothing but trees and bushes between there and here. So where the hell had the guy walked from and how far had he come? And why did he cross the road at this particular point?

Then Temple spotted a small side road about twenty yards back. It was half hidden by bushes and he hadn't noticed it when they drove past.

'What's through there?' he asked.

Mrs Larkin turned and followed his gaze.

'It leads to a small industrial estate,' she said. 'Most of the units are vacant, though.'

Temple wondered if maybe it was a good place to leave a car or bike. It was just a short walk from the bridge and hidden away from the passing traffic. Definitely worth checking out, he thought. He shoved the car into gear and said, 'Can you show me exactly where you next saw the man?'

He drove onto the bridge. A bunch of people had gathered to look at the flowers and stare down at the motorway. The westbound carriageway was still littered with debris and groups of people in high visibility jackets were busy clearing up. He saw three police cars and a fire engine, plus a tow truck.

Mrs Larkin told him she saw the man standing at about the centre of the bridge looking over the railings at the oncoming traffic.

'He was by himself,' she said. 'I didn't see any other pedestrians.'

Temple stayed on the bridge just long enough to take in the surroundings. The embankment was still cordoned off and SOC officers were carrying out a fingertip search around the bushes in the hope that daylight would undercover some vital evidence. The embankment was steeper than Temple thought and there was much more vegetation. But there was nothing unusual about the spot. It was just an ordinary motorway overpass, like hundreds of others across the country. He wondered why the shooter had decided to come here. Was it a random choice or was the location significant? Had he planned it weeks in advance or was it a spur of the moment decision?

He took Mrs Larkin back to her house, thanked her and gave her one of his cards.

'If you remember anything else about the guy then please give me a call on my mobile, day or night.'

He drove straight back to the little lane leading to the industrial estate. The tarmac surface looked almost unused. So did the units. He reached them after about twenty yards. The prefabricated buildings were small and squat and windowless. There were six of them in all and four had 'to let' signs out front. Only one seemed to be in use and the sign above the entrance read Global Imports. There were two small vans parked outside with the Global Imports logo on the sides.

Temple stopped the car in a small parking area on the other side of the road and took out his phone. He called the incident room and got someone to run a quick check for him. He wanted to know if the estate had been visited by either a detective or a uniform.

After a short wait he was told that armed officers had searched the grounds last night during their sweep of the area and hadn't found anything. A uniformed officer also went there later but all the units were locked up. However, the officer noted that the buildings all had video surveillance cameras. It was therefore on their list of places to visit today.

'Well, I've beaten them to it,' Temple said. 'Tell them I'll check it out and report back.'

He switched off his phone and got out of the car. The security camera on the Global Imports unit wasn't that easy to spot. It was positioned in one corner just below the roof and angled so that it covered the front of the building and part of the approach road.

Temple had a quick look round and saw that there was no activity at any of the other units. Then he walked across the road to Global Imports. He tried the front door and as it opened a bell rang somewhere inside.

He stepped into a small reception area with

a desk and a couple of cheap looking armchairs. There was a pile of cardboard boxes in one corner. An inside door opened and a man stepped through, short, thin and somewhere in his thirties. He wore jeans and a purple T-shirt and his arms were covered in tattoos.

'Hello, there. Can I help you? I'm Michael.'

Temple waved his warrant card and introduced himself.

'Is this about what happened on the motorway?' Michael said. 'I saw all the police as I drove in this morning.'

'I'm afraid it is,' Temple said. 'Are you here by yourself?'

Michael frowned. 'No. My partner's out back packing boxes. We import domestic cleaning products. There's just the two of us.'

'And is this the only unit that's occupied?'

Michael nodded. 'It is now. Two were vacated last year and the others have been empty since the estate opened.'

'Were you or your partner here around five last evening?'

Michael shook his head. 'No way. We always knock off at three. Times are tough so we both have second jobs.'

'What about the security camera out front? Is it on?'

'It should be. We never turn it off.'

'Does it record?'

'For sure. Wouldn't be much use to us if it didn't.'

'In that case I need a favour,' Temple said.

A few minutes later he was in a small storeroom out the back where the camera's digital video recorder was kept. Michael's partner Barry had to be called on to work the equipment. He was an overweight nerdy type with rimless glasses, a tan sweater and wild curly hair. He seemed to relish the opportunity to show off his skills. He explained that the camera was in record mode day and night and footage was stored on a hard drive for a week.

'I'm curious to know if anyone came on to the estate around five o'clock yesterday afternoon,' Temple said. 'Either on foot or in a car.'

Barry raised his brows. 'You think maybe the sniper did?'

'Let's find out, shall we?'

Barry took the tape back to three o'clock to show Temple when he and Michael had left the unit in their vans. The high-resolution picture was surprisingly clear and in colour. They watched as the vans pulled away from the building and disappeared down the lane.

Barry then spun slowly through the tape and as darkness descended the infrared facility kicked in. Nothing happened until just before five. Then a car appeared briefly on the lane as it came onto the estate. It drove straight past the camera. It looked to Temple like a Ford Fiesta, but the figure beyond the windscreen was just a dark shape. The three of them continued staring at the screen until someone walked into shot.

A man.

With what looked like a rucksack on his back.

'Jesus, I don't believe it,' Michael said. 'Is that the bloke?'

The guy had his back to them so they couldn't see his face. He looked to be of average height and build and was wearing some kind of parka, just as Mrs Larkin had said.

They watched, transfixed, as he walked along the lane and out of shot.

'Spin forward again,' Temple said. 'Let's see if he comes back.'

It was no surprise to Temple when the guy reappeared. The time code on the tape read 18.02, which was just after the motorway shootings.

To the detective's immense frustration they still couldn't see his face because he kept his head down without once looking up. But when the Fiesta drove into shot again on its way off the estate they had better luck. Temple got Barry to freeze a frame and zoom in on the rear number plate.

'Well, what do you know?' he said, barely able to contain his excitement.

The vehicle registration was clearly visible.

14

Temple phoned in the registration on his way back to the incident room. By the time he got there the team had discovered that the vehicle — a six-year-old Fiesta — had been reported stolen three days earlier from a street in Eastleigh near Southampton.

Two detectives were on their way to talk to the owner who, according to the DVLA, was a 50-year-old woman named Susan Kline. A nationwide alert for the car was triggered and Temple told the press office to put out a news release. He also wanted to know immediately if it turned up on other CCTV footage in the area.

Then he got the team together for another briefing and asked Chief Superintendent Beresford to attend. He told them about his meeting with Mrs Larkin. Then he showed them the footage from the Global Imports security camera which Barry had obligingly transferred to a memory stick.

'This has to be our man,' Temple said. 'He parked the car as near to the bridge as he could. He must have known the industrial estate would be deserted. Look at the rucksack he's carrying. It's big enough to accommodate one of those rifles that fold up.'

It was the kind of breakthrough that detectives hope for on any investigation and it generated an enthusiastic buzz in the room.

'I can't believe he didn't spot the camera,' Beresford said.

'Maybe he did,' Temple said. 'He knew we wouldn't be able to identify him from the footage. Showing himself like this might be part of his game. He's playing with us.'

Beresford nodded. 'He's obviously an attention-seeker. Why else leave the message under the bridge?'

'Well, he's about to get a bucket-load of attention,' Temple said. 'I want this footage on every TV channel. And I want images from it plastered all over tomorrow's papers.'

The security footage was a big boost to morale. There'd been no other significant developments during the morning. If they were lucky someone might recognize the man from his walk. Or maybe the rucksack would jog a memory. What they really needed was a shot of the bastard's face.

Nevertheless Temple told the team they had good reason to be pleased. Only eighteen hours after the shootings and they already had CCTV footage of a likely suspect. That was in addition to the forensic evidence

— the bullets and the shoe prints. It didn't amount to much, but it was more than they often had this early on in a major inquiry.

He listened to various updates. Provisional postmortem reports confirmed that only two of the drivers had died from bullet wounds, the others from injuries caused by the crash. There appeared to be no link between any of the victims. They were just ordinary people: random targets. Two had lived in Southampton, one in the New Forest, one in Winchester and one along the coast in Bournemouth. A total of eight children had become orphans as a result of the crash. Calls had been flooding in from members of the public. Some were claiming they knew the identity of the shooter, others asking whether it was safe to use the motorways. This came as no surprise to Temple. A crime on this scale was bound to encourage people to pick up the phone. Most would feel they had something important to pass on. But a sick minority would be intent on wasting police time. All the calls had to be followed up because you never knew which of them would turn into a credible lead.

When the meeting broke up, Temple returned to his shoebox of an office which had a view over the docks. There were no personal effects other than a framed photograph of his daughter Tanya. She was living in London now, having left university. She'd got a job as an account manager in an ad agency. He hadn't seen her for three months and had yet to meet the new boyfriend she was sharing a flat with.

He sat behind his desk and fired up his computer. He wanted to flesh out some vague memories he had of sniper attacks in other countries.

And it didn't take him long to find what he was looking for. There were dozens of news reports and features.

> *1992 Lyons, France ... A sniper had opened fire on drivers travelling along a motorway crowded with holiday makers. A dozen vehicles were hit by bullets. One person was shot and wounded and three others were injured by broken glass.*
>
> *2004 Ohio, USA ... A man hunted for a deadly string of motorway sniper attacks had been captured in a Las Vegas hotel. He was believed to have carried out twelve random shootings along Interstate 270.*
>
> *2011 The Netherlands ... A man armed with a rifle fired at cars on the A4*

motorway near Rotterdam. The public prosecutor put up a 10,000 euro reward for information that proved helpful in catching the gunman.

Temple then came across a series of articles on the infamous Washington snipers. A dozen people had been killed and others critically injured in 2002 when two men carried out rifle attacks in Washington DC and along Interstate 95. He remembered there was widespread fear and commotion. Rewards totalling a million dollars were offered and eventually the killers were caught and convicted. But not before they'd established themselves as two of the most notorious criminals in American history.

Temple sat back in his chair and released a long, loud breath. It all made for depressing reading. Random attacks of this nature were easy to commit and bloody hard to solve. What's more, UK motorways were at saturation point. Hundreds of thousands of vehicles thundered along them every day. A nutcase armed with a high-powered rifle could cause mayhem. For the most part the roads ran through rural areas — trees, fields, wooded embankments: a million places to hide and wait and fire at unsuspecting motorists.

His mobile rang — a sharp, crisp chirp. It came as a welcome distraction. He snatched it from his pocket and checked the caller ID. It was DC Marsh.

'Hello, detective,' he said. 'Did you manage to drop in at the hospital?'

'I did, sir. That's why I'm ringing. It's Angel. She's not too good.'

There was a sudden tightening in Temple's throat.

'What's wrong?'

'They won't tell me, sir. But they've just whisked her away for some tests. She was complaining of a bad headache. I thought you ought to know.'

'I'll be right there.'

15

Temple told the incident room coordinator that he had to go somewhere in a hurry. He didn't say where. Just that he could be reached on his mobile. Then he rushed out of the office and down to his car.

Fifteen minutes later DC Marsh met him outside the general hospital's main entrance. She looked utterly exhausted as well as anxious. Her cheeks were flushed and she had dark semicircles beneath her eyes. She filled him in as they hurried up the stairs.

'Angel was awake when I got here,' she said. 'She seemed happy to see me and we talked for a while. She was worried about her car and wanted to know if it was a write-off. I said I'd find out. But she suddenly started complaining about a severe headache so I called the nurse. Then a doctor came. I was ushered out of the room and they rushed her off to have a CT scan.'

I should never have left her, Temple told himself. *I should have stayed with her until she was over the worst of it.*

'I'm sure she'll be all right, sir,' Marsh said. 'Angel is a tough lady.'

Temple turned to look at her. For the first time it struck him that Fiona Marsh was very much like Angel. They were both bright, confident women. Savvy enough to hold their own in the male-dominated world of the police. It was good that they had become firm friends.

'I'm really glad you were here,' he said. 'But you look tired. I think you should go home now and get some rest.'

'I don't mind staying, sir.'

'I know and I appreciate it, but you've been up all night. I'm here now so you can go and recharge your batteries. You're needed on this sniper investigation.'

She bit into her bottom lip. 'Well, if you're sure. But call me if you need me.'

'I will.'

He flashed her a smile and moved swiftly towards Angel's room. The nurse he'd met that morning came out from behind her station. When she saw how worried he was, she took his arm and steered him into the little waiting room. There she told him that Angel was having more scans because there was concern about the headache.

'I must stress that this is not uncommon in patients who've suffered concussion,' she said. 'We just need to find out if there are any problems that didn't show up last night.'

'When will you know?'

'Very soon. If you wait here, I'll come and get you when they bring her back up.'

The moment he was left alone he had an anxiety attack. Adrenaline fizzed through his body and his heart felt like it was beating out of control. He was forced to sit down and take a series of deep breaths.

He told himself to be positive and not to jump to conclusions. He knew from experience that most people recovered from head injuries, even those injuries that were life-threatening.

When the nurse came back into the room he tensed, feeling an alarm blast through him.

'Miss Metcalfe is back in her bed,' she said with a wide, professional smile. 'You can see her now.'

He could feel the blood fill his cheeks as he strode along the corridor, one step behind the nurse. When he entered Angel's private room he was surprised to see that she was sitting up against the pillows, wide awake. Her face broke into a gentle smile when she saw him.

'Fiona called me,' he said. 'So I came right away.'

The nurse left them to it and he stepped up to the bed. He kissed her on the mouth and took one of her hands in his.

'So what did the scan show?'

As if on cue, a doctor came into the room. One he hadn't seen before. He stood on the other side of the bed to Temple and introduced himself as Dr Malcolm Fuller. He was forty-odd and had a round, square-jawed face. His eyes were the colour of pale slate.

To Angel, he said, 'We have an explanation for the headache, Miss Metcalfe. I'm afraid you have a blood clot. It's located in the right transverse sinus, that's a large vein between your brain and your skull, just behind your right ear.'

Temple felt a clutch of apprehension. He squeezed Angel's hand and listened intently, his breathing suspended.

'It was almost certainly triggered by the concussion,' the doctor said. 'If untreated it could prevent blood from draining out of your brain, leading to a stroke.'

Temple felt his stomach twist like a corkscrew and Angel drew in a sharp breath.

'So what can be done?' she asked.

'Well, this type of clot we treat with anticoagulants, or blood thinners,' the doctor said. 'To begin with it'll be administered through an intravenous drip in the arm. Once everything is stable we switch to an oral medicine and the drip is removed. The aim is to stop the clot from spreading. Your body should then dissolve it by itself.'

'How long will that take?' Angel said.

The doctor shrugged. 'No way of knowing for sure. You'll probably be on the medicine for several weeks after being discharged.'

'So what's the prognosis?' Temple asked. 'She's going to be all right isn't she?'

The doctor held his breath, then released it slowly.

'She'll be fine provided there are no complications in the next few days,' he said. 'That's why we'll be monitoring her carefully.'

Temple suddenly found himself choking back an eruption of raw anger that was levelled against the sicko who had caused this. He wanted to rip the bastard apart — tear off his limbs. It would be nothing more than he deserved for what he'd done to Angel. And for what he'd done to all those other people.

It took all Temple's will power to stay quiet and calm. He pressed his lips together and felt a beat at the back of his throat.

When the doctor left the room Angel said, 'I'm scared, Jeff.'

He pulled a chair up to the bed.

'At least they know what's wrong and they can treat it,' he said.

She winced from a dart of pain in her ribs.

'That doesn't mean it can't get worse. Even in the best-case scenario it could be weeks or months before I can get back to work. And maybe I never will.'

'You shouldn't be thinking like that.'

'It's hard not to.'

'You'll be fine.'

'But you don't know that. Nobody does.'

'Well, the doctor didn't seem overly concerned,' Temple said.

'That's because he doesn't want to alarm me, but he said there's a risk of complications developing. You heard him.'

In an effort to stop her becoming increasingly despondent he tried to distract her by talking about the case. He told her about the CCTV footage and the lines of inquiry they were chasing up. And he said he wouldn't rest until he'd caught the sniper.

He wasn't sure she was listening, though. She just stared at the ceiling, her features pale and drawn. Eventually she succumbed to fatigue and drifted off to sleep.

Temple kissed her hand and dabbed at the film of perspiration on her forehead with a tissue. Then he sank back into the chair and looked at his watch. It was 3.30 already. The time had flown by and he knew he ought to get going.

He felt a great wave of tiredness pull at him

and closed his eyes. From outside came the mournful sound of a siren. Then voices reached him from the corridor.

The last thing he heard before falling asleep was his own laboured breathing.

16

Rush hour on the M3 in Hampshire.

It was 5.15 p.m. and already dark. He took up a position on a wooded embankment between junctions eight and nine, south of Basingstoke.

He looked down on the northbound carriageway, facing an endless procession of blazing headlights. It was a cold, dry evening with the traffic flowing freely at an average speed of 80mph. Vehicles were nose to tail; thousands of people cocooned in their metal shells, oblivious to his presence.

Most were no doubt going home from work. To put their feet up and watch television. Their Tuesday night dose of Emmerdale and Eastenders. But some of them wouldn't make it. This would be their last journey and this motorway their final destination.

He'd arrived half an hour ago and spent the first ten minutes leaving another message for the cops to find. Then he walked through the bushes to the spot he'd chosen a week ago.

Now he lay on his belly with the rifle

resting on the bipod. He gazed through the scope, preparing to acquire his first target. The magnified optics threw up the traffic ten times normal size. The night vision aspect turned everything but the headlights into fishbowl green.

The vehicles looked close enough to touch. He could see dark shapes beyond the windscreens. He decided to strike at a range of 300 yards. The shells would move faster than the speed of sound so that the actual pile-up would occur about 150 yards away. Perfect.

He clamped his teeth together and made subtle adjustments to his grip and body position. The crosshairs trembled in the scope and he started to breathe slowly in rhythm with the beat of his heart. He did a quick calculation in his mind, accounting for speed and distance. There was no wind to speak of. Then he selected his target. A lorry travelling in the middle lane. He centred the crosshairs on the driver's silhouette and held steady for one . . . two . . . three seconds.

Then he squeezed the trigger and the rifle kicked back, but the blast was muted by the suppressor. A heartbeat later he saw the lorry's windscreen shatter. The huge vehicle swerved into the fast lane, crushing a car against the central barrier before tipping on to its side and sliding along the tarmac. More cars smashed into it and one of them flipped over on top of a motorcyclist. Even from up here he could hear the grinding of metal and the howling of tyres.

He opened the bolt and the spent shell fell out. He quickly lined up another target. This time a car that was about a hundred yards behind the lorry. It was braking hard along with most other vehicles. He centred the crosshairs as before on the driver and pulled the trigger.

The car veered violently to the left and cartwheeled out of control. It collided with a van and rolled into the path of a four-by-four.

The knock-on effect was spectacular. Cars, vans, coaches and motorcycles crashed into each other with tremendous force. Even those drivers who managed to apply their brakes were rammed from behind.

The sniper couldn't help but smile. Two well-aimed shots was all it took to cause bloody mayhem. So fucking easy.

But he hadn't finished. He wanted to ramp things up this time. Get the message across that he meant business. That he was not a one-hit wonder.

So he lowered the rifle and let his senses feast on the havoc he'd caused. The chaos of lights. The hideous noise. The flying debris.

The pulverized vehicles.

It seemed an eternity before the collisions finally stopped. For several long seconds everything went quiet. The carriageway was blocked by wrecked and overturned vehicles. He saw pockets of smoke. One car burst into flames. Steam hissed from broken radiators.

And then he saw someone on the hard shoulder. A small dark figure moving towards the front. Then another figure appeared further back.

He looked through the scope and saw they were both male. They appeared to be uninjured and were probably looking to help those who were. He left it a further thirty seconds, by which time more people were moving around down there on the motorway. Through the scope they made big, fat, easy targets.

He chose two at random. A middle-aged man and a young woman. Both were clearly distressed. Their startled faces were caught in the harsh beams of light. He lined up the crosshairs and shot them both. Their heads exploded in puffs of red.

Even before their bodies hit the ground he was on the move, scurrying towards the footbridge that was his escape route.

He knew the police would by now be on their way. But by the time they arrived he'd be long gone.

17

Temple awoke suddenly, his mind dragged unwillingly from sleep by the grating shriek of his mobile phone.

For a second he didn't know where he was. His head felt like it was filled with concrete and his eyes took an age to focus. Then he saw Angel and he jolted upright, heart racing. She was sitting up in bed watching him. The sight of the bandages and IV lines brought the whole sorry situation flooding back.

'I think you'd better answer that,' she said.

His brain was slow to react and he struggled to retrieve the phone from the inside pocket of his jacket.

'That you, guv?' It was DS Vaughan. He sounded breathless.

'Yeah, it's me, Dave. What's up?'

'There's been another shooting,' Vaughan said. 'This time on the M3 near Basingstoke.'

Temple was so taken aback his breath caught in his throat.

'It happened a few minutes ago,' Vaughan said. 'Highways Agency cameras picked up a multiple crash. Now calls are flooding in from motorists caught up in it.'

'So how do they know it's not just an accident? Who says it's a sniper attack?'

'A couple of the callers are claiming that several people were gunned down when they got out of their vehicles. There are bodies on the motorway.'

'Jesus.'

'Firearms units have been dispatched and every available chopper is being scrambled. It sounds really bad.'

'Does Beresford know?'

'He and everyone else is being contacted as we speak, including the Anti-Terrorism Command. Where are you, guv?'

'I'm at the hospital with Angel.'

'Then I'll meet you at the scene. Christ knows how long it'll take us to get there. Traffic will be backed up for miles.'

Temple switched off his phone and stood up. His heartbeat drummed against his ribs and he felt a rush of heat in his chest.

'The sniper has struck again,' he said. 'Only this time he's also shot people outside their cars.'

Angel stifled a gasp. 'You'd better go then.'

'Will you be OK? I feel I should stay here with you.'

She forced a weak smile. 'I'd rather you didn't. I don't think I'll get any rest if you sit in that chair snoring like a trooper all evening.'

18

A growing number of UK hospitals have their own helipads. The one at Southampton General was built above the car park at a cost of £1.2m.

As Temple hurried towards his Mazda, he spotted the air ambulance up there on the pad. The helicopter looked as though it was being prepared for take-off. The pilot was climbing on board and a second crew member was just passing through the gate.

Temple had a sudden thought. He dashed over to the gate and showed his ID. He asked the crew member if they'd been called out to the M3. He said they had.

'Then I'd like to hitch a ride,' Temple said.

Under normal circumstances they told him they'd have said no. But these weren't normal circumstances. So the guy made a quick call to the hospital's director of major trauma operations. He was the official who needed to authorize it, and he did after Temple spoke to him.

Five minutes later the chopper was airborne with Temple strapped into the passenger seat.

The M3 starts in Southampton and heads north towards London. The chopper followed the trajectory of the motorway as it rolled across the dark Hampshire countryside. A traffic jam many miles long had already built up on the northbound carriageway. Temple stared down through the window at the unbroken ribbon of headlights, a feeling of dread building up inside him. They covered the forty miles to the crash scene in just over fifteen minutes. On the approach they could see vehicles on fire and plumes of smoke rising above the motorway.

As the chopper began its slow descent towards the carriageway, Temple was shocked by the devastation. He tried to swallow but had almost no saliva.

Scores of vehicles had ploughed into each other. The road had been turned into a raging inferno of cars, vans and lorries. And there were distressed people everywhere.

It was like landing in the middle of a war zone.

* * *

It was far more horrific than the scene Temple had encountered on the M27, no doubt because he was among the first to arrive.

There were only two police cars already there, one fire engine and a Mercedes Sprinter, its lights strobing in the gloom.

The chopper was put down on the carriageway about forty yards back from the carnage. Temple was the first out the door on to the tarmac and he was struck by the searing heat and the foul odour of oily smoke.

The police, fearing the sniper might still be up on the embankment, were urging people to climb over the central barrier onto the southbound carriageway, which was itself crammed with vehicles that had ground to a halt, bumpers grinding bumpers.

Temple ran to the nearest police car and identified himself to an ashen-faced officer who was on his radio. He had to shout to make himself heard above all the commotion.

'I was told people had been shot? Is that true?'

The officer, a young man who looked to be in a state of shock, raised an arm and pointed.

'Over there and over there,' he said. 'A male and a female. Both shot in the head. They're the only ones we've come across.'

Temple saw two bodies lying on the carriageway. They were being ignored by the paramedics and fire fighters whose first duty was to help the injured and those trapped in their vehicles.

'I need a jacket,' Temple said.

The officer jerked his thumb towards the back of the car.

'Help yourself, sir.'

As Temple slipped on a fluorescent jacket he felt his phone vibrate against his chest. He took it out, checked the ID, and answered it.

'It's me, boss,' he said.

Beresford wanted to know where he was and when Temple told him the Chief Super was rendered speechless.

'I was at the hospital when the call came through,' he explained. 'I hitched a ride with the air ambulance.'

Temple described the scene and told Beresford about the bodies in the road.

'It's total fucking mayhem here,' he said. 'Quite a few of the vehicles are on fire so we might not know for ages how many drivers have been shot.'

As he spoke more emergency vehicles began to arrive and two helicopters appeared overhead.

'For your information the Chief Constable has already spoken to the Home Secretary and the head of the Anti-Terrorism Command,' Beresford said. 'So brace yourself for a big announcement either tonight or tomorrow. This investigation is about to go national.'

'Understood,' Temple said. 'Keep me posted.'

He pocketed his phone and walked over to the first of the sniper's victims. The dead woman was wearing jeans and a dark sweater. The right side of her face had been blown away and blood and brain matter had pooled around her head.

Temple had seen plenty of gunshot wounds in his time. He was pretty sure that it was a high velocity bullet that had killed her. The man's body lay about fifteen feet away. He was wearing a suit and looked quite old. He'd been shot in the back of the head and there wasn't much left of his skull.

Temple felt physically sick at the stark injustice of it. A wave of impotent rage swept his body. It made no sense to him that these two people should be gunned down for no apparent reason. The only thing that connected them was their availability as targets. They were in the wrong place at the wrong time.

He looked up as more fire fighters rushed past him towards the belching smoke and burning wrecks. Behind him lights were popping and sirens blaring. A police helicopter roared overhead as it shone a light on the wooded embankment.

There was still no sign of the armed-response team. They should have been here by now. But Temple doubted that the sniper was still around. Surely he would have scarpered as soon as he heard the sirens and saw the choppers approaching.

He decided to venture up onto the embankment. That must have been where the shots had come from. It would have provided an elevated position, lots of bushes and cover of darkness. Then he noticed a footbridge spanning the carriageway about a hundred yards away. The sniper could just as easily have fired from there with a long-range rifle.

He looked back at the destruction and let out a breath he hadn't been aware he was holding. He saw fire fighters battling with flames and paramedics tending to the injured. And he saw police officers leading people away from the chaos. A shard of guilt twisted in his chest because he wasn't doing anything to help them.

He had to remind himself that he had a different, but no less important job to do.

* * *

The embankment rose about thirty feet above the carriageway. There were clusters of thick bushes with open areas of long grass in between. The ground was soft and damp and

Temple found it hard going in his slip-on shoes.

It didn't take him long to get to the top and thanks to a full moon he could see that there was a small area of woodland beyond the embankment. Through the trees he glimpsed flashing blue lights.

It helped him get his bearings. The air ambulance pilot had told him that the location of the pile-up was close to the village of Popham. The busy A33 road ran parallel with the motorway at this point and only about sixty yards separated them.

The sniper had chosen the perfect location. From where he stood Temple could see that the footbridge that crossed the motorway continued through the wooded area to the A-road. The sniper had probably parked his car or motorbike over there to ensure he had a speedy avenue of escape.

Temple trudged towards the footbridge, poking his key-ring torch between the bushes. He stopped a couple of times to look down on the motorway and saw that from a number of positions the sniper would have had a clear view of traffic coming towards him on the northbound carriageway. He didn't come across anything the sniper had left behind. No impressions in the grass or spent shell casings. But he wasn't equipped to carry out a thorough search. That would be up to the SOCOs.

He came to the iron footbridge and climbed over the railing. Then he walked out across the motorway and stared down at the scene below. There were many more emergency vehicles now and some of the fires had been brought under control. It was still chaotic, though, and Temple found it hard to believe that someone would cause so much damage and distress for no good reason.

As he stood there, his face grew rigid and white with anger. He wished that he hadn't given up smoking. For the first time in ages he craved a cigarette to help calm his nerves and slow his pulse. At that moment a helicopter appeared in the sky above him, its rotor blades whirring frantically. Temple turned away from the fierce beam of light that shone down on him.

As he did so something caught his eye on the floor of the footbridge. A few words scrawled in red paint. He knew instantly that it was another message from the sniper.

As he read it, he felt his blood slowly turn to ice.

19

And so began a long and distressing night on the M3.

Temple played his part by coordinating the efforts of his team of detectives and scene of crime officers. He also liaised with the armed response unit when they finally arrived.

The footbridge and part of the embankment were cordoned off and the search for evidence started in earnest. Blankets were laid over the bodies on the carriageway and the paramedics and fire fighters were told to look out for casualties with gunshot wounds.

The motorway was the scene of frenzied activity: flashing lights, radio static, prostrate forms on stretchers, shouting, crying, vomiting. Those people who hadn't been injured were confused and distraught. Some were draped in foil blankets while they waited to be taken to hospital. Others were consoled by shell-shocked police officers.

Fire fighters spent hours cutting drivers and passengers from wrecked vehicles. By midnight all the fires had been put out and all the vehicles involved in the collisions checked.

The death-toll had reached seven. Matherson, the pathologist, was on hand to determine how many of the dead had been shot. It turned out that four of them had — the two who'd been standing on the carriageway and two others who'd been driving at the time of their deaths. Three more people had serious injuries, one of them a child aged eight.

A lot of drivers had had lucky escapes. Several emerged from smashed-up cars virtually unscathed. One motorcyclist was thrown thirty feet through the air onto the hard shoulder and lived to tell the tale.

Clearing the backed-up traffic was an enormous task in itself. It led to massive congestion on roads throughout the area. As dawn broke the M3 was still closed and littered with blackened wrecks.

And Temple still had no idea why it had happened and how the hell they could stop it happening again.

20

Temple left the scene when there was nothing more he could do there. By that time the smoke was burning his throat and his mind was fogged by fatigue and adrenaline.

DS Vaughan took him home in a pool car and waited while he showered and changed. Vaughan then dropped him off at the hospital so he could pick up his car.

He popped inside to check on Angel, but she was asleep and he chose not to wake her. The nurse told him that she was comfortable and her condition was unchanged.

The incident room was packed and noisy when he got there, and the atmosphere was charged. It was barely twenty-four hours since the last major briefing, but there had been a significant shift in mood and attitude. Everyone was aware that the second sniper attack had turned the investigation into one that would attract worldwide attention. Twelve people had now been killed — six of them shot dead by the sniper. Ten others — including Angel — were in hospital with serious injuries. This was now the biggest case any of the detectives had ever worked on.

The challenge was immense. They had no motive: no promising leads and no clue as to the identity of the sniper, save for the fuzzy image on the security footage. And at the same time the pressure was building. The M3 attack had increased fears among drivers who travelled on motorways. One question being posed in the media was why the motorways attacked were both in Hampshire. Were they picked at random or were they part of a pattern that had yet to emerge?

Temple spent half an hour bringing himself up to date. There were reports to read, calls to return. He also viewed the footage from the traffic cameras on the M3. Although they showed the actual pile-up the picture was poor, even with image enhancement.

First a lorry lost control and then a car. It led to a shunt involving more than fifty vehicles. There was no lighting along that stretch of motorway so both embankments were in total darkness. The sniper wasn't visible and there was no sign of a muzzle flash from a rifle.

A couple of minutes after the crash two figures could be seen walking onto the carriageway after getting out of their cars. Temple's heart gave a horrified lurch when he watched them suddenly fall to the ground having been shot.

He viewed the tape twice more and then spread the word that the briefing was about to begin. He set up two whiteboards with photos and maps and a list of subjects to be covered.

Chief Superintendent Beresford came down along with half the press office. As Temple got things going he wasn't surprised to see lots of red, puffy eyes in the room. Very few of the detectives had had any sleep. They'd spent the night out on the motorway or in the office logging calls and writing up telephone interviews.

Temple had never seen his team so tense and solemn. Fiona Marsh was gnawing at her nails like there was no tomorrow. Dave Vaughan's forehead had deeper creases than the Grand Canyon. And Beresford was chewing frantically on nicotine gum.

There was none of the usual banter and telling of crude jokes. No one tried to lighten the mood with an insult or gratuitous remark. They all understood that this case called for the highest degree of professionalism and the utmost concentration.

'So here's what we have,' Temple said. 'The sniper was up on the embankment just in front of the footbridge that runs between the M3 and the A33.' He pointed to a map that was pinned to one of the boards. 'Last night

SOCOs found four shell casings just here. For the second time the sniper didn't bother to take them with him. Ballistics have confirmed that they match the bullets used in the previous attack.

'Once again he shot two people while they were driving. The bullets went straight through the windscreens. His intention must have been to cause another multiple collision. But this time he also shot two drivers who got out of their cars. All four were struck in the head. That can't have been by accident. This guy is a first-class marksman. And according to ballistics he's using a top-notch sniper rifle.'

Temple produced a sheet of paper that had just been faxed over from the National Ballistics Intelligence Service.

'The experts are a hundred per cent certain that the bullets were fired from a rifle used by the British army,' he said. 'It's the L115A3, also known in the military as the 'silent assassin'.'

Most of the team had heard about the weapon which had earned a deadly reputation in Afghanistan, but they weren't familiar with the details contained in the report.

'The rifle has a folding stock so it can be carried in a backpack or rucksack,' Temple said, reading from the document. 'It has a telescopic sight that can magnify targets up to twenty-five times. It has a five-round magazine and a suppressor that reduces noise and muzzle flash. And it has an effective range of over a thousand yards.'

'That's an impressive piece of kit,' DS Vaughan said.

'Too bloody right it is,' Temple said. 'And it's not the kind of rifle you'd expect an amateur to be using. So there's a good chance the guy is military or ex-military.'

Temple was told that they were still waiting for the Ministry of Defence to get back to them. The team had asked for a list of trained army snipers and military personnel who were currently in the UK. They also wanted details of any servicemen and women who were considered high risk, perhaps because they had a history of mental illness.

'We need that information now,' Temple said. 'So chase up the MOD. If you think they're dragging their feet intentionally then let me know.'

Temple then opened up the meeting to questions and ideas. He wanted to hear their thoughts and theories.

'We should check out the traffic cameras on the A33,' someone said.

Fiona Marsh pointed out that this was in hand.

'Unfortunately, there are no cameras for several miles in either direction from the spot where it happened,' she said. 'And it's a busy road, especially during the rush hour.'

'Should we try to communicate with the sniper?' DS Vaughan said. 'If we can open a line of communication perhaps we'll understand why he's doing it.'

'It's something we should consider,' Temple said. 'We could make a direct appeal during the next press conference.'

This was a cue for the press office people to raise a bunch of issues. They said the media were clamouring for more information. A press conference had already been scheduled for later that morning. There were a dozen requests for interviews and motoring organizations were demanding to know what was being done to keep drivers safe.

Beresford spoke up for the first time at this point, his voice was high-pitched with urgency.

'You don't need me to tell you that these attacks have shocked the nation,' he said. 'If there's another during this evening's rush hour, fear will really get out of hand. Motorways are vital arteries. They keep the country running. If people stop using them then the financial implications will be enormous.'

He paused for a few moments and worked his jaw in circles as though in thought. There were small spots of perspiration on his forehead.

'From the sniper's point of view motorways are easy targets, especially in the dark and when they are busy,' he said. 'Drivers can't see anything beyond the hard shoulders on unlit sections. All the sniper has to do is lie in wait and strike when he's good and ready.

'He also has plenty of time to make good his escape. Motorways are usually surrounded by countryside. The sniper might well be the only pedestrian around for miles. And unless choppers get to the scene within minutes of an attack there's no hope of catching him.'

A low murmur swept through the room. The Chief Super was spelling out a stark reality which most of them hadn't yet come to terms with.

'I've just heard that the Prime Minister intends to convene an emergency meeting later today of the COBRA Committee,' Beresford said. 'The Chief Constable has been asked to attend so that he can brief them on the investigation.'

For Temple this was not an unexpected development. COBRA meets to formulate government responses to national crises. In recent years it had been convened for the London bombings, the fuel strike and the knife attack on the soldier in Woolwich.

'Downing Street wants to be seen to be doing all it can to find this maniac,' Beresford said. 'The sniper's latest message has generated a high degree of concern and it seems certain that the investigation will now be led from London. But that doesn't mean we stop what we're doing.'

Beresford moistened his lips and turned to Temple, 'I gather that only a few of us are aware of what was in the message. I think it's time everyone was told.'

Temple cleared his throat and explained for those who didn't already know that the sniper had sprayed another message in red paint on the floor of the footbridge.

'He must have done it just minutes before he started shooting,' Temple said. 'He would have known that the footbridge would be one of the first places we'd check.'

Temple decided to write the short message on one of the whiteboards so that it would have more impact. He used a black marker pen and wrote it out in big bold letters.

THIS WON'T STOP UNTIL I'M DEAD

Then he stepped back and let everyone see why even the Prime Minister was now quaking in his boots.

21

The sniper's latest message was so alarming that they feared it alone could lead to widespread panic. For that reason Temple did not want it in the public domain.

Much to his annoyance, though, someone went and leaked it to the media. He was tipped off about it just before he faced the second press conference, which meant he at least had time to prepare himself.

'We are indeed taking the message seriously,' he said in answer to a journalist's question. 'As you would expect we're doubling our efforts to catch the sniper. And I'd urge the public to remain vigilant and report anyone they see acting suspiciously close to a motorway.'

'What exactly do you mean by doubling your efforts?' asked a reporter from Sky News.

Temple leaned forward across the table and pinched the bridge of his nose between forefinger and thumb. He kept his voice flat as he spoke into a collection of microphones.

'Aerial surveillance is being stepped up along all motorways,' he said. 'That means more helicopters in the sky during the busiest periods, all with night vision capability. From today we're also putting out more police traffic patrols and we're increasing the number of officers working on the investigation to fifty.'

'Do you believe the sniper will launch another attack during the rush hour this evening?' This from a young female reporter with CNN.

'We really don't know,' Temple said.

'But it's obviously possible,' she persisted. 'In which case what's your advice to drivers planning to travel home from work on motorways? Should they avoid them and use other roads?'

This was a tricky one so Temple didn't respond immediately. He ran his tongue around his mouth in the hope that Beresford, who was sitting next to him, would feel obliged to answer it. But he didn't. So Temple said, 'We can't allow what's happening to affect the way we live our lives. People have to go about their normal business and that includes travelling on all major roads. The sniper can't be everywhere at once so the chances of becoming a victim are miniscule.'

He knew it was a feeble answer, but then he couldn't think what else to say. The last thing he wanted to do was encourage drivers to shun motorways. That would surely lead to chaos on a massive scale. Other roads would become gridlocked, causing heavy lorries to thunder through towns and villages that were ill-equipped to cope with them.

He moved on to talk about the security footage showing the man with the rucksack. The tape — which included shots of the car — had already been widely circulated along with photographs.

'This man is our prime suspect,' he said. 'The car he used was stolen and he parked it as close to the M27 as he could. It's possible he was carrying a weapon in the rucksack. We'd like to hear from anyone who thinks they might know him.'

Temple then gave a description of the L115A3 sniper rifle and pointed out that it was used by the British army, but was also available via the internet.

'This is a very distinctive and powerful weapon,' he said. 'We believe it's what the sniper is using. So we want to know who has one. It could be someone's friend or neighbour. Or a dealer who sold one recently or in the past. Any information we receive will be treated in the strictest confidence.'

The questions continued at a blistering rate and several referred to the government's decision to convene a meeting of the COBRA

Committee. Beresford answered those and said that the investigation was now too big for Hampshire police to conduct alone. He said officers from the Anti-Terrorism Command were already working alongside his own team.

Finally Temple got around to appealing directly to the sniper.

'We have no idea why you're carrying out these shameful attacks,' he said to the cameras lined up in front of the table. 'We'd like you to tell us. You've murdered twelve innocent people. So surely there has to be a point to it. Get in touch and speak to us.'

He knew the appeal would generate numerous hoax calls, but he also knew there was a small chance they'd hear from the sniper himself — if only so he could boast about what he'd done and what he planned to do next.

* * *

After the press conference, Temple retreated to his office and tried to pull his thoughts together. His brain felt splintered and dread lined his stomach.

He viewed yet again the video footage of the pile-ups and the sequence showing the man and woman being gunned down. They'd been identified as Joanna Frome, a 31-year-old secretary, and Phil Kavanagh, a 45-year-old solicitor and father of three. The two drivers murdered in their cars were both men in their fifties.

Temple then read through all the statements that were taken at both scenes and discovered what he already knew: nobody had seen anything, but that was hardly surprising given the circumstances.

Next he turned on his PC and went to Google maps. Using the satellite gizmo he studied the locations of both shootings. He was able to view the motorways and the bridges from various angles, and get a bird's eye view of the areas around them. He could even put himself in POV mode and approach the crime scenes just as though he was driving a car.

What struck Temple was how easy it would have been for the sniper. His victims wouldn't have seen him. The roar of the traffic would have smothered the sound of the shots. And having delivered death to the motorways, he would have been able to leave the scenes at a leisurely pace.

Temple found himself wondering why this hadn't happened before. Had it really not occurred to terror groups like Al-Qaeda that it would be easier to target motorways than planes, tubes and government buildings? A high-powered rifle could do as much damage as a bomb, especially if used to cause a multiple collision involving vehicles travelling at high speed.

Temple picked up a folder containing all the details of those who'd died. He read the names and stared at the photos, his stomach knotting like a ball of twine. He wondered about the sniper. Was he indeed an ex-military man? Someone who'd been trained to kill for a living? Someone who had learned to become emotionally detached from what he did? Someone who was insane or having a breakdown? The fact that he was using a British army sniper rifle suggested he could be, but that didn't narrow the field by much since there were hundreds of military guys out there whose minds had been warped by conflict. The prisons were full of soldiers who'd snapped. In fact former servicemen were significantly over-represented in the prison system when it came to violent crime.

Temple's eyes were suddenly drawn to the TV in the corner of the office. He saw himself speaking earlier at the press conference. Then there was a brief interview with the Home Secretary outside the Cabinet Offices in London where the COBRA Committee meeting was about to start. The volume was turned down so Temple couldn't hear what he was saying.

'I didn't know you could lip read, guv.'

It was DC Marsh. She was standing in the doorway with a quizzical expression on her face.

Temple grinned. 'I'm not really watching it. I'll be out shortly.'

'Well, I've come to tell you that I've just had a call from the MOD,' she said. 'They've arranged for us to meet a senior officer with the Royal Military Police's Special Investigations Branch. He's got information to impart.'

'About bloody time. Is he coming here?'

'No. We're going to him.'

'Oh, right. Where is he?'

'Bulford in Wiltshire. It's where the RMP are quartered.'

22

The day was still grey and washed out as Temple and Fiona Marsh headed north in a pool car.

Marsh checked the internet via her mobile phone for information on the Royal Military Police HQ in Bulford.

'It's on Salisbury Plain, close to Bulford Army Camp,' she said. 'About forty miles from Southampton.'

The RMP were more commonly known as the Red Caps. Their responsibility was the policing of service personnel in the UK and abroad. The Special Investigations Branch dealt with serious crimes and operated in a similar way to the mainstream CID.

'Who's the guy we're going to see?' Temple asked.

'His name is Greg Savage. He's one of their senior investigators.'

'Did you speak to him?'

'No. I took the call from the MOD in London.'

'So you don't know what he's going to tell us.'

'They just said that he's the officer who's

been assigned to respond to our questions.'

'Well, let's hope he's not going to waste our time. It's a long way to go for no good reason.'

They discussed various ideas and theories. She told him that the view among the team was that the sniper was probably not a terrorist. He was more likely a lone psychopath who was either ex-military or an amateur gun fanatic. Someone with a grudge. Or a very loose screw.

'It's amazingly easy for any nutter to lay his hands on a high-calibre rifle,' Marsh said. 'I did a quick search of the internet after the briefing and found three of those army sniper rifles for sale within a few minutes.'

That didn't surprise Temple. Anything could be bought on the highly encrypted section of the internet known as the 'Dark Web'. Thousands of illegal and untraceable transactions took place every day. A whole new dynamic had been added to the business of buying and selling firearms.

'I also didn't realize just how many guns are stolen from the British army,' she said. 'According to one official report more than four hundred weapons have gone missing since 2006 from barracks and depots.'

'What kind of weapons?'

'Mostly rifles and machine guns. Squaddies

sell them on the black market.'

It was a frightening statistic, but Temple wondered just how accurate it was. Whenever figures were released that reflected badly on the armed forces you could be sure they'd been doctored by the MOD.

The true number of missing weapons was probably much higher.

* * *

RMP headquarters. A squat L-shaped building just south of the Bulford Army Base in Wiltshire. Temple and Marsh were met at the gate and escorted to Greg Savage's office.

There they were greeted by a curvy, middle-aged woman with a hint of blush on the apples of her cheeks. Her name was Gaynor and she wore large horn-rimmed glasses that gave her an erudite look.

'Mr Savage is expecting you,' she said. 'I'll bring in coffee and tea so you can take your pick.'

Senior Investigator Greg Savage was sitting behind his desk in an office that looked too small for him. As he stood up to introduce himself Temple saw that he was built like a rugby scrum half. Broad-shouldered and heavy-chested. He was fortyish with a shaved head and a florid face. Temple was surprised he was wearing a sombre grey suit and not a uniform.

He shook their hands and invited them to sit across the desk from him. The office smelled of wax polish and dried flowers. There were photographs on the walls of Red Caps on parade and in combat situations.

'Let me start by thanking you for travelling up from Southampton,' Savage said as he straightened his tie. 'I would have driven down, but I have to attend a court martial at the base in a little while.'

'It's no problem,' Temple said. 'I just hope that what you have to tell us will be helpful to the investigation.'

'I hope so too,' Savage said. 'This really is a bad business. And I'm sure you must be dreading the prospect of further attacks.'

'Damn right we are,' Temple said. 'And since the killer appears to be good at what he's doing we suspect he's a proficient marksman. Which is why we need information on military personnel past and present who've had sniper training.'

'I completely understand,' Savage said. 'But as you can probably appreciate there are scores of people who fall into that category.'

'Well, you can rule out anyone who's overseas at the moment,' Marsh said.

Savage nodded. 'Even so the list of names

is pretty daunting. But we've had a team working on it throughout the night to come up with a shortlist. I asked them to start with men who live or are based in the south of England. Having seen the security footage you released of the man with the rucksack I told them to forget about women. I also told them to flag up guys whom we know have psychological issues, including those who've served time in prison for any reason.'

He tapped a buff-coloured folder on his desk.

'So far they've come up with eight names. I was given the list earlier and I've spent the last two hours going through it. They've done a good job and drew my attention to one man in particular who stands out.'

Temple felt a spurt of adrenaline and wanted to leap up from the chair and grab the folder.

'Who is he?' he asked.

'His name is Cole Renner,' Savage said. 'Lance Corporal Cole Renner. He's a sniper with Four Battalion, the Rifles, which happens to be based here at Bulford.'

'So why does he stand out?' Temple said.

Savage leaned forward across his desk. His breath reeked of peppermint. 'Renner has gone AWOL,' he said. 'He was supposed to report back here for pre-deployment training nearly two months ago. But he didn't show up and we've no idea where he is. Plus I discovered a note that was put on his file three weeks ago. It refers to a phone call we received from one of his former colleagues, a guy named Ryan Addison. Addison wanted us to know that Renner phoned him out of the blue whilst apparently off his head on drink or drugs. Anyway, he told Addison that he was pissed off with the world and wanted to take it out on someone. Addison felt duty bound to report it.'

'So what was done about it?'

'We renewed our efforts to find him, but to no avail.'

'Well, it sounds promising,' Temple said.

Savage sucked in a breath. 'But there's more. Renner was last stationed here in November before he went on leave. That same month one of our large calibre sniper rifles went missing. And it still hasn't turned up.'

23

Savage stopped speaking when his office door opened and Gaynor wheeled in a trolley with flasks of tea and coffee.

'No need to pour them,' Savage said. 'I can do that.'

As Gaynor stepped back out of the office, Savage got up and asked Temple and Marsh what they wanted. They both opted for coffee and while he filled their cups, Temple said, 'The rifle that went missing. Was it an L115A3?'

Savage nodded. 'Indeed it was.'

'We believe the motorway sniper is using one,' Temple said.

Savage raised his eyebrows. 'Then that makes Lance Corporal Cole Renner even more interesting, doesn't it?'

Savage served up the coffee and sat back behind his desk.

'So what can you tell us about him?' Temple said.

Savage stretched out a kink in his neck and picked up the folder. He took out eight sheets of paper, each with a colour photograph attached. He selected one and unclipped the photo, which he passed across the desk to Temple.

'That's him,' Savage said. 'Twenty-eight and single. His parents live in Romsey near Southampton and his father is an army veteran who also served as a rifleman.'

It was a head and shoulders photo of Cole Renner. He had a military-style buzz haircut and a hard face with a thick neck. His eyes were set close together and his nose looked as though it had been broken at some time in the past. His skin was fair and there was a shadow of stubble along his jaw.

Is this the bastard who put Angel in hospital? Temple wondered, feeling the blood stiffen in his veins.

'He's been a sniper for the past four years and is highly rated,' Savage said, reading from the sheet of paper. 'In Afghanistan he killed no less than thirty insurgents. But he's been disciplined twice for fighting and according to his commanding officer he's recently been showing early signs of post-traumatic stress disorder.'

'What signs are those?' Marsh asked.

'Nightmares, flashbacks, difficulty sleeping. He'd been to see a medical officer and was referred to a trauma risk management specialist, but he went AWOL before the meeting took place.'

'So was he considered dangerous?' Temple asked.

'Not at all. PTSD is pretty common in the Forces. Very few people actually flip and become dangerous to themselves and others.'

'But I know from experience that it happens.'

'Of course it does. That's why there are programmes in place to help those who are having problems.'

'And was Renner going to be put on one of those programmes?'

'That would have depended on his assessment.'

Temple thought about it for a moment and became aware that his heart was beating a little faster. But then why wouldn't it? This was a significant development. He sipped at his coffee and felt the pleasing warmth of its passage down his throat.

Then he said, 'Does Cole Renner have an address?'

'He was living with his parents until November,' Savage said. 'He left there after an argument with his dad and that was when he disappeared. Our investigator went to see the couple when Renner failed to show up for training. They insisted they had no idea where he was. The father told us he'd fallen out with his son. Turns out he himself was

151

medically discharged from the army nine years ago because of depression and emotional difficulties. If you want to go and see the parents I can give you their address.'

'Thanks. We'd like to talk to this bloke Addison as well.'

'He lives in Portsmouth. I've got his address too and his file complete with a photo.'

'Is he a close friend of Renner?'

'At one time maybe. But Addison was made redundant from the army eighteen months ago. I'm not sure if they stayed in touch.'

'Have you talked to Addison?'

'No. I dug out his contact details, but I thought you'd probably want to interview him yourselves.'

'And what have you done to find Renner?' Marsh asked.

Savage played with the knot in his tie. 'What we always do with absentees and deserters. We've liaised with the police, circulated his picture, red-flagged his credit card and bank account. He was withdrawing money from his account at ATMs in Southampton until very recently so we think he's probably still in the area. You have to bear in mind that there are scores of deserters out there and we can only do so much with limited resources.'

Savage then ran through the other names on the list his team had come up with and Temple and Marsh looked at the photographs.

'I'd like you to fax this lot over to our incident room,' Temple said. 'The team can get to work on it while DC Marsh and I follow up on Renner.'

'Consider it done,' Savage said. 'Just give me the number.'

Temple gave him the fax number and told him to mark it for the attention of Detective Sergeant Vaughan.

'We have all their prints and DNA on file,' Savage said. 'I'll send those over as well.'

'I appreciate your help,' Temple said, getting to his feet. 'If Renner turns out to be our man, I'll make sure the RMP get the credit.'

'That won't be necessary, but feel free to involve my team if you need more bodies on the ground.'

'I might have to take you up on that offer,' Temple said.

When they got back in the car Temple phoned DS Vaughan and told him about their conversation with Savage.

'You'll get a fax shortly,' he said. 'Start checking the names. And tell Beresford what's going on.'

'What about you, guv? Where will you be?'

'DC Marsh and I will drive to Romsey to talk to Renner's parents. See what they know.'

'You really think this Renner might be the sniper?' Vaughan said.

'It's no more than a credible lead at this stage, Dave. For all we know the guy could be out of the country and he may have had nothing to do with the rifle that went missing from the camp.'

'Well, at least we've got something to get our teeth into at last. There's fuck all else happening.'

'Has there been much response to the press conference appeal?'

'We've been inundated with calls,' Vaughan said. 'We're sifting through them as fast as we can, but it's already obvious that a lot of them are from time-wasters.'

'Any updates on the COBRA meeting in London?'

'Not yet, guv, but it's added fuel to the media firestorm, that's for sure. There's blanket coverage now. Every TV news channel is reporting on the sniper attacks and speculating on whether there'll be another one this evening. And a big haulage company has put up the first reward. One of its drivers was among those badly injured.'

'What are they offering?' Temple asked.

'A £100,000.'

'Well, let's hope it provokes a response,' Temple said.

'I'm sure it will, guv. And if there are more attacks I reckon we'll see even bigger sums put forward by companies who stand to lose business. Did you know that more than two million tons of freight are transported every day on UK motorways?'

'No I didn't,' Temple said.

'Well, that's just one of the statistics being quoted by talking heads on TV. And it's all adding to the hysteria that's being whipped up ahead of this evening's rush hour.'

Temple felt a tightening in his gut.

'If the sniper's objective is to cause panic then he's doing a bloody good job of it,' Vaughn said.

24

Romsey is a small market town about eight miles northwest of Southampton and two miles from junction three of the M27.

Temple knew it well. In fact it was where he and his wife Erin spent their last day out together before the cancer confined her to a bed. The memory surfaced as he drove past the town's famous Norman Abbey where on that day they attended the Sunday service. He remembered how the tears welled in his eyes when Erin knelt before the altar to say a silent prayer. It was a long time ago, but still painfully vivid in his mind.

Dawn and Martin Renner lived half a mile from the Abbey in an end-of-terrace council house with a shabby front garden. There were no cars on the concrete drive which was stained with oil and sprouting weeds. The rundown street was narrow and backed on to wintry skeletal woodland.

Temple parked with two wheels on the pavement. As he and DC Marsh got out of the car he was struck by the sudden drop in temperature. It now felt quite cold. Bruised clouds hung low and fat above the estate.

They walked up the path and rang the bell. The door was opened almost immediately by a skinny woman wearing a short, black skirt and an off-white cardigan. She was somewhere in her early fifties with lack-lustre blonde hair and a harelip.

In one hand she held a mug of something hot and a lighted cigarette.

'Mrs Renner?' Temple said.

She frowned at him, eyebrows almost meeting in the middle.

'Who wants to know?' she said, her voice reedy and high.

He showed his card. 'I'm Detective Chief Inspector Temple and this is my colleague, Detective Constable Marsh. We'd like to talk to you about your son.'

'Does that mean you've finally caught up with him?'

'I'm afraid not. May we come in? We need to ask you some questions.'

She sighed and a tremor passed over her lower lip.

'I suppose so,' she said. 'But you'll have to excuse the state of the place. I've just finished work and haven't had time to clear up.'

She turned and gestured for them to follow her along the hallway. She led them into the living room where the walls were painted a morose shade of grey and the carpet was old and faded. But the sofa looked fairly new and so did the flat-screen television which was showing some confessional talk show, the sound barely above a whisper.

Mrs Renner sat on one of two armchairs and invited them to sit on the sofa. She took a pull on her cigarette and let smoke out in thin jets between her teeth. The smell of tobacco pervaded the room and Temple felt it pinch the back of his throat.

'If you've come to ask me whether I've seen or heard from Cole the answer's no,' she said. 'He hasn't phoned or written to me since he buggered off.'

'Have you tried to call him?'

'I did at first, but then the line was dead so he must have changed his phone and number.'

'Then you have no idea where he is?'

'Not a clue. A couple of people have told me they've seen him around, but that's all.'

'Did those people speak to him?'

'I doubt it. If they did they didn't say.'

'When was the last sighting?'

'I can't remember. Couple of weeks ago maybe. One of the neighbours told me her son saw him in a pub in Southampton.'

She switched her gaze from Temple to DC Marsh and back again. 'So come on,' she said. 'What's all this about? Why the sudden interest again in Cole? Has something happened?'

'We'd like to speak to your husband as well, Mrs Renner?' Temple said. 'Is he around?'

She gave a mirthless grin, showing teeth that were small and sharp.

'I sent him packing just before Christmas,' she said. 'The bastard hit me once too often. Decided I wasn't gonna take any more.'

Temple and Marsh exchanged glances. Temple said, 'Do you know where he is?'

She took another drag on the cigarette and it sparked a phlegmy cough that lasted all of fifteen seconds.

'He's renting some shitty flat across town,' she said. 'But I can tell you now that he's the last person Cole would get in touch with. They fell out big time.'

'Why?'

She turned down the corners of her mouth and shrugged. 'Martin came home drunk as usual. He started slapping me around and Cole tried to stop him. There was a fight and Cole was given a hiding. He's never been a match for his dad. Anyway, that night Cole packed up all his belongings, told me he'd had enough and moved out. That's the last I saw of him. I didn't know he'd done a runner from the army until the military police came

159

here. But it didn't surprise me.'

'Why's that?' Temple said.

'He was stressed out and dreading going back to the base,' she said. 'He was also drinking too much and having mood swings. I sometimes heard him crying in his bedroom. He was never the same after his last tour of duty in Afghanistan. It fucked up his mind.'

'Did he tell you what happened over there?'

'No. He would never talk about it. I tried to help him but he pushed me away.'

'Did he become violent?' Temple asked.

'He was far more aggressive than he'd ever been. And that was a shame because I'd hoped he wouldn't take after his father.'

'Do you think your son is capable of killing anyone, Mrs Renner?'

The question surprised her. Her eyes narrowed as she thought about it. Then she shook her head. 'The honest answer is I don't know. I sometimes thought he was a ticking time bomb. That at any minute he could explode.'

'Were you told that he might have been suffering from post-traumatic stress disorder?' Marsh asked.

Mrs Renner nodded. 'That's what his dad reckoned was wrong with him. Martin was in the army too before they kicked him out.'

Temple found himself feeling a little sorry

for her. She was probably a decent woman whose life had been indirectly ravaged by senseless wars in far-flung places.

'Could your son be staying with a relative?' he asked her. 'Or a friend perhaps?'

'He's got no relatives other than me and his dad. And I don't know any of his friends. Truth is I hardly know my son. He's spent most of the past few years away from home.'

Temple knew it to be a familiar story where a son or daughter served in the Forces. Thousands of young men and women were sent to fight in Iraq and Afghanistan and many of them came back injured. The official Army advice to soldiers was to 'communicate' their feelings, but many of them chose to suffer in silence, thus creating within society a volcano of suppressed emotions.

'You haven't answered my question,' Mrs Renner said. 'Why the renewed interest in Cole?'

'We never lost interest in him,' Temple said. 'But we now want to ask him what he's been doing since he went AWOL. We believe he may be involved in a criminal activity.'

She furrowed her brow. 'What's he supposed to have done then?'

'I'm not at liberty to go into details,' he said. 'But it's important that we find him.'

'Well, as I said, I haven't seen him and I

don't know where he's staying.'

Temple stood up and took out one of his cards, which he handed to Mrs Renner. She scrunched up her eyes and examined it closely.

'If you hear from him or you find out where he is will you please call me?' he said.

She dropped her cigarette butt into an ashtray on the floor next to the armchair and got to her feet.

'Are you going to talk to Martin?' she asked.

Temple nodded. 'Have you got his new address and phone number?'

'They're in the kitchen. I have a terrible memory so I have to write everything down.'

'I'll make a note of them if I may. Does your husband work?'

'I doubt it,' she said. 'In addition to being a wife beater he's also a lazy bastard.'

'Is this the first time you've lived apart?' Temple asked as he followed her into the kitchen.

'It most certainly is,' she said. 'After twenty-eight years of marriage I finally came to my senses.'

25

They left Mrs Renner's house armed with her husband's new address and phone number. His flat was apparently just a mile away.

'When we put out Cole Renner's picture I'd like you to give his mum a call,' Temple said when they were in the car. 'I don't want it to come as a complete shock to her.'

DC Marsh nodded. 'Of course, guv. So what do you think?'

Temple started the engine. 'I think she was telling the truth. She doesn't know where her son is. Or if she does then she's a bloody good liar.'

'What about the stuff she told us?'

'Well, it tallies with the information Savage gave us. Cole Renner sounds like he's cracking up: mood swings, aggression. What he experienced on the battlefield may well have unhinged him. Could be he's angry and has decided to exact revenge on the world at large.'

'I had a friend who was in the army,' Marsh said. 'He enjoyed the camaraderie and lapped up the danger, but when he came back he struggled to adapt to civilian life.'

'What happened to him?'

'He was diagnosed with something called acute stress reaction and ended up in a psychiatric hospital. I lost touch with him after that so I don't know how he got on.'

'It's a big problem,' Temple said. 'You can't help feeling sorry for them. They risk their lives and go through the most appalling experiences. Then they return to a country that seems indifferent to their suffering.'

'I agree, guv. Thank God most soldiers don't respond by going on a killing spree.'

★　★　★

They found Martin Renner's address easily enough using the pool car's sat nav. The flat was above a newsagents and had its own side entrance in a narrow alley.

Temple left the car round the corner in a pay and display car park. Then they walked back to the flat and rang the bell. There was no answer.

'Try calling him, guv,' Marsh said.

He tapped into his mobile phone the number Mrs Renner had given him. But the call went straight to voicemail.

'Shit. He's not picking up.'

The newsagents was open so they went inside and asked the Asian guy behind the counter if he knew who owned the flat upstairs. He said he didn't, but he had seen the new tenant.

'He comes in here to buy his paper,' he said. 'Scruffy bloke. Told me he's just separated from his wife.'

'Have you seen him today?'

'Yeah, early this morning. He got his paper and some cigarettes. But we didn't speak to each other because I had a queue.'

Outside on the street DC Marsh said, 'We could go and see Ryan Addison. Then come back here afterwards.'

'I've got a better idea,' Temple said. 'There's a pub across the road. Let's go have some lunch. I don't know about you but I'm starving.'

The pub was small and cosy, all flagstone and dark wood. There was a roaring blaze going in a large inglenook fireplace and the black beams on the ceiling were hung with chamber pots and pretty plates. The only thing that didn't fit with the rustic theme was a fifty-inch television on one wall that was showing the Sky news channel.

They chose sandwiches from the blackboard menu above the bar. Temple ordered half a pint of lager and Marsh opted for a diet Coke.

They took the drinks to a corner table close

to one of the front windows. Temple positioned his chair so he could see the alley across the road and the front door to Martin Renner's flat. With any luck he'd soon return home.

As he took a sip of his lager, he thought about Angel and decided to give the hospital a call, but just as he was reaching for his phone, Marsh drew his attention to the television.

'I think you need to see this, guv,' she said.

Temple turned to the screen. The scrolling headline read: *Terror squad to take charge of sniper investigation.*

'So now it's official,' Temple said.

The newsreader handed over to a reporter outside the Cabinet Offices in Westminster.

The reporter went straight into a piece-to-camera: 'The Prime Minister has just announced that a special task force is being set up to take over the investigation into the motorway shootings. It follows a meeting of the COBRA Emergency Committee here in London. Detective Chief Superintendent Owen Vickery of the Counter Terrorism Command will lead the task force.'

The reporter explained that the COBRA Committee had been presented with strong evidence to suggest that the motorway shootings were the work of a terrorist with links to Al Qaeda.

Temple arched his eyebrows and wondered where the line about Al Qaeda had come from.

On screen the reporter linked to a short sound-bite from the Prime Minister who spoke in solemn tones.

'These are sickening and barbaric acts of terrorism and they will not go unpunished,' he said. 'We will do everything possible to find the person or persons responsible and I would urge the public to stay calm. Meanwhile our thoughts and prayers are with the families of the victims.'

The reporter then said that DCS Vickery was about to make a statement. The shot changed again to show a sharp-suited black guy standing before a bevy of microphones. Temple had never come across Vickery before. He was in his forties, tall and trim, with an arrogance in his bearing.

Vickery cleared his throat, adjusted his tie, spoke without the aid of notes.

'The Counter Terrorism Command welcomes the opportunity to spearhead a task force that will investigate the motorway shootings,' he said. 'Evidence we put before the COBRA Committee has convinced members that these crimes are the work of terrorists; we believe those responsible have links to Al Qaeda.

'I'm not at liberty to go into details at this stage, but I can tell you that we won't tolerate a reign of terror. This task force will have access to considerable manpower and resources. The Chief Constable of Hampshire has assured me of the support of his team of detectives who are already working on the case. I'll be liaising with them as soon as possible.

'I want to reassure the public: we are determined to catch those responsible for these attacks. Since I've only just received orders regarding the task force I'm not in a position to answer questions, but as soon as the team is in place I'll release more information. Thank you.'

Vickery turned on his heels and walked away from the media scrum to a car that was waiting to whisk him back to New Scotland Yard. Temple felt his spirit shrivel inside him. He turned away from the screen and looked at Marsh.

'So what do you make of it all, guv?' she said.

At that moment the barman arrived and placed their sandwiches on the table.

Temple was no longer hungry. His heart was pumping hard and he was anxious to get going.

He gestured towards the sandwiches. 'If you want yours then you'd better bring it with you.'

He stood up and headed for the door, leaving his own sandwich behind. On the way to the car they checked to see if Martin Renner had returned to his flat. He hadn't so Temple put one of his cards through the letter box. On the back he'd scrawled a message: *Mr Renner. Call me asap.*

26

Temple's phone rang as soon as they set off for Southampton. He took it from his pocket and gave it to DC Marsh, telling her to answer it.

'It's the Chief Super,' she said. 'He wants to speak to you.'

'Tell him I'm driving. And tell him I've heard the news.'

Marsh relayed the message, listened to what Beresford had to say, then said, 'He's arranged a video conference call with DCS Vickery in half an hour. He'd like you to be there, guv.'

'Tell him I wouldn't miss it for the world.'

The phone rang again thirty seconds later. It was DS Vaughan, wanting to know what was happening. Marsh told him about the conference call and Temple said he'd hold a team briefing afterwards to put them all in the picture.

As they sped south along the A36 at just over the speed limit Temple tried to focus his mind on the likely outcome of the new development.

He was keen to know exactly what

evidence had been put before the COBRA Committee. Did it really link Al Qaeda to the shootings? And if it did then why the fuck hadn't they told him about it earlier?

★ ★ ★

Beresford's office was a fair reflection of the man himself — tidy, meticulous, functional. The walls were bare and nothing was out of place.

The burly Welshman was behind his desk when Temple got there, his mouth working hard at a piece of nicotine gum. His expression was grim and he was holding the weight of the world on his shoulders.

'Sit down, Jeff,' he said. 'I'm sorry I wasn't able to tell you about the task force before you heard it elsewhere. The Chief Constable phoned me after the COBRA meeting. But it's what we expected.'

'So what's this terrorist angle?' Temple said. 'And why didn't they bring it to our attention first?'

'That's what we're about to find out. DCS Vickery will be calling any second.'

'What do you know about him?'

Beresford shrugged. 'Not much. He's a high flyer with the Counter Terrorism Command — moved over from the Serious

Organised Crime Agency two years ago —
has a reputation for getting things done.'

Temple was about to brief Beresford on his
meeting with Greg Savage when the call from
Vickery was put through. The DCS appeared
on Beresford's computer screen a moment
later and Beresford adjusted it so he and
Temple were framed by the in-built camera.

Vickery was sitting behind a big desk in
London and it looked to Temple as though he
was puffed up with self-importance. He'd
removed his jacket and loosened his silk tie
and his eyes peered over a pair of designer
glasses.

After brief introductions, Vickery said, 'I
won't beat about the bush, gents. This
investigation has moved up a gear and I need
to get to grips with it fast. I don't expect you
to be happy about losing control, but that's
the way it is. So if it's going to be a problem
then tell me now.'

Temple felt his hackles rise, but decided to
rein in an audible sigh. He saw no point in
getting off on the wrong foot just because
Vickery wanted to establish at the outset that
he was the boss.

'We don't have a problem with it,'
Beresford said. 'You can expect our full
cooperation.'

Vickery nodded, satisfied. 'Good. That's

exactly what I wanted to hear. So let's get straight down to business.'

'Before we do there's just one thing I'd like to know,' Temple said.

A frown wrinkled Vickery's forehead. 'Go on.'

Temple pursed his lips and said, 'Why weren't we given the heads-up before an announcement was made on television?'

'There was no time,' Vickery said. 'I didn't know myself until after I presented evidence to the COBRA Committee. They decided then and there that it was the best way to deal with the threat posed by the sniper. And your Chief Constable was in full agreement. He also went along with the decision to announce it straight away — before you guys had been informed.'

Temple stuck out his bottom lip. 'So shouldn't you have let me know about this evidence first? I was in charge of this case up to an hour ago.'

Vickery blew out his cheeks. 'Until late last night there was nothing I could have told you. We received information and my commander referred it directly to the Home Secretary. He then convened COBRA and I was told to attend.'

Temple shrugged. 'So what is this evidence?'

Vickery cleared his throat and sat back in his chair. Then he waited a few beats before speaking.

'We were told by one of the sniper's accomplices that a terror campaign had been launched to target motorways,' he said.

Temple and Beresford were thrown by this revelation. It wasn't what either of them had expected to hear and the shock was evident in their expressions.

'I think it's time we were put in the picture,' Beresford said.

27

'Three months ago rumours started circulating in certain Muslim communities that a small Al Qaeda cell in the UK was planning a terror attack,' Vickery said. 'We'd been expecting something to happen because things had been too quiet for too long. Plus the Al Qaeda online propaganda magazine, *Inspire*, has been urging its followers to inflict maximum damage with whatever means at their disposal. In other words: just do something.

'Then one of our people in Pakistan was told about an English national named Yousef Hussain who'd recently spent several weeks at a terrorist training camp outside Islamabad. He'd never appeared on our radar which is why he wasn't flagged up when he returned to the UK. It was soon obvious that he had become a radicalized Muslim and that he was preparing himself for some kind of jihadist mission in London.

'We traced him to a flat in Stratford which he shared with two other men — one from Somalia and the other from Algeria. Both were known to MI5, but were considered low risk. So we put them all under surveillance.

'None of them went to work, but they had plenty of cash and could afford to run a car. We eavesdropped on a few of their conversations and managed to hack into an email account they were all using.

'A familiar story emerged. All three had been brainwashed to kill in the name of a perverted politicized version of Islam. They talked about striking terror in the capital and several times one or the other said it was going to happen imminently. It got us worried so we decided to move in.'

'Is this to do with the arrests you guys made early last week?' Temple asked.

'That's right. We raided the flat when we thought all three were there, but unfortunately we cocked up because Hussain had slipped away.'

'I remember,' Temple said. 'You circulated his picture.'

Vickery nodded. 'That's right. We had no idea what he was up to. After their arrests his two accomplices didn't say a word. Then suddenly the Somali guy asked to see me last night. He said he had something to say and took great pleasure in telling me that Hussain was the sniper and that despite our efforts their mission was being carried out as planned.'

'And you believe him?' Temple said.

'No reason not to. He describes himself as a soldier and is keen to claim responsibility for the attacks on behalf of Al Qaeda.'

'So was there anything in the flat to support his claim?'

'We found three forged passports and some explosive substances, including sulphur powder and potassium nitrate. Plus two pistols, a number of knives and a book on how to make a Semtex bomb.'

'What about maps of motorways or rifle cartridges?'

'Nothing like that, but the Somali guy said they kept that stuff somewhere else.'

'Did you manage to seize their laptop?' Beresford asked.

Vickery nodded. 'We did and we came across an email account they'd been using. A few of the messages referred to a job that was underway in London.'

They lapsed into silence for a spell as Temple and Beresford took in what Vickery had told them. And there was a lot to take in. Temple knew that there were followers of Islam living in Britain who might be prepared to carry out murder in the name of jihad. Many of their most spectacular plots had been foiled by the security services in recent years. More 'lone wolf' fanatics with links to

Al Qaeda were acting on their own initiative — and coming up with increasingly ingenious ways to inflict terror.

'If Yousef Hussain is indeed the sniper then his undoubted aim will be to kill as many people as he can and cause turmoil across the country,' Vickery said. 'He knows the attacks will trigger an avalanche of national and worldwide publicity. It's the kind of exposure they yearn for. So you can see why COBRA felt it was necessary to set up a task force. If we don't find this guy then God knows what the final death toll will be.'

Temple shook his head. 'I get all that, but despite what you've said I'm not sure we should put all our eggs in one basket?'

Vickery's eyebrows shot up. 'So you think the Somali guy lied?'

'I honestly don't know,' Temple said.

'Well, I was the one who spoke to him and I happen to think he was telling the truth. He wants the world to know that they've found a new way to strike terror.'

'But he might be claiming credit because you scuppered their real mission when you raided the flat and arrested them,' Temple said. 'For all you know Hussain might have fled to Pakistan.'

'That's unlikely. For me it's too much of a coincidence. The three of them have clearly

178

been planning something. Then just a week after one of them disappears, motorways come under attack.'

'Coincidences do happen,' Temple pointed out.

Vickery's eyes narrowed and Temple could see that he was not happy explaining himself.

'Well, as far as I'm concerned Hussain is the number one suspect,' Vickery said. 'His height and build even match the hooded guy in the security footage you put out. So until we can put someone else in the frame this task force will focus on him.'

'We do have someone else in the frame as a credible suspect,' Temple said.

Vickery tilted his head sideways. 'Are you serious? Your Chief Constable told me you had no suspects.'

'He doesn't know yet,' Temple said. 'The guy's name emerged this morning. He's Cole Renner and he's a trained army sniper who's gone AWOL. It's also possible that he stole a rifle from his camp in Wiltshire. The same kind of rifle being used by the sniper.'

Vickery twisted his lips in thought and gave a slight nod.

'OK, you'd better tell me more,' he said.

So Temple filled him in on what he was told by Greg Savage and by Renner's mother. And Vickery chewed on his lower lip as he listened. When Temple had finished Vickery worked his jaw in circles as he thought it through. Then he agreed — reluctantly it seemed to Temple — that it was a lead worth pursuing.

'Just hold back for now on releasing Renner's photo,' he said. 'We're about to circulate a picture of Hussain and I don't want to confuse the issue, but do all you can to trace Renner, if only to rule him out.'

'It'll speed things up if we can release his picture,' Temple said.

'It'll also divert attention away from Hussain and I don't want that. You've only just been alerted to Renner so you might run him down by this time tomorrow and find out he's a poor fucked up soldier who's done nothing wrong.'

Temple swallowed a sharp retort and said nothing.

'Meanwhile send me everything you've gathered so far,' Vickery said. 'I want to get this task force mobilized as quickly as possible.'

'What happens if there's another attack this evening?' Beresford asked.

'We play it by ear,' Vickery said. 'If it's in your region then you'll have to respond. If it's outside Hampshire I'll work with the local Force. At some point I'll bring everyone together for a meeting, probably in London.'

They talked for another ten minutes about various aspects of the case and Vickery provided some background information on Yousef Hussain and his accomplices. Then, as he drew the meeting to a close, Vickery said, 'I've been told that one of your officers, DI Angelica Metcalfe, was among those injured in the first attack on the M27.'

Temple creased his brow and said, 'That's right. She's in hospital.'

'How is she?'

'She's got a punctured lung, a couple of fractured ribs and a blood clot in her head,' Temple said. 'But I'm hopeful she'll make a full recovery. Thank you for asking.'

Vickery nodded. 'You probably don't know this, but DI Metcalfe and I worked together on a case about a year ago. That was just before she left the Met to move to Southampton.'

'Really? What was the case?'

'The Joseph Roth murder. You might recall that he was the police officer who posed as a Muslim convert and helped us uncover a plot to blow up four London hotels. He was shot dead in the crossfire when we tried to arrest them.'

'I remember the case,' Temple said. 'In fact Angel mentioned it just the other day.

181

Something about a memorial service. She said she was hoping to go along to it.'

'That's right. The mayor of London has arranged a special gathering at a church in Catford this Friday to mark the first anniversary of Roth's death. I'll be attending myself if I can.'

'Well, Angel won't be going I'm afraid.'

'And that's a shame. It would have been good to see her again. She's a nice person and a fine detective. I hope she soon recovers and I'd appreciate it if you would pass on my best to her.'

'I'll be glad to,' Temple said and a second later the screen went blank.

28

The M25.

That man-made monstrosity that inspired the Chris Rea hit song *Road to Hell*.

One hundred and seventeen miles of grey tarmac encircling London. It's the busiest motorway in Europe and since opening in 1986 it's been a nightmare for drivers — constant congestion, endless road works, more traffic than it can cope with.

This evening's rush hour was as busy as ever despite the hysteria over the first two attacks. The sniper had positioned himself at a spot between junctions eight and nine, just south of Epsom Downs.

He was standing behind a clump of bushes on a low embankment, out of reach of the lights on the central reservation. It was an isolated spot, chosen after careful thought. There were a couple of farms in the area, but they were some distance off and concealed by trees and hedges.

To his right was an area of thick woodland as black as tar. Behind him the embankment descended steeply to a minor country lane that passed beneath the motorway. That was where he'd left the Suzuki motorcycle that would whisk him away from here as soon as the deed was done. He could make good his escape by heading north or south and be miles away before the first emergency crews arrived on the scene.

A heavy frost was beginning to settle, but despite the cold his back felt warm and wet with sweat. He looked up at the sky, at faint clusters of stars, and he felt his heart beating rapidly.

He took a long, deep breath and emptied his mind of everything, everything except the job at hand. He looked down on the traffic moving west to east. All four lanes were flowing fast with only about ten yards between most of the glaring sets of headlights.

As he raised the rifle he felt completely at ease. These killings had become routine. He was just going through the motions; one deadly step at a time until he'd reached his goal. He didn't feel a thing for his victims. He didn't know them. They were just a means to an end.

He flipped the lens cap off the scope and pressed his left eye against it. He willed his heart to slow, breathed out, kept his lungs empty.

He stared through the scope until the

crosshairs settled on a car windscreen. Then he focused on the vague shape beyond it. He counted his heartbeat, corrected for the wind . . . and pulled the trigger.

The rifle cracked and bucked against his shoulder.

Then he flicked the bolt, jacking out the spent cartridge, before homing in on another target.

29

It was 5.30 p.m. when Temple finished briefing the troops. The session had lasted a solid hour because there'd been a lot to get through.

He told them about Cole Renner and relayed the conversation with DCS Vickery about Yousef Hussain. There was a lukewarm response to the setting up of the task force, but that didn't surprise him. Like him, the team were wary of losing control of the investigation, but they all understood the reason for it.

He listened to the various updates and reports. He learned that they were sifting through no less than twenty-four hours' worth of CCTV footage taken from cameras around the crime scenes on the M27 and M3. They were now trying to make contact with the other men on the list that Greg Savage had produced. But it was slow going under intense pressure.

After the briefing, Temple called the hospital and was told that Angel was asleep. He asked them to tell her he'd be along later. He didn't know what time, of course, because that would depend on the sniper.

Like everyone else Temple was on edge, wondering if there would be another attack on another motorway.

He had to wait until just after 6 p.m. to find out.

⋆   ⋆   ⋆

This time it was the M25 in Surrey.

The incident room became as still as a cemetery when the news broke. Within seconds every television monitor was tuned to a news channel.

There was a mixture of shock and relief among the detectives. Shock that it had actually happened and relief that it wasn't in Hampshire so they didn't have to rush out to another distressing scene.

At first the reports just said there had been a serious accident on the motorway. Then it became a multiple crash with many vehicles. Then confirmation that shots had been fired and eyewitnesses were reporting bodies on the carriageway.

As Temple watched he felt a cold shiver wash over him. How many people would die this time? he wondered. How many wives and husbands would lose their spouses? How many more children would be orphaned? A dark rage flared inside him, like a hard, burning flame.

'We need to catch this bastard,' DC Marsh said as she stepped up beside him. 'This is beyond a joke.'

He turned to look at her. Her face was strained and there were dark smudges of tiredness under her eyes.

Like everyone else she was totally exhausted. The case was wearing her down and eating into her soul. The job of a murder detective is a test of sanity at the best of times, but this went beyond that. There were so many victims. So many completely pointless deaths. It was impossible to remain professionally detached.

Beresford came down to the incident room to inform Temple that Vickery was on his way to the M25 where he'd be joining officers from Surrey Police.

'We're on stand-by,' he said. 'If Vickery needs us we'll respond. In the meantime we crack on with our own enquiries.'

On TV the newscasters were telling viewers that there was gridlock on the M25 and warning drivers to steer clear of the area. At the same time they were asking the questions that everyone wanted answers to.

How many people were dead? How many had been shot? Had the sniper got away? How many vehicles were involved?

Within fifty minutes of the pile-up the first aerial footage was relayed live from a news helicopter. It was a familiar scene: flashing lights, burning cars, heavy smoke, overturned lorries and emergency crews in reflective yellow jackets.

Then came details about the exact location. Roughly halfway between junctions eight and nine. The eastbound carriageway. South of Epsom downs.

DS Vaughan ran a search on Google and called Temple over to his computer. They looked first at the map showing the location and then switched to the satellite image. It looked as though the sniper had been positioned on a wooded embankment next to an underpass. They moved on to the ground-level POV image and saw that it was an isolated spot surrounded by woods.

'He's picked another good place,' Vaughan said. 'Well concealed and quiet. Escape routes to the north and south. He'll be miles away by now.'

Information came in throughout the evening direct from officers at the scene and from the TV news teams. By 9 p.m. it was clear that it was the worst attack yet in terms of casualty numbers.

At least twelve had died — four gunned down when they got out of their vehicles and two shot whilst driving. A family of three had perished in one car when it burst into flames after being hit by a lorry and three others had died when their vehicles collided.

More than thirty people had been injured, some seriously, and about a hundred vehicles had been involved in the pile-up.

Beresford took a call from Vickery. The DCS wanted them to know that the sniper had left another message. It was sprayed on a wall of the underpass. It read: *Until the next time.*

30

Angel's room was filled with soft white light. The air was warm and static and smelled of eucalyptus. As Temple approached the bed, her freckled cheeks lifted with a gentle smile.

'I'm sorry I couldn't get here sooner,' he said. 'But it was impossible to get away.'

He kissed her gently and tasted toothpaste on her lips.

'I've been following the news,' she said. 'I can hardly believe what's happening.'

He turned to look at the small TV screen. It was showing a map of the M25. The crawler caption at the bottom read: *Third sniper attack. More drivers shot.*

'They're saying he shot people outside their cars again,' Angel said.

Temple turned back to her. 'This guy's a fucking monster,' he said. 'He's now killed a total of twenty-four people. Twelve of them shot dead.'

Angel reached for his hand and squeezed his fingers.

'I can see it's getting to you,' she said.

He couldn't deny it so he just nodded. He was a hard-bitten detective with many years' experience, but this case was proving to be the biggest challenge of his life. It was twisting him up inside and making him question his faith in humanity. He'd hunted serial killers before. He'd brought rapists and child murderers to justice. But no case had ever crawled under his skin like this one. Nothing he'd encountered in the past had prepared him for what he was now witnessing.

And it was beginning to show. He cut a dishevelled, rather mournful figure. His eyes were bloodshot and his face was wrinkled with stress lines. His white shirt was crumpled, the tie drooping from the unbuttoned collar.

'How are you feeling, sweetheart?' he asked her.

'My ribs catch every now and then and it hurts like hell, but the medicine's a godsend.'

'And the blood clot?'

'I had another scan this morning. It's unchanged.'

'That's a relief.'

She creased her brow. 'You look tired, Jeff. You need to sleep.'

In fact he was so tired it felt like sludge was running through his veins. His muscles were heavy and weak and a dull weariness that went beyond exhaustion pervaded his body.

'Have you met your new boss yet?' she asked.

'You mean Vickery?'

She nodded.

'We had a conversation via video link,' he said. 'He told me you two know each other and he sends his best wishes.'

'We worked together on the Joseph Roth case,' Angel said.

'I know. Vickery told me. He said he was hoping to see you at Roth's memorial service.'

'That's right. This Friday. I had planned to go. It'll be a big event. Roth was well liked and it was thanks to him that the terrorists were caught.'

'And what was it like working with Vickery?'

'He was OK. A bit cocky, and very direct. But a good copper. What about you? What was your impression?'

Temple shrugged. 'I think I've already put his back up.'

'Why?'

'He's convinced the sniper is an Al Qaeda terrorist. I'm not.'

He pulled over a chair and sat down. Then he brought her up to date on everything. This time she was more responsive. She listened to what he said and nodded a couple of times.

He took this to be a good sign.

'They're both credible suspects,' she said. 'But Vickery's bound to focus on Hussain because that's the reason he's been brought in to head up the task force. I think you're right to be wary though. His accomplice might be lying in order to achieve some notoriety.'

'That occurred to me too,' he said. 'But I'm also bothered by the messages that have been left. Terrorists don't usually leave messages. And when they do it usually refers to a jihad or something.'

'Have you raised that with Vickery?'

'Not yet. But I will when we talk next.'

'Then again it might be neither of them,' Angel said.

'That's the problem. It could be just about anyone who knows how to fire a rifle — including a screwed-up police marksman.'

★   ★   ★

The first thing Temple did when he got home was to pour a large, neat whisky. He downed it in one go and felt his cheeks warming as it spread into his bloodstream. Then he made himself a cheese sandwich and munched on it in front of the television.

Coverage of the latest attack continued.

194

There were sound bites from emergency crews and survivors. Journalists were reporting live from the motorway and from outside several hospitals. DCS Vickery gave a brief interview in which he described the scene on the motorway as horrendous. He also said he believed the attacks were part of a terror campaign backed by Al Qaeda.

There were maps and graphics and images showing where the pile-up had occurred and the likely location of the sniper. They ran footage showing armed police on the embankment and in the woods. And there were talking heads in the studio discussing the knock-on effect for drivers and businesses.

Temple felt a pressure forming behind his eyes. He finished his sandwich and poured another whisky. He thought about what he would do tomorrow and made some notes. He would go and see Renner's father and also Ryan Addison, the friend whom Renner had called to say he was pissed off with the world and wanted to take it out on someone. Temple needed to forge ahead with this line of inquiry if only to determine whether or not he was wasting his time.

After a while it was a struggle to stay awake. His thoughts became jumbled and he became aware of a dull ache at the back of his skull. He closed his eyes and slumped back on the sofa. He could still hear the TV and told himself he ought to get up and switch it off before going to bed. But he never got to do it because he quickly slipped into the black treacle of unconsciousness.

31

Thursday morning and Temple was driving past the spot on the M27 where the sniper had carried out his first attack. The inside lane was closed as repairs were still underway and a sheet of tarpaulin covered the spray-painted message under the bridge. A single police car was parked next to it, with an officer inside. Another was standing on the embankment with a couple of men in suits.

For Temple it was a surreal experience, especially as he was listening to the news on the radio about the latest attack on the M25. That stretch of motorway was still shut down and there was traffic chaos. Hundreds of thousands of vehicles were being diverted on to minor roads, causing gridlock in towns and villages.

The M27 was relatively quiet. It was 10 a.m. so the rush hour was over and Temple was making good time. He had decided to go by himself to Portsmouth to interview Ryan Addison. He'd called his number before leaving home and luckily the former soldier had picked up and agreed to meet him in a café around the corner from his flat.

Temple had managed just a couple of hours of fragmented sleep on the sofa, but he felt refreshed after a shower and some toast. He still wasn't sure what to make of the terrorist theory that was gaining momentum. A photo of Yousef Hussain had been released: he was clean-shaven with shoulder-length dark hair and an olive complexion. He was wearing John Lennon glasses and a wry smile. DCS Vickery was telling the media that Hussain was wanted for questioning in connection with the shootings. Temple wasn't convinced; though he was well aware that terrorists were increasingly varying their tactics in order to heighten the level of shock, these attacks did not bear the hallmarks of an Islamic fundamentalist. Of course this didn't mean they weren't being committed by an individual inspired by Al Qaeda ideology.

Vickery had also announced that more reward money was now being offered for information leading to the sniper. Scotland Yard had agreed to set up a centralized fund into which it could all be put. Contributions had come from businesses, national newspapers, anonymous donors and even the parents of Joseph Roth, the police officer whose memorial service was taking place on Friday.

They had offered to put £2,000 into the pot which had already reached a staggering £500,000.

Temple knew that a big reward would generate a lot of interest and focus the minds of the public. But rewards were also an indication that the police were desperate for help and struggling to move forward with a case.

* * *

The café was close to the naval base in Portsmouth. It was a greasy spoon establishment with lino on the floor and blue plastic tablecloths.

There were half a dozen customers, including Ryan Addison, who was sitting next to the window. Temple recognized him immediately from the photograph Greg Savage had provided. In the picture he was in uniform and sporting a crew cut. But now he was wearing a padded lumberjack shirt and his hair looked like it was a month overdue for a trim.

'You must be Mr Addison,' Temple said as he approached the table.

The young man was already on his feet and Temple guessed he must be about five foot eight and twelve stone or so.

'That's me,' Addison said.

Temple held out his hand and Addison took it. His grip was firm and his palm felt calloused.

'Thanks for taking the time to see me,' Temple said.

'D'you want a cuppa?'

'Coffee would be great.'

Addison got the attention of the woman behind the counter and ordered a coffee and a tea.

Temple studied him for a moment. He had a lean, wolfish look and there was a dark, brooding intensity in his sunken eyes. Temple had seen the expression in the eyes of other soldiers whose minds had been marked by the horrors of war. It was as though they were reliving the hideous experiences over and over again inside their heads.

According to Savage's notes, Addison was twenty-nine and had served three tours of duty in Helmand Province with Four Rifles. He'd received various commendations and seen plenty of action on the front line. Eighteen months ago he'd been made redundant from the army as part of a major cost-cutting exercise by the MOD.

Temple pulled out a chair and sat down. Addison furrowed his brow and said, 'So what's this about, Inspector? You were pretty cagey on the phone.'

Temple had told him only that he wanted to discuss a former colleague from the army.

'I'm trying to trace Cole Renner,' Temple said. 'I know he phoned you after he went AWOL and that you were concerned enough to alert the Military Police.'

'That was the first time he called,' Addison said. 'He's phoned me a few times since then and we even met up for a drink.'

Temple felt his pulse quicken. 'Why the hell didn't you inform the RMP?'

'Cole asked me not to,' Addison said defensively.

'So when did you meet him?'

Addison licked his lips and narrowed his eyes a little. 'About two weeks ago, I think. He was desperate to borrow money. I had a couple of hundred put by so I gave him some.'

'Where did this meeting take place?'

'The Fortress pub in Southampton.'

'Was it just you and him?'

Addison nodded. 'Yeah, but look, if you're after nicking me because I didn't turn him in . . .'

'No, you're not in trouble,' Temple said. 'But Renner might be. So I need you to tell me where I can find him.'

Addison hunched his shoulders. 'I've got

no idea. Honest. I don't even have his phone number. He calls me when he wants to chat and it's usually from a public phone.'

'So he hasn't told you where he's living?'

'No. And I haven't asked him.'

'When was the last time he called?'

Addison sucked his lips in thought. 'Last Wednesday I think. He rang when I was in the jobcentre so I couldn't speak to him for long.'

'What did he want?'

'Nothing really. Just a chat — and to tell me he's hoping to pay me back soon. I don't think he has anyone else to talk to. And he's paranoid, thinks all his friends are under surveillance.'

'What did you talk about when you met?'

'He told me he was lodging in Southampton, but needed money to pay the rent. He said he was hoping to do some off-the-cards work. He was really down and sounded desperate.'

'In the earlier call he said he was pissed off with the world and wanted to take it out on someone. Is that right?'

'Yeah, he was pretty angry then. And he was still pissed off the last time we spoke.'

'So do you think he's having some kind of mental breakdown?'

Addison sucked on his bottom lip. 'I'm not

sure about that. But I do think he needs help.'

'What do you mean?'

The tea and coffee arrived so Addison waited for the woman to retreat before answering.

'Cole spent too much time on the front line,' he said. 'He killed a lot of people and saw a lot of his friends die. It got to him like it gets to most of us. He couldn't face the prospect of another tour so he deserted. But now he can't hack it on civvy street. He's like a lost soul. It doesn't help that he gets no support from his family, especially his dad who's a violent bully.'

'So what's Renner like?' Temple said.

Addison blew on his tea and thought about it.

'He can be moody and he has a temper,' he said, 'but he's a good mate. When I was made redundant I was given a derisory pay-off. I felt this crippling sense of abandonment and betrayal. The army didn't give a fuck and the only person who stayed in contact was Cole. Before he went AWOL he even asked me if I needed money. That's why I was prepared to help him. And it's why I got worried when he phoned me in a state. I thought that if the RMP could find him they might be able to help.'

'What was Renner like as a soldier?'

Addison drank some tea before replying. 'He was in his element during the first two tours. He was one of the regiment's best snipers and killing seemed to come naturally to him. But during the third tour he became disillusioned, as did most of us. The whole thing began to seem pointless and then to make things worse the government announced mass redundancies. Can you imagine what that did to morale?'

'Why wasn't Renner made redundant?'

'Because he was a trained sniper and the MOD decided they wanted to keep people like him on board at least for a bit longer.'

Temple sipped at his coffee and reflected briefly on just how badly the government had treated all the soldiers who fought bravely in Afghanistan. Thousands had lost their jobs on their return and were now struggling to make ends meet. He couldn't help feeling sorry for men like Addison and he could well understand why they felt aggrieved.

'Do you know if Renner is in possession of any weapons?' Temple asked.

Addison lifted his head. 'Why do you ask?'

'We've reason to believe that he might have stolen a rifle from the Bulford Camp the last time he was there. If so then he poses a major threat to the public. We need to find him and we need to know for certain whether he's armed with a rifle.'

The muscles in Addison's neck visibly tightened and his eyes grew wide.

'I think I know where you're going with this,' he blurted. 'The motorway sniper! You think it might be Cole.'

Temple cast his eyes around the café to see if any of the other customers had overheard, but it didn't appear so.

'It's true, isn't it?' Addison said. 'That's what this is all about.'

'We're anxious to rule out everyone who's had sniper training,' Temple said. 'And Renner is of particular interest because he's disappeared — and because of what he said to you.'

'But on the news they're blaming a terrorist. They're even showing some bloke's picture.'

'That man is one of a number of suspects,' Temple said. 'As is Renner.'

Addison broke off eye contact with Temple for a few moments and stared off into the middle distance. Then he shook his head.

'Look, I don't know if Cole has a rifle,' he said. 'He's never mentioned it to me. But I can tell you that it's fairly easy to swipe weapons from army bases. Believe it or not it happens all the time.'

'So I've heard,' Temple said.

Addison bit down on his bottom lip and his face stiffened.

'I've just thought of something he mentioned to me,' he said. 'It might be helpful.'

'What is it?'

'Well, when he told me about not being able to pay his rent he said that he was being hounded for it by his landlady and that she was pregnant. And he said he thought he was paying over the odds for a tiny flat in a not very nice house in Southampton.'

'Did he say anything else about this woman?'

Addison thought about it for a moment and shook his head.

'I'm afraid not.'

Temple noted this down. There can't be that many pregnant landladies in Southampton, he thought.

'Can you remember anything else about the conversation?' he asked.

Addison shook his head. 'I'm sorry, no.'

'Well, contact me if anything comes to mind,' Temple said. 'The sooner we can track down Lance Corporal Renner the sooner we can rule him out of our inquiries.'

'Or arrest him for mass murder,' Addison said.

Temple said nothing, just shifted his shoulders in a slow shrug.

206

32

Something Addison had said played on Temple's mind as he drove back along the M27 towards Southampton.

'He was one of the regiment's best snipers and killing seemed to come naturally to him.'

Did that mean Renner was a natural-born killer? Was he just as capable of committing cold-blooded murder outside the theatre of war? These were questions that could probably only be answered with the benefit of hindsight. Right now the only thing that seemed certain was that Lance Corporal Cole Renner had some serious mental problems; Greg Savage, Ryan Addison and even Renner's own mother had described him as a deeply disturbed man — a 'lost soul' filled with anger and resentment, and perhaps consumed by a warped sense of injustice.

Temple realized these were probably the same motivating factors that had turned Yousef Hussain into a terrorist.

Another obvious comparison between the two men was their education: Hussain had travelled to a terrorist training camp in Pakistan to learn how to commit mass

207

murder and Renner had, for several years, been used as a killing machine by the British army. Temple could visualize both men on a motorway embankment aiming a rifle at the traffic.

He called the incident room on his hands-free and spoke to DS Vaughan. He told him about his conversation with Addison.

'See if you can track down a pregnant landlady,' he said. 'It's a long shot, but it might pay off. She's apparently renting out a flat to Renner in Southampton.'

'Will do, guv. Are you on your way back?'

'I'm about to phone Renner's father. If he's around I'll head over to Romsey.'

'Well, for your information the Chief Super was here a few minutes ago asking for you. There's a task-force meeting in London at 4 p.m. this afternoon and he wants you to go.'

'I've been expecting to be summoned at some point,' Temple said. 'Do you know where it's taking place?'

'The Yard.'

'Then tell Beresford I'll be there.'

Temple hung up and rang the number Mrs Renner had given him for her husband. It rang six times before it was answered.

'Hello.'

'Is that Mr Martin Renner?' Temple asked.

'Yeah. Who's this?'

'I'm Detective Chief Inspector Temple of Hampshire police.'

'I got your card. I was going to get in touch later today.'

'Well, I'd like to talk to you about your son, Mr Renner.'

'I figured as much. I saw you on the telly last night at that press conference.'

'Then you know that because Cole is a trained sniper he's on the list of people we need to interview.'

'I told the Red Caps weeks ago that I don't know where he is. I still don't.'

'Nevertheless anything you can tell us about him might be of assistance. You see we believe that your son may have obtained a firearm illegally and we're therefore treating him as a serious suspect in the shootings.'

There was a long pause during which Temple could hear the other man breathing into the phone.

'If you have information about Cole then I need you to give it to me,' Temple said. 'People are being murdered at an alarming rate and if your son is responsible then he has to be stopped.'

After a moment, Renner cleared his throat and said, 'I don't believe for a minute that he is the person who's doing this, Inspector, but I do know he stole a rifle from the army base in Wiltshire a while ago.'

'How do you know?'

'Because he told me.'

Temple felt his muscles go rigid.

'Are you at home, Mr Renner?'

'I am.'

'Then stay put. I'll be there in fifteen minutes.'

33

Martin Renner's flat was small and shabby — the furniture was old and the carpets worn. Damp patches stained the walls.

The man himself was overweight and anaemic. His eyes were glazed and rheumy and there was a map of blood vessels in his cheeks.

Temple followed him into his tiny living room where Renner lit a cigarette. They sat opposite each other on armchairs. Temple noticed an open copy of the *Mail* on the coffee table. On the front page was a large picture of the carnage on the M27 and a smaller picture of the hooded man in the security video from the industrial unit. The image was blurred and no identifying features were visible.

Renner sucked so hard on his cigarette it made his cheekbones bulge. Then he coughed, rattling phlegm in his throat.

'I gave up for a time,' he said, as though he felt the need to explain himself. 'But when I get stressed I light up. It's hard not to.'

'I know the feeling,' Temple said. 'I was a smoker for years. I still struggle at times to lay off them.'

'But at least you've got a job. You don't have to sit around all day with nothing to do but feel sorry for yourself. That's when the nicotine beckons.'

'I can imagine it does,' Temple said.

Renner sat back in his chair and sucked in a tight breath. Temple noticed a fanged snakehead tattoo on his neck. It's mouth seemed to open and close as Renner moved his head.

'So, let's get this over with, Inspector,' he said. 'Cole and I don't get on, but he is my son and I'm not comfortable with grassing him up. And if this wasn't such a serious business I wouldn't.'

Temple fished out his notebook and rested it on his knee. He jotted down the date and time at the top of the page and then said, 'The RMP told me that a rifle had gone missing from the army base. They suspected that your son might have stolen it. What do you know about this?'

Renner pressed his lips into a tight line that barely moved when he spoke.

'I told Cole he was out of his mind to steal a rifle like that,' he said. 'I told him to get rid of it. But he ignored me.'

'Did he show you the gun?' Temple asked.

Renner shook his head. 'He said he'd stashed it in a safe place.'

'So why did he tell you about it?'

'Because he thought I might know someone who'd buy it. A few years ago I got involved in that stuff. I sold a few stolen weapons. It's not something I'm proud of, but I wasn't the only one doing it. Nowadays it's common practice.'

'So what did you tell Cole when he mentioned it to you?'

Renner shrugged. 'That I wasn't into that anymore. I'd lost contact with the dealers and I didn't want to get involved.'

Renner blew a plume of smoke to the right. The smell of burning tobacco made Temple yearn for a cigarette.

'When was the last time you talked to your son?' Temple asked.

Renner clenched the cigarette between his teeth, eyes screwed up against the smoke.

'Not since we had a bust-up and he stormed out,' he said. 'After that things got bad at home and the missus told me to go. That's why I'm in this dump, but you probably already know that.'

'I saw your wife yesterday,' Temple said. 'She told me that Cole has psychiatric issues.'

Renner nodded. 'Post-traumatic stress for sure. He's badly fucked up. Like a lot of guys who've been through that shit. Me included.'

'So would you say he's capable of

murdering people at random? After all, killing from a distance is what he spent his time doing in Afghanistan.'

'That was different,' Renner said. 'It was war. Soldiers who kill in combat don't always become addicted to it.'

Temple gestured towards the newspaper on the coffee table.

'You must have seen the footage of the suspect caught on a CCTV camera,' he said. 'Could that guy be your son?'

Renner picked up the paper and stared at the picture for several seconds.

'It's impossible to tell,' he said. 'I've seen the video a couple of times, but it's blurred and the guy doesn't turn towards the camera at any point. But I do know that Cole was never in the habit of wearing a hood.'

'Does this man have the same height and build?'

Renner squinted at the picture. 'I suppose so. Cole's five eight and fairly slim.'

'Did you ever see him with a rucksack like that?'

'He did have a rucksack when he was living at home,' Renner said. 'But I've no idea if it's the same type. It's not at all clear.'

'I spoke earlier to one of Cole's old army pals,' Temple said. 'Guy named Addison.'

Renner nodded. 'Ryan Addison. I met him

once. He'd just lost his job and was miserable as sin.'

'Well, Mr Addison has been talking to Cole on the phone. They even met for a drink.'

Renner shrugged. 'Doesn't surprise me. Cole doesn't like his own company much. And he probably didn't think there was much risk of being spotted by the police.'

'Cole told Mr Addison that he's renting a room in Southampton and that his landlady is pregnant. Does that ring any bells?'

Renner pursed his lips and shook his head. 'I don't know any landladies and I don't know anyone who's pregnant.'

Temple looked at his watch and realized that he was pressed for time. It was almost noon. There was a train from the city centre station to Victoria at two and he had to be on it if he was to make the task-force meeting.

'I'm afraid I have to go, Mr Renner,' he said. 'But please call me if you think of anything else that could be useful or if your son does contact you.'

As Temple got to his feet, Renner said, 'I know my son better than anyone, Inspector. And I'm convinced he's not the motorway sniper. There's no way he would kill anyone outside a combat situation.'

★ ★ ★

Temple hurried back to police headquarters in Southampton. The incident room was buzzing. He quickly brought the team up to date on what he'd learned during the morning.

'We now have confirmation that Cole Renner acquired a high-velocity rifle,' he said. 'This lends significant weight to the theory that he — and not Yousef Hussain — is the motorway sniper. So, this afternoon at the task-force meeting in London, I'll urge DCS Vickery to reassess his approach to the investigation.'

He instructed the detectives to focus their efforts on finding Renner.

'It seems likely he's still in the Southampton area. According to his friend Addison, Renner is renting a room in a house and his landlady is pregnant. I want a trawl of all privately rented accommodation and estate agents. Make sure that every uniform patrol has a photo of him. And try to track down all his known associates just in case he's staying with one of them.'

He listened briefly to what else had happened during the morning. All the other army snipers on the list from the RMP had been ruled out as possible suspects. The M3 had finally reopened to traffic, but a two-mile section of the M25 remained closed, causing traffic chaos.

Finally, in the last hour, it had been announced that the reward pot for information leading to the sniper's arrest had reached £1 million.

34

The central railway station in Southampton is only a few minutes on foot from police headquarters. Temple arrived there just in time to catch the 2 p.m. train to Victoria.

There was plenty of room in the second-class carriage. He took off his overcoat, placed it on the empty seat next to him, and settled down for the eighty minute journey to London. He intended to make use of the time by reading through his notes and checking his emails, but first he phoned the hospital to speak to Angel.

Her bedside phone was answered by a nurse who told him that Angel was sleeping, but that he shouldn't worry because she was making good progress. He left a message that he'd call later and then tapped the mail icon on his phone. He had two dozen emails, mainly from members of his team who had been told to copy him in on all correspondence. There were also messages from the Scientific Services Department with forensic reports attached.

The Chief Super had forwarded a note from Vickery about the task-force meeting and a list of the people who were going to attend. They included officers from Surrey Police and the Counter-Terrorism Command, as well as representatives from the Home Office and Highways Agency. Temple didn't expect much to come of the meeting. It was no doubt aimed at bringing the relevant parties together so that Vickery could assign tasks and make clear the various areas of responsibility. It would also give him an opportunity to stamp his authority on the operation.

As Temple started to surf the Web on his phone he saw how the story was dominating the news agenda. There were photographs and video clips of the crash scenes: chilling images of the devastation and banner headlines that were sure to instil fear in drivers.

Politicians were lining up to condemn the killings, along with some of the business leaders who'd contributed to the reward fund. The owner of one haulage company had ordered his drivers to stop using the motorways. Many of the stories focused on the victims. Friends and relatives of those who'd died spoke about their loss, while the injured told of their experiences from their hospital beds.

Temple found it freakish to think that

another attack was probably imminent. Rush hour was rapidly approaching and traffic would then pour onto the motorways.

The message left by the sniper under the bridge on the M3 flashed in his mind.

This won't stop until I'm dead.

★ ★ ★

It was dark by the time the train reached London. Temple climbed in a black cab outside the station and told the driver to take him to New Scotland Yard. It was a while since he'd been there. Two years in fact, but he knew it well enough from frequent visits over the years.

Traffic was heavy and there was a light drizzle. It took over twenty minutes to get to the Yard. He was directed to one of the many briefing rooms where ten people sat around a long glass conference table, their faces grim and strained. DCS Vickery was not among them and someone explained that he'd had to rush off to take a call.

Temple introduced himself to the others and as soon as he sat down Vickery came back into the room. He was out of breath, his face flushed.

'I'm sorry, gentlemen,' he said. 'But we have to postpone the meeting. A man carrying a rucksack has been spotted by a motorist beneath a bridge on the M4 outside London. A chopper's on its way along with vehicle patrols. I need to get out there right now.'

'I'd like to come with you,' Temple said, without thinking.

Vickery looked at him and considered the request for just a second before nodding. 'Why not? We need to talk anyway. I gather you have new info on the runaway soldier.'

Temple got swiftly to his feet. 'That's right. We now know for certain that he stole a high-calibre rifle from the army base in Wiltshire. He told his father.'

Vickery raised his brow. 'Well, grab your coat and let's go. If luck is on our side we might soon know if the sniper is a soldier or a terrorist. Or someone else altogether.'

35

He realized suddenly that he should have played safe and fled the scene, but it was too late. He could see the helicopter approaching fast from the east and he could hear the wail of sirens speeding along the motorway towards his position.

Five minutes had elapsed since a car stopped briefly on the hard shoulder only yards from where he was standing. He'd stepped back behind the concrete bridge support the moment he saw it, and relief had surged through him when nobody got out and it went on its way after less than a minute. He'd been sure that the driver hadn't seen him and had probably stopped simply to answer a mobile phone. So he'd finished spray-painting his message on the wall before climbing to the top of the embankment, intent on carrying out another attack.

But now he knew it wasn't going to happen. The cops were coming for him. He was sure of it. Whoever was in the car must have spotted him and raised the alarm.

He was not sure how to react and a bolt of fear rippled down his spine. In a few seconds the helicopter would be directly overhead and the pilot would have no trouble seeing him.

His bike was about a hundred yards behind him on a country road and in front of him, beyond some low bushes, was the M4. The rush hour was just getting under way and traffic was pouring out of London onto the westbound carriageway.

He tightened his grip on the rifle as the helicopter reached the opposite embankment and hovered about two hundred feet above the trees.

The pilot switched on the searchlight and directed the beam onto the bridge. Slowly the big bird moved towards him across the motorway, a wave of shuddering air beneath its rotor blades, the roar of its engine drowned out the sound of the traffic.

He forced himself to stay calm, breathing slowly as he quickly considered his limited options. After a couple of anxious heartbeats he knew what he must do. He had to take down the helicopter. He wouldn't be able to outrun it and once it pinpointed his position the cops on the ground would know where to go.

So he lifted the rifle and took aim. It was a big, easy target. When it was about forty yards away he pulled the trigger.

The first shell smashed through the front window and as the 'copter veered dramatically to the left the second shell punched a hole in the fuselage.

The 'copter gained height briefly, then spun out of control as he let rip three more rounds, emptying the magazine.

The 'copter spiralled downwards towards the motorway with smoke billowing from its engines. Its blades clipped the side of the bridge, gouging out great lumps of concrete. The traffic below started to brake and he could hear shrieks of tortured rubber.

But a number of cars and vans were directly beneath the 'copter as it crashed onto the westbound carriageway. The drivers and passengers didn't stand a chance as their vehicles were consumed by a giant ball of fire.

The searing heat from the explosion reached up the embankment along with the sound of imploding glass and grinding metal. It was as though a bomb had dropped on the motorway.

The sniper couldn't hold back a grin and the hairs quivered on the back of his neck. He'd managed to salvage the situation and complete his mission, despite an unforeseen setback. The death and destruction down on the motorway was more than he could have hoped for. The impact on the public and the authorities would be enormous.

There was no time to savour the moment.

He wasn't out of the woods yet. More cops would soon descend on the area, in helicopters and in cars, along with all the other emergency services. He needed to get away from there fast.

He started to dismantle the rifle as he headed back through the bushes towards the road. His escape route was all worked out. He'd follow the road south through Datchet and Windsor to the M25. From there it would take him about an hour to get home.

He came to a wooden fence and climbed over it. The narrow road was still deserted, but he knew it wouldn't be for long. To his right was the bridge over the M4 and a shower of ash from the fire below rained down on it.

He turned left and dashed towards a small clump of trees on a grass verge at the side of the road. That was where he'd left the motorbike after making sure it was well concealed from passing traffic.

But when he got there he stopped suddenly and stared in confusion. He thought that maybe he'd got it wrong, that this wasn't the right spot.

But then it dawned on him and his heart sank.

This was definitely where he'd left the bike.

The problem was it was no longer there.

36

The two detectives saw the explosion. They were travelling towards the M4 in one of the Met's air support helicopters when the blast lit up the sky in the distance.

Moments earlier they'd heard the pilot's panicked voice over the emergency channel, yelling that he and his observer were under fire from the ground.

It didn't take a great stretch of the imagination for Temple and Vickery to realize what had happened. The sniper, having been spotted on the motorway embankment, must have shot at the helicopter, causing it to crash to the ground.

The rifle he'd been using was powerful enough to do the job, and the chopper would have presented an easier target than any of the cars on the motorway.

Temple felt a tightening in his gut. He found it hard to take in the sheer brutal reality of what had happened. Yet at the same time his heart rate spiked at the prospect of closing in on the sniper. The bastard had made his first big mistake and it was likely that he was still at or near the scene. Every patrol car in the area had been alerted. They knew the exact location thanks to the motorist who had happened to stop on the hard shoulder to send a text on his mobile phone. He'd apparently spotted a hooded man under the bridge acting suspiciously and had called 999.

The bridge straddled the motorway at Slough, a few miles west of London. The road that crossed it went south towards Windsor and north towards Farnham and Uxbridge.

Temple and Vickery were going to be among the first police officers on the scene. The carnage on the motorway would delay most of the patrol cars. Below them tailbacks were already stacking up along the westbound carriageway.

Neither man spoke as the helicopter moved rapidly across the urban landscape. He was dreading what they were going to find when they reached their destination. In fact it turned out to be far worse than he'd imagined.

The fire was still raging on the motorway where the police helicopter had come down on traffic. A number of cars and vans were ablaze. Several had been crushed. A lorry had smashed through the central reservation onto the eastbound carriageway. It had toppled over, causing a second multiple pile-up.

The devastation was widespread and as they hovered above the scene Temple knew for sure that the death toll would be in double figures.

Vickery leaned forward and put his hand on the pilot's shoulder.

'We need to circle the area,' he said. 'See if we can spot the sniper.'

The pilot was hesitant. 'But if he's still around he might start shooting at us.'

'Then we need to keep our eyes peeled,' Vickery said. 'We can't pull out now. I know there's a risk, but if the bastard gets away there'll be more scenes like this and more deaths.'

The pilot nodded beneath his helmet. 'Then I reckon it's a risk worth taking.'

The helicopter banked sharply to the left and swept in low over the bridge. Temple saw that one side of the bridge was damaged and the road itself was littered with ash and debris.

He also saw movement down on the motorway. A few people had got out of their vehicles and were fleeing the scene on foot. Others were standing amidst the wreckage staring at the flames. No doubt their senses were so scrambled they didn't know how to respond.

A moment later the scene below the

helicopter changed. The inferno was replaced by trees and bushes and an unlit road that rolled northwards through countryside. The pilot switched on the thermal image sensor and continued to stare down through the window. Vickery watched the black and white picture on a small monitor in front of him and Temple.

His eyes followed the progress of the helicopter's searchlight as it brushed over the landscape. They were about a hundred feet above the ground and Temple prayed that they weren't about to come under attack. There was no way of knowing if the sniper had them in his sights and would try to bring them down too, but his gut told him it was more likely the man was already putting distance between himself and the scene. There was no sign of life along the embankment.

It was easy to see why the sniper had chosen this spot from which to launch his fourth attack. The unlit road provided an escape route and clumps of bushes along the top of the embankment provided cover. There were no properties in the immediate area and Temple could see no traffic on the road. It was a quiet, rural location, just like the others the sniper had chosen.

'What's that?' Vickery shouted suddenly.

Temple turned to look at the monitor. The picture was clear and there was very little vibration thanks to the stabilizing gyroscopes beneath the undercarriage. He saw a small ghostlike figure moving along the road.

'It looks like someone running,' Temple said. 'Can we zoom in?'

Vickery adjusted the controls and the picture was magnified.

'Jesus Christ,' Vickery said. 'It must be him.'

The figure was that of a man and it was as though he was lit up from within. He was wearing a short jacket and he appeared to be carrying something on his back, possibly a rucksack.

The pilot began shouting directions into his radio and word came back that at least one police patrol car was closing in on the road. Others were screaming towards the crash scene on the motorway.

The man was running north along the road away from the bridge towards a built-up area.

'Hold back a little,' Vickery told the pilot. 'Just in case he stops and decides to take a pot shot at us.'

Vickery was right to be cautious, Temple thought. The guy was still a serious threat. But he wouldn't be for long. A patrol car could already be seen on the screen at the far end of the road.

The man carried on running and every few seconds he twisted his body to look up at the helicopter, his face a white smudge. Then suddenly he veered off to the right and scrambled over a fence into a field.

And that's where he finally ran out of steam and collapsed on the ground.

On the monitor they watched him roll on to his back and stare up at the sky. Thankfully he didn't produce his rifle to make a last, desperate stand. Instead he seemed to accept his fate as police officers on foot entered the field and moved cautiously towards him.

'We've got him,' Vickery said in a breathless whisper. 'We've got the murdering bastard.'

37

The pilot managed to put the helicopter down in the same field. By the time Temple and Vickery stepped out onto the grass, their quarry was in handcuffs and surrounded by half a dozen police officers.

Temple could barely contain his excitement as he ran towards the cluster of high-visibility jackets. They were only about two hundred yards from the motorway and they could hear the sirens and see the glow from the fires.

Temple was sure he could also hear screams. He had to force himself not to think about what was happening beyond the embankment. It was likely that people were dead and dying — some perhaps being burned alive in their vehicles.

He experienced a frisson of guilt because he wasn't doing anything to save them. He had to tell himself that he had no choice but to pursue the man responsible. And that man was just yards ahead, sitting on the ground with his hands behind his back.

Vickery got to him first and pushed the uniformed officers out of the way so he could get a close look.

'Thought you could outrun us, did you?' he yelled at the man in a voice that shook with rage.

Then he snatched a torch from the hand of one of the officers and shone it on the man's face.

Both Vickery and Temple were shocked to discover that it wasn't Yousef Hussain or Cole Renner. This guy was unfamiliar to them. He was younger, in his late teens. He had a mop of black curly hair and a hollowed-out face. His eyes were wide with alarm and sweat glistened on his forehead.

He was wearing a brown leather jacket and jeans and next to him on the grass lay a black sports rucksack.

Vickery picked it up and peered inside.

'There's no fucking rifle,' he blurted out as he reached in the bag and pulled out a motorcycle crash helmet. 'He must have dropped it.'

Temple stepped forward and stared down at the young man. He had to resist a powerful urge to beat the shit out of him. After all, this was the deranged bastard who had launched a killing spree against innocent people. The animal who had put Angel in hospital and struck fear into the hearts and minds of motorists across the country.

And yet he didn't look like the devil

incarnate. He looked like a pathetic, terrified loser.

'Where's the rifle?' Temple demanded, his voice sharp and hoarse.

The guy shook his head. 'I don't know what you're talking about. I don't have a rifle.'

Vickery reached forward, grabbed the man's jacket by the collar and wrenched him to his feet.

'You're a bloody liar,' he shouted. 'You've just shot down a police helicopter and killed God knows how many people on the motorway. What have you done with the rifle?'

The man looked from Vickery to Temple and shook his head again. 'I swear I didn't do that. I saw the helicopter come down and heard the explosion. That's why I left the motorbike and legged it. I knew something bad had happened and I didn't want to get roped in.'

Temple frowned. 'What do you mean, you left the motorbike?'

The guy swallowed hard and spluttered his words. 'I couldn't ride it because I haven't got the key. I was pushing it along the road and I knew it would hold me up. So I dropped it and started running.'

'So why haven't you got the key?'

'It's not my bike,' he said. 'I saw it at the side of the road when I walked over the bridge. I thought it had been dumped because there was nobody around. So I took it. I was going to push it home.'

'Where's home?' Vickery asked.

The man pointed with his chin. 'About half a mile that way. I live with my parents.'

'So where were you coming from?' Temple said.

'The pub. It's just over the bridge. I was with some mates. They're still there. You can check. And the landlord knows me. His name's Thomas Mosby.'

Vickery and Temple exchanged anxious looks. This wasn't good. Could it really be that he wasn't the sniper? That they had chased the wrong man?

'What's your name?' Temple asked.

'Paul. Paul Whitman.'

Temple stepped forward and searched his pockets. He found a wallet and mobile phone. There was a driving licence in his wallet along with a couple of credit cards and the name on them was Paul Whitman. He handed the licence to Vickery.

'So where's the motorbike?' Temple said.

'It's back there next to the road,' Whitman replied.

'Then show us.'

They marched Whitman back the way he'd come. The motorbike was on its side in front of a hedge. It was a Suzuki and the engine was still warm.

'So you're saying that you came across this machine just minutes ago?' Vickery said, his voice tight with tension.

Whitman nodded.

'And the helmet?'

'It was lying next to it.'

'All right,' Vickery said. 'Now show us where you claim you found the bike. And move your fucking arse.'

The spot was thirty-odd yards further back along the road. It was behind some trees a short walk from the embankment.

'I only saw it because I was walking,' Whitman said. 'It was well hidden. If I'd been in a car I would never have spotted it.'

Vickery came to a sudden decision and instructed the uniforms to take Whitman in, after first making a note of his address and home phone number.

'Get the techies to carry out forensic swabs on his hands,' he instructed. 'And I want search teams up here to go over every inch of this road and the surrounding area, including the embankment. If the rifle's been dumped then we need to find it.'

He also instructed the officers to secure the

motorbike and the area around it.

As Whitman was being bundled into the patrol car, Vickery turned to Temple and said, 'We need to check out this lad's story, but I've a horrible feeling he's telling the truth.'

'Me too,' Temple said. 'And he doesn't strike me as a mass murderer.'

Vickery wiped sweat from his brow with his sleeve and nodded. 'But if he's not our man then the sniper may still be close by.'

38

Out of desperation he clambered down the embankment between the bushes towards the motorway. The bridge was to his right, the blazing helicopter just beyond it.

On this side of the bridge the carriageway was packed with people who had managed to get out of their vehicles and out of harm's way. They were standing around, shocked and dazed, the glow from the fires revealing the stark terror on their faces.

Several cars had parked haphazardly along the road, their drivers having stopped on the carriageway after seeing the explosion in their rear-view mirrors.

The police and paramedics had yet to arrive so there was complete chaos. People were screaming, shouting, crying, running. The heat from the fires was intense and the noise deafening.

But it meant the sniper was able to step onto the hard shoulder and then onto the carriageway without drawing attention to himself. Nobody looked at him, despite the fact that he was carrying a rucksack on his back and he was out of breath after running like the clappers from the spot where his motorbike should have been.

He had no choice but to head for the motorway as soon as he saw the second helicopter. There was nowhere else to run. In the woods and fields he would have been picked up by searchlight or heat-seeking sensors.

At least now he stood a chance. The helicopter was out of sight and in all the confusion he could get away, but he had to stay calm and in control. He couldn't afford to panic.

He stood on the edge of the carriageway to get his bearings. The place was ringing with the roars of pain and despair. He saw a blue flashing light up on the bridge and he could hear sirens approaching fast. He watched as a woman staggered away from the carnage with her clothes on fire. Two men rushed over to help her. And then he saw a small boy wandering along the bottom of the embankment, lost and frightened.

And suddenly every cell in his body seemed to freeze as a wave of guilt washed over him. He was never meant to get this close to his victims. He never wanted to see their faces or hear their screams. The plan had always been to keep his distance, remain detached from the suffering he'd caused. So being here in the midst of the mayhem was not good. The images prodded his conscience and he could do without that. He had to shake himself mentally in order to get a grip.

Then, wielding a fierce look of determination, he started to jog away from the bridge along the westbound carriageway.

He wasn't alone. Others were running too while some were sitting on the tarmac waiting for help to arrive. There were quite a few parked vehicles along the hard shoulder. All of them were empty, their drivers playing at being good Samaritans.

He spotted a BMW 3 Series with its driver's door open. No one was standing next to it. He peered inside and saw the key in the ignition. He looked around. No one was watching him. So he threw his rucksack onto the front passenger seat and then quickly slipped behind the wheel.

He switched on the ignition. The engine rumbled into life and the headlights snapped on. Then he moved along the motorway at 15 mph, past groups of bewildered people; most of them had stepped over the central barrier from the gridlocked eastbound carriageway.

He pushed down on the accelerator when he saw that the road ahead was clear. Within minutes he was approaching the junction 6 exit.

He had a moment of panic. Should he leave the motorway here or stay on it? The police would be bound to look out for him. But had they had time to mobilize their patrols and get road blocks into position? He doubted it. And the sooner he got off the M4 the better.

So he turned onto the slip road which brought him to a large roundabout. There was a police car parked at the kerb, but it looked as though it had only just arrived and the officers were spreading traffic cones across the road. One of them waved him through and with a sigh of relief he turned left onto the A355 towards Windsor.

He continued driving for about ten minutes, then fished out his mobile and made a call.

'It's me,' he said when it was answered. 'There's been a problem and I need help.'

There was a sharp intake of breath on the other end of the line. But before the other person could respond he revealed that he'd been forced to shoot down a helicopter and that his motorbike had been taken.

'I had to steal a car,' he said. 'But I have to dump it as soon as I can. So I need you to pick me up.'

He didn't wait for a reply. Instead he gave the location from where he wanted to be picked up. Then he turned off his phone and concentrated on the road ahead as he tried to ignore the acid feeling in his stomach.

He'd had a close shave, but he felt confident that he'd soon be home and dry. And he consoled himself with the thought that, despite the set-back, he was one step nearer to achieving his goal.

39

The two detectives knew that a full-blown search of the area was going to have to wait. Rescuing survivors and making the carriageways safe was the first priority for the emergency crews.

So Temple and Vickery decided to do what they could until more detectives arrived. Vickery called the task force HQ and told them to arrange for Slough police to send someone to Whitman's address. The pair then split up. Temple set off for the pub to check out Whitman's alibi while Vickery went back up in the chopper to scour the landscape.

Temple had to cross the bridge to get to the pub and when he looked down at the appalling scene on the motorway he felt nauseous. The first fire tender had turned up but the wrecked helicopter was still ablaze. And so too were several cars. He wanted to go down and do what he could to help, but he resisted the impulse because he knew that catching the sniper was the only way to stop this happening again.

So he dragged his gaze away from the carnage and pressed onwards over the bridge.

Within seconds he saw that a police Range Rover had closed off the road ahead, just this side of the pub. Several people had gathered there, no doubt curious to know what was going on.

The pub was called The King's Head — it was small and quaint with a car park out front. Temple flashed his ID to the uniformed officer standing next to the Rover and hurried inside the pub. There were about half a dozen male customers around the bar talking in hushed tones. Temple walked straight over to them and introduced himself. The man behind the bar was tall and overweight with a shiny bald head. He said he was the landlord and that his name was Thomas Mosby. He went on to confirm Paul Whitman's story that he'd been drinking in the pub until just before five. Temple also managed to elicit a few more facts about Whitman. He'd lost his job as a car mechanic eighteen months previously and had served a term of community service for stealing a car. Thomas also revealed that Whitman had been in the pub the previous evening — around the time of the sniper attack on the M25.

Temple stepped outside the pub and called Vickery on his mobile phone.

'So while we were chasing that fucking idiot the sniper slipped away,' Vickery said

244

above the rumble of the chopper.

'We weren't to know,' Temple said. 'He was running away from the scene. We had no option.'

'Tell that to the people he kills on his next outing.'

They arranged to meet back in the field where they'd cornered Whitman. Temple was waiting when the helicopter landed. By this time the area was swarming with police and patrol cars were backed up along the road. Below on the motorway the fires were being brought under control and casualties were being taken to ambulances. Gradually the extent of the damage was becoming evident. Eight cars and two vans were crushed or burned when the helicopter was brought down. Fifteen other cars had shunted together, forming a barricade of wrecks, and two lorries had overturned. There was total gridlock on both carriageways stretching for miles in each direction.

The two detectives kept themselves busy while they waited for reinforcements. Vickery arranged for the abandoned motorbike to be towed away after calling in the registration number so it could be checked. Together they went down to have a look under the bridge where the hooded man had been spotted by the motorist. Sure enough the sniper had left another message. It had been sprayed on the concrete slabs in red paint.

It read: *This is fun. Long may it last.*

* * *

A mobile command centre arrived after an hour and parked on the road close to the bridge. The vehicle was as big as a coach and filled with monitors, work stations, a small conference room and even a toilet.

Vickery and Temple stationed themselves inside and as detectives and scene-of-crime officers arrived the two officers dispatched them to search for clues.

Temple was impressed by the way Vickery managed things; his instructions were always clear and concise and he never lost his cool. If he was daunted by the task facing him, he didn't show it. It made Temple realize why he'd been put in charge of the task force. He might have been arrogant, but he was also bloody good at his job.

Information flowed in during the evening. They were told that Paul Whitman's parents had vouched for their son and could not believe he was suspected of being the sniper. They were now at the local nick waiting to find out what was going to happen to him. Then SOC officers reported back from the

246

embankment that they'd found the spot from where the sniper had fired at the helicopter — five brass shell casings had been discovered lying in the grass.

Then news came in about a motorist who'd stopped on the westbound carriageway to see if he could be of help. When he tried to return to his car — a BMW — he found that it had gone. This immediately gave rise to the suspicion that the sniper had stolen it in order to make good his escape. Vickery at once ordered an ANPR (Automatic Number Plate Recognition) check. This would draw data from the CCTV network and hopefully track the vehicle's movements.

The information they'd all been dreading reached them at 9 p.m. It was the list of casualties. Six people had been killed, including the two helicopter crew members, and seven had been injured, two of them seriously. It came as a shock to Temple even though he'd been bracing himself for bad news. But an even bigger shock came shortly after when vehicle licensing sent through the identity of the person who owned the motorcycle.

It was none other than Martin Renner, the nicotine-addicted father who'd claimed his missing son was in possession of a stolen sniper rifle.

40

Temple wasted no time calling the incident room in Southampton. It was still being manned despite the hour and DC Fiona Marsh was the senior detective on duty.

Temple told her about the motorcycle found near the scene of the latest incident and the fact that it belonged to Martin Renner.

'Get to his flat in Romsey right away,' he said. 'We believe he may have stolen a car so he's probably home already. If he is then arrest him. If there's no answer, I want you to break in. And send someone to his wife's house as well, just in case he goes there.'

'I'm on it, guv.'

'Be sure to take an armed response team with you.'

Temple hung up the phone and as he turned to Vickery, his face bunched up in a grimace.

'I can't believe it,' he said. 'I was with the guy this afternoon.'

'Maybe he's gone psycho,' Vickery said. 'His life is fucked up right now. His wife kicked him out of the family home and he's living in a pokey flat. He doesn't have a job and he's fallen out with his son. This might be his way of getting even with the world for what he's going through. Did he strike you as a psychotic killer?'

'Of course not, but psychotic killers are usually very good at pretending they're perfectly normal people.'

'So why did he tell you his son stole the rifle?'

'Probably because it's true and he wants us to think that Cole is the sniper.'

Vickery shook his head. 'But we're not talking about one or two victims here. Thirty people have been killed, for God's sake. Surely someone like Renner wouldn't commit murder on such a massive scale just because he's having a hard time of it.'

'Isn't that usually why people go on killing sprees?' Temple said. 'Look at all those school shootings in the States. From Sandy Hook to Virginia Tech, there's never a credible motive behind them. The killer almost always turns out to be a pissed-off student who wants to vent his rage over some trivial incident or perceived grievance.'

'But this isn't a one-off atrocity that can be explained away so easily,' Vickery said. 'This is a fucking campaign of terror that's been carefully planned. The sniper wants to unsettle the whole country. Not just kill people. That's why he's launching his attacks during rush hour and on motorways. He knows he'll scare the hell out of us all.'

'But based on the facts, Martin Renner fits the bill,' Temple said. 'He was in the army so he knows how to use a weapon. We also know that his son stole a rifle — the same rifle that's being used by the sniper. Then to cap it all a motorbike that's registered to him turns up at the crime scene after the latest attack.'

Vickery heaved his shoulders. 'I can see where you're coming from and I have to admit it is pretty convincing, but even so we can't just ignore what Yousef Hussain's accomplice told us. He said Al Qaeda were behind this.'

'And he may have been talking bollocks,' Temple said. 'It could be that he just wants you to *think* they're behind it. He wouldn't be the first terrorist to falsely claim responsibility for an attack.'

At that moment Temple's phone rang. It was Fiona Marsh. She was at Martin Renner's flat in Romsey and it was empty.

'We've started searching the place,' she said. 'And I've got officers watching outside in case he turns up. All his clothes are here and it doesn't look as though he left in a hurry.'

'Have you heard back from his wife?'

'DS Vaughan is there now, guv, and apparently there's no sign of Renner.'

'OK. Stay put then and keep me informed.'

As he hung up, he and Vickery moved over to the conference table where they were joined by a couple of other detectives and one of the SOCOs. It was time to take stock of what they had and decide how many officers needed to stay at the scene into the night. But just as the discussion was starting Vickery took an urgent call from Scotland Yard. As he listened his face tightened and then he suddenly shot to his feet as though his legs were spring-loaded.

'Get them to take him to Paddington Green,' he barked into the phone. 'We'll go there right away.'

When he hung up he looked at Temple and said, 'Police at Heathrow have made an arrest.'

Temple drew in a ragged breath. He knew the airport was just a couple of miles from where they were sitting. He immediately assumed that Martin Renner had driven there in the stolen BMW ready to fly out of the country.

But he was wrong.

'It's Yousef Hussain,' Vickery said. 'He was trying to board a flight to Karachi. He was using a fake passport. A sharp-eyed customs officer spotted the bastard.'

251

41

Temple and Vickery were soon haring across London in a patrol car. Their destination was Paddington Green nick, the most important high-security police station in the country, where prisoners suspected of terrorism are held for questioning.

It had certainly been an evening of high drama, Temple reflected as he stared dreamily through the window at the busy streets of the capital. It had begun the moment he arrived at New Scotland Yard and since then it had been one shock after another.

He didn't know what to make of this latest development, though. Was it coincidence that Yousef Hussain had suddenly turned up at Heathrow? Or had he fled there from the scene of the latest motorway attack? And if so did that mean that he was somehow connected with Martin Renner?

Temple wanted to talk it through with Vickery, but the DCS spent the entire journey making and receiving calls on his mobile. He spoke to the Met's Operational Command Unit at Heathrow and told them to check all their CCTV cameras to see how

Hussain arrived at the airport. He gave them the registration of the stolen BMW and asked them to retrieve Hussain's luggage if he had any.

He also took calls from the Home Secretary and the head of the Counter-Terrorism Command, both wanting to know what was happening. Vickery told them he was on his way to question Hussain, but added that there was now some doubt as to whether he was the sniper.

'To be honest, events are taking us in two different directions,' he said at one point. 'It remains to be seen where we'll end up.'

*　　*　　*

Paddington Green police station is just ten minutes from London's Oxford Street. It's a grim 1960s building with sixteen cells located below ground level, plus CCTV cameras throughout.

It's the only purpose-built unit in the country for suspected terrorists and over the years the cells have housed dozens of suicide bombers and IRA activists.

Temple had been there on only one occasion in the past and that was to interview an Islamic fundamentalist who had been involved in a plot to blow up an oil refinery near Southampton.

It hadn't changed much since then, except that the walls had been painted a brighter colour and the floors were polished to a shine.

He and Vickery were expected and were told that Yousef Hussain had already arrived. He'd been accompanied by two officers from Aviation Security at the airport and was in the process of being checked over in the sterile medical examination room.

Hussain had been carrying a large rucksack when he was apprehended at the departure gate. The contents had been emptied out on a table for Vickery to examine, along with his clothes. The DCS slipped on a pair of latex gloves before he touched anything.

Hussain's passport was in the name of Imran Rehman. It looked genuine and in the picture Hussain had a beard and his hair had been shaved off.

'It's a crude but effective disguise,' Vickery said.

One of the Aviation Security officers said they'd become suspicious because Hussain looked nervous and started sweating when he was asked questions by a customs officer. So they pulled him over and quickly discovered his true identity.

Hussain's rucksack also contained his one-way flight ticket to Pakistan which had been purchased at 7 p.m. that very evening at the airport using a credit card assigned to Imran Rehman. There was also a dog-eared copy of the Koran, a wallet with £500 cash in it and a small prayer mat. There were no spare clothes and nothing to link him to the motorway shootings. The clothes he'd been wearing consisted of a leather jacket, denim jeans and a polo sweater.

In one of the coat pockets there was a balled-up receipt from a MacDonald's restaurant in Catford two evenings ago.

'Even terrorists can't resist the allure of a Big Mac,' Vickery said.

'What do you reckon he was doing in Catford?' Temple asked.

Vickery shrugged. 'Maybe that's where he's been staying since he left the flat he shared with his accomplices. We need to find out.'

Vickery asked for everything to be sealed in plastic bags and sent to the lab for analysis.

He then collared one of the Paddington Green CID officers and showed him the MacDonald's receipt.

'Check this out,' he said. 'Looks like Hussain was there only two nights ago and MacDonald's are bound to have security cameras. See if you can pick him up before and after his visit. We're desperate to trace his movements.'

Vickery and Temple then grabbed a coffee and sandwich in the canteen and Vickery started bashing his mobile phone again. Temple felt exhausted. He rubbed his eyes hard enough to make them water, then popped a couple of caffeine pills into his mouth. It was often the only way he managed to keep on top of things when he'd had hardly any sleep.

He made a quick call to DC Marsh. She was still at Martin Renner's flat and he hadn't turned up and neither had the BMW that had disappeared from the motorway. Temple then called the hospital and was told that Angel was asleep, but doing OK. She hadn't had any more seizures, thank God.

It was almost midnight when the two detectives were led along a corridor and into an interview room. A harsh fluorescent light painted everything a dull yellow. There was a table with two chairs on either side. A microphone hung from the ceiling ready to record the proceedings and there were video cameras on two of the walls, plus a large two-way mirror on another.

They sat at the table and Temple's stomach was cramped with anticipation. While they waited for Hussain to be brought in the DCS said that he would lead the interrogation.

'I don't expect him to be very forthcoming,' Vickery said. 'Often as not the only way to get a straight answer from these fuckers is to torture them.'

A few minutes later Hussain was ushered into the room. He was handcuffed and wearing a grey cotton jumpsuit.

With the shaved head and beard he looked nothing like the man in the photograph that had been shown in newspapers and on the television. He was just under six feet tall and olive-skinned. His eyes were black beads in a round face. He sat opposite Vickery and curled his lips in a mirthless grin.

Vickery wasted no time. He switched on the recorder and said aloud the date and time.

'This interview is being recorded,' he went on. 'I am Detective Chief Superintendent Owen Vickery of the Counter-Terrorism Command. The other officer present is Detective Chief Inspector Jeff Temple of Hampshire's Major Investigations Team. We are in the interview room of Paddington Green police station and we are interviewing Mr Yousef Hussain.'

He paused there to see if Hussain would react, but he just sat there, motionless, staring straight ahead.

'I understand you've waived your rights to be represented by the duty solicitor,' Vickery said. 'Is that correct?'

Hussain spoke in a voice that was hoarse and gravelly and without emotion. There was just the faint trace of an accent.

'I don't need a solicitor,' he said. 'I've done nothing wrong.'

Vickery leaned towards him across the table. 'Then why were you about to flee the country?'

Hussain looked from Vickery to Temple and then back again. He moistened dry lips with a sharp, pink tongue.

'I was going to Karachi to see my family,' he said. 'There's no law against that, is there?'

'So why get a one-way ticket?' Vickery said. 'And why use a fake passport?'

Hussain shifted in his chair and pumped out his chest. A vein started to tick on the side of his forehead.

'No comment,' he said, after a second.

Vickery jabbed a finger at him. 'I think you were going to Karachi because you panicked after things went wrong with your latest attack on the M4. You stole a car, drove to the airport, bought a ticket. If you hadn't been rumbled at customs you'd be in the air now.'

Hussain laughed. 'I haven't been anywhere near the M4. And for your information I'm not the sniper, despite what the papers say.'

'So how did you get to the airport?'

'By Tube from central London.'

'Then how come there's no Tube ticket amongst your belongings?'

'I threw it away.'

'So where in Central London did you get on the tube?'

'I can't remember. What does it matter anyway?'

Temple listened to the exchange with interest, content to be an observer. He was struck by Hussain's presence. He had an aura about him, a sense of calm malevolence that was quite disturbing. In that respect he was like other terrorists Temple had come into contact with. Even when the world was falling in on them they remained arrogant and defiant. It was as though they were able to withdraw behind a protective shield that could not be penetrated by threats and intimidation.

'I really don't see the point of dragging this out,' Vickery said. 'Why not make a full confession? We already have enough on you to make sure you go to prison for a very long time.'

'You know nothing.' Hussain spat the words. 'You only *think* you do.'

'You're wrong,' Vickery said. 'We know you have links to Al Qaeda and that you've been running a terrorist cell in this country since you returned from a training camp in

Pakistan. We found bomb-making equipment in the flat where you stayed. We have incriminating emails and recorded phone conversations about an imminent operaton, which your Somali accomplice told us refers to the sniper attacks.'

'And you believed him?' Hussain said with raised eyebrows.

'Why would he lie to us?'

Hussain gave a short, stunted laugh. 'Because it's what he wanted you to think. He was playing with you, claiming credit for something he wasn't involved in just to confuse you. And obviously you fell for it.'

'If that's true then what have you really been up to?'

Hussain puffed out his lips and shook his head.

'No comment.'

'Grow up, for fuck's sake,' Vickery snapped. 'We'll find out soon enough anyway so you might as well tell us now. And if you cooperate it'll work in your favour when you eventually face trial.'

'*If* there's a trial,' Hussain said.

'Oh, there's no doubt about that, my son. You'll face trial and be convicted. And even your beloved Allah won't be able to help you there no matter how many times you pray to him.'

Hussain gave Vickery a sneering look of contempt. 'I've changed my mind about a solicitor,' he said. 'I'm not saying another word until I get one.'

Vickery drilled into him with his eyes. 'If that's how you want to proceed then I'll go and sort it.'

'But not the clown on duty. I want my own solicitor.'

Vickery's nostrils flared. 'What's the name and number?'

'I'll call him myself,' Hussain said. 'I know I'm entitled to one phone call.'

Vickery gave a resigned shrug and announced for the benefit of the recorder that he was suspending the interview. Then he flicked the machine off.

'I'll have a phone brought in,' he said to Hussain. 'But tell your brief to get his arse over here pronto.'

Vickery then got to his feet and signalled for Temple to follow him out of the interview room. In the corridor the DCS struggled to hold in his anger and frustration.

'So what do you think?' he said.

'I think he'll be a hard nut to crack,' Temple answered.

'That's what I think,' Vickery said. 'We need to trace his movements. Find out how he got to the airport for starters. If he arrived

261

in the stolen BMW then he's our man. If he travelled on the Tube then he's probably not. The airport and the Underground are saturated with CCTV cameras. It shouldn't take us long to pick him out.'

At that moment Temple's phone rang. He snatched it from his pocket. It was DC Marsh with the latest news about Martin Renner.

'He's just turned up at his flat, guv,' she said. 'And he's in a right state.'

'What do you mean?'

'He's pissed. Completely legless. Somehow he's managed to stagger home from wherever he was.'

'What's he got to say for himself?'

'Nothing. He collapsed outside his front door. He was sick all over one of the uniforms and he reeks of booze. He won't be answering questions for a while I'm afraid.'

'What have you done with him?'

'There's an ambulance on its way. We'll take him to the hospital for a check-up and then let him sleep it off.'

'Make sure you get his clothes to the lab and check his hands for gun residue.'

'Will do.'

'And turn his flat over. Seize every bit of clothing. Get the SOC officers to pore over every inch of the place. Is that clear?'

'As daylight, sir.'

'And I don't want him questioned until I get there, which will be later this morning.'

'Understood, guv.'

Temple hung up and gave Vickery the news.

'This calls for a change of plan,' Vickery said. 'You need to get back to Southampton right away and follow up on Martin Renner. I'll arrange for a car to take you. Meanwhile I'll keep pressing Hussain and try to get him to open up.'

'Do you believe what he said about not being the sniper?'

'I'm not entirely sure,' Vickery said. 'But I am convinced he's been up to something. And if his mission wasn't to kill people on motorways then we need to find out what the hell it was.'

42

Temple managed to get an hour's nap in the back of the unmarked police car that took him to Southampton.

He arrived home just after four in the morning. It was still dark and a light frost was twinkling on the ground. The central heating was on the night-time setting so the house was freezing. He flicked the override switch and made himself a cup of tea. He drank it at the breakfast bar whilst watching a 24-hour news channel on the small TV.

The carnage on the M4 was the main story around the world. There was intense coverage on all the networks and the same horrific pictures were being transmitted, along with the out-of-date photograph of Yousef Hussain.

It was now public knowledge that he had been arrested and several reporters were reporting live from outside Paddington Green police station. There was no mention of Martin Renner's motorbike and Temple was pleased about that. He didn't want a media army camped outside police headquarters when they started to question him.

On screen two people were reviewing the morning papers in a studio. The M4 attack was emblazoned across every front page. There were several editorials criticizing the police for not catching the sniper. A number of stories reflected the growing concern among motoring organizations and business leaders. Tens of millions of pounds were being lost each day because of delays caused by the shootings.

The sniper had created such a state of fear that hundreds of thousands of drivers were choosing not to use motorways, according to the Highways Agency. The impact was most severe in the south of England where deliveries of goods to supermarkets and warehouses were being severely disrupted.

The reward pot for information leading to the sniper's arrest had soared in the last twenty-four hours and now stood at £2.5m. Temple was sure it was now one of the highest rewards ever offered in the UK. But then the shootings were among the most heinous crimes ever committed. Even now, after everything that had happened, he found it hard to take it all in. The chaos, the bloodshed, the sheer randomness of the attacks. How could the sniper possibly justify what he had done?

Sitting there Temple trawled through the

past few days in his head. Everything that had happened seemed unreal. From the discovery of Angel's blood-spattered car on the M27 to the sight of the crashed helicopter on the M4. Thirty people dead and many more injured. Hundreds of vehicles wrecked and scores of lives destroyed. It had been a hellish week so far. Four days of carnage.

But maybe it was finally over, he thought. Two viable suspects were in custody: a jihadist with links to Al Qaeda who had been planning an attack for weeks. And an army veteran whose son had stolen a sniper rifle from an army base before going AWOL.

Temple felt the evidence against Martin Renner was the most compelling. Surely he had to be the sniper. Why else would his motorbike have been at the scene of the latest attack?

He must have left it at the side of the road whilst he took up position on the embankment. When things went wrong and he tried to escape he discovered that it'd been taken. So he made his way onto the carriageway and took a car that was parked on the hard shoulder. It all seemed straightforward. There were still too many unanswered questions swimming around in Temple's head. Was Renner acting alone? Why did he reveal that his son stole a sniper rifle from the army camp? Surely it would have been wiser not to mention it. Or did he hate his son so much that he wanted to shift the blame onto him?

And then there was Yousef Hussain. Could he possibly have been in collusion with Renner? If not then what had he and his fellow conspirators been plotting?

Temple was hoping that all or some of the answers would be forthcoming during the day ahead.

He got up and switched off the TV. His eyes were dry and heavy and he could feel a dull ache growing at the base of his skull. He rolled his head and massaged the back of his neck, then went upstairs. A hot shower partially revived him and he felt the tension leave his shoulders. He felt even better after putting on some clean clothes.

He made coffee and toast and was about to leave the house when he remembered he'd left his car at the station. So he rang for a taxi and while he was waiting he called the incident room. A detective named Brannigan answered the phone. He was one of the newer recruits to MIT. He said that Martin Renner had been brought back from the hospital and was asleep in one of the cells. DC Marsh had gone over to Renner's flat to join the scene of crime team who were still there.

'I spoke to DC Marsh about twenty

minutes ago, sir. She said they hadn't so far found anything incriminating.'

Temple clucked his tongue in disappointment.

'Did she manage to get any sense out of Renner at all?'

'I gather not. He was too pissed apparently.'

'So we don't yet know where he was before he turned up at the flat.'

'No, we don't.'

Brannigan also had an update on the stolen BMW. It had been found abandoned on a layby on the A34 close to Southampton. The keys were in the ignition and a forensic team were on their way to examine the car and the area around it.

Temple felt his pulse surge. It was a significant development and almost certainly meant that Hussain had not driven to Heathrow in that particular car. So it was a fair bet that Martin Renner had taken it and driven to the layby. But how had he got from the layby to Romsey? And where had he spent the rest of the evening?

Brannigan assured him that they were looking into all the various possibilities and were already rounding up CCTV footage from the area.

'Is there anything else?' Temple asked,

more in hope than expectation.

'Nothing yet, sir. But it's early. There are only a few of us in.'

'Well, I'll be in after I've visited the hospital to check on Angel. Call me on my mobile if something comes up.'

★ ★ ★

Temple got a shock when he walked into Angel's room at the hospital. It was 7 a.m. and he was expecting her to be sitting up in bed.

Instead she was lying back against the pillows with an oxygen mask on her face. Dr Fuller stood on one side of the bed consulting his notes and a nurse stood on the other checking IV lines.

Temple felt a sudden panic and his body went rigid.

'What's going on?' he gasped.

'Now stay calm, Mr Temple,' the doctor said, turning towards him. 'We had a bit of an emergency earlier, but it's OK now.'

Temple listened, his body numb, as the doctor explained that Angel had suffered a seizure in the early hours caused by the blood clot.

'It's not uncommon in these circumstances,' the doctor said. 'Fortunately she was here and we were able to react immediately. She's fine now and under sedation.'

'Does this mean she'll have more seizures?' Temple said.

The doctor shook his head. 'Not necessarily. Once the clot starts to shrink as a result of the thinners the threat should quickly recede.'

Temple stepped up to the bed and put a hand on Angel's forehead. It was warm and clammy. He felt gutted for her. He knew that when she came round she'd be worried sick and convinced that her life plan had been demolished.

'How serious was the seizure?' he asked.

The doctor hung the clipboard containing the notes on a hook on the bed frame.

'All seizures are serious,' he said. 'But in this case it wasn't life-threatening. We've already carried out another scan on Miss Metcalfe's head and there's been no change.'

'So what now?'

'We continue to administer the medicine and monitor her progress.'

'When will she wake up?'

'Not for some hours yet.' The doctor paused for a beat before adding, 'I know from watching the news that you've got your hands full investigating these sniper attacks, Mr Temple. So let me assure you that there's no need to stay here. We can call you when Miss

Metcalfe is conscious.'

Temple was torn. Angel's seizure had changed his perspective on things. He was even less inclined now to leave her alone. He wanted to be around when she woke up.

But at the same time he needed to interview Renner and bring the investigation to a close.

The doctor, sensing that he was struggling with the dilemma, said, 'I'll make it my business to check on her every few minutes, Mr Temple. If I thought her condition was likely to deteriorate rapidly then trust me I would tell you. But I don't.'

Temple found reassurance in the doctor's words and came to a decision.

'Just phone me if there's a change,' he said.

★   ★   ★

Temple's mobile rang as he was exiting the hospital. It was Vickery and it sounded as though he was in a squad car with the siren going.

'Can you hear me, Jeff?' he said, almost shouting.

'Just about. What's up?'

'It's about Hussain. I want you to know that I think I've got to the bottom of what he and his accomplices have been plotting.'

271

Temple stopped walking and pressed the phone hard against his ear.

'Go on,' he said. 'I'm listening.'

'Do you remember the MacDonald's receipt we found in his pocket?' Vickery said.

'The one from the restaurant in Catford?'

'That's right. Well as you know I got someone to follow it up.'

'And?'

'We got lucky. Hussain was caught on the restaurant security camera having a meal there two evenings ago. He had a rucksack with him and he looked furtive. When he left the place we were able to pick him up on two more street cameras. He walked about three hundred yards from MacDonald's and turned into a road called Fraser Hill.'

'Should that mean something to me?' Temple said.

'It's where St Mary's Church is located. And St Mary's Church is where they're due to hold the memorial service for Joseph Roth in a little while.'

'Wasn't this the service you and Angel were going to attend?'

'Yeah, along with the mayor of London, the police commissioner and a bunch of other dignitaries.'

'So what are you saying, guv?'

'Don't you see? I reckon the memorial

service has been Hussain's target all along. Why else would he go there late in the evening? The bastard could be out for revenge for what happened a year ago when the Al Qaeda bomb plot was foiled and Roth was killed. I'm on my way to the church now.'

'So did CCTV show him going into the church?'

'No, but it does show him climbing a wall into the grounds.'

'Bloody hell. It sounds plausible.'

'Damn right. And I wanted you to know about it before you question Renner. If I'm right about this then Renner has to be the sniper.'

'I'll be talking to him shortly,' Temple said.

'Then keep me updated and I'll let you know what we find at the church.'

'Good luck,' Temple said.

43

The incident room was positively bursting at the seams by the time Temple got there. There was a constant trilling of telephones and a barking of orders; he only recognized half the faces. They'd been drafted in from all over Hampshire. He'd called ahead to tell them he wanted a full briefing before he began interrogating Martin Renner.

The restless chatter died down as soon as he called for quiet. He gave a brief summary of the M4 attack and the interview with Hussain, then told them about the conversation he'd just had with Vickery.

'I'll update you when I know more,' he said. 'Meanwhile we've got our hands full at this end with Martin Renner. So before we grill him I want status reports on everything.'

A SOCO named James Frost was first up. He said that Renner's motorbike was now at the lab being examined. Various sets of prints had turned up on it and these were now being processed. They needed to eliminate those given by the lad who tried to steal the bike.

'The latest information from Renner's flat

is that nothing much of interest has been found there,' he said. 'No weapon, no ammunition, no maps of motorways. We're still checking over his clothes and shoes, but I can confirm there was no gun residue on his hands, which doesn't mean he didn't fire a rifle. He probably wore gloves.'

'Anything from the team on the M4?' Temple asked.

'I had a conversation with one of the officers there an hour ago,' Frost said. 'Shells similar to those found at the other scenes have been discovered on the embankment. And it's believed the paint used for the message under the bridge is also a match. So no surprises there.'

'And the BMW stolen from the motorway?'

'It's been towed to the lab, but I'm told the steering wheel and door handles have been wiped clean of prints. So I wouldn't expect much to come of it.'

Next up was DC Marsh, who had also just returned from Renner's flat above the shop in Romsey. She looked tired and her skin seemed grey and somehow shrunken. She began by confirming what Frost had said about the lack of forensic evidence at the flat.

'We've found nothing that links him to the shootings,' she said. 'And neighbours say they've never seen him riding a motorbike.

They didn't even know he had one.'

'Has anyone spoken to him this morning?' Temple asked.

'I popped down to see if he was awake when I got back,' she said. 'He's just been given some breakfast and he's moaning that he's got a hangover.'

'What a fucking shame,' someone piped up.

'You told me not to start questioning him about the shootings so I said he was brought in for being drunk and disorderly in a public place,' she said. 'I also asked him where he spent most of last evening.'

'What did he say?'

'He reckons he was at a pub in Romsey. The Green Man. I've spoken by phone to the landlord. He knows Renner and confirms he was there. But he didn't arrive until after nine o'clock, which would have given him plenty of time to get from the M4 to Southampton.'

'What else did the landlord say?' Temple asked.

'He said Renner was already inebriated when he turned up. He sat at a table by himself drinking spirits until closing time. When he left the pub he was plastered.'

'And what time was that?'

'Eleven.'

'But he didn't turn up at his flat until around midnight.'

'Renner says he lost his way after leaving the pub. And maybe that's not surprising if he was in such a state.'

DS Vaughan then explained that the layby where the BMW was found was close to a built-up area, but not covered by CCTV. Vaughan then went on to say that there was still no sign of Martin Renner's son Cole.

'He told his squaddie friend Ryan Addison that he was living in Southampton and renting from a pregnant landlady,' Vaughan said. 'We've been trawling estate agents but so far no joy.'

Temple asked if there was any news on the stolen car that was captured on the CCTV camera close to the scene of the first attack on the M27. He was told that it still hadn't turned up and neither had the hooded man who'd been driving it.

'Could that guy have been Martin Renner?' someone asked.

Temple nodded. 'Renner senior is about the same height and has the same build, but then so does his son apparently.'

There were a few more status reports and then Beresford updated everyone on the wider picture. He mentioned the multi-million pound reward and said the task force hotline in London had been inundated with so many calls that more operators had been brought in to help.

He said a ten-mile section of the M4 was still closed and there was traffic chaos on roads in the area. The pressure to catch the sniper was growing by the minute and politicians were critical of the police for letting him slip away.

'The impact is being felt across the whole country and not just in London and the South,' Beresford said. 'People are genuinely afraid to drive on motorways, even outside the rush hours. Police forces are trying to maintain a high profile with traffic patrols and helicopters, but it's a real struggle on current levels of manpower and resources. If the man we've apprehended turns out not to be the sniper then I dread to think how bad it's going to get.'

Temple wound up the meeting and asked Vaughan to join him for the interview. The pair were about to head out of the office when DC Marsh suddenly drew everyone's attention to one of the office televisions.

Temple stopped and looked up at the wall-mounted screen. A news reader was reporting on a breaking story. She was saying that there had been an explosion in a church cemetery near Catford in South London — the same church where a memorial service was being held for a police officer who'd been gunned down by terrorists a year ago.

And, according to initial reports, there were casualties.

44

Temple's heart thumped like a Zulu drum.
He pulled out his mobile and called Vickery,
but his call went straight through to
voicemail.

Several other detectives grabbed desk
phones and within two minutes they learned
that a bomb had gone off in the grounds of St
Mary's church, but it was too early for
details. Ambulances had been called to the
scene and the local hospital alerted. But no
one knew how many people had been hurt or
whether anyone had been killed.

Temple was tempted to hold off on
interviewing Renner until he knew more, but
Beresford persuaded him not to.

'Whatever has happened, there's nothing
you can do about it,' Beresford said. 'So crack
on with Renner and I'll keep you informed of
what's happening.'

Temple didn't argue. Beresford was right.
He couldn't do anything and however bad the
news was it could wait.

He and Vaughan hurried along to the
interview room where Martin Renner was
waiting for them with the duty solicitor, a

decent enough brief named Paul Sweeney who looked stiff and formal in a suit and tie.

Temple was shocked by the sight of Renner who was wearing pristine white overalls because his clothes were being tested. He seemed to have aged several years since yesterday at his flat. His face was lined and gaunt. He had a lean, grizzled expression and his eyes were sunken with tiredness and dehydration. He sat slumped in the chair, his hands resting unnaturally on the table in front of him.

As Temple sat down he had a brief mental snapshot of the man crouching behind a bush on a motorway whilst aiming a rifle at the traffic. It sent his pulse soaring.

'What the fuck is going on?' Renner yelled. 'Why am I still here? All I did was get pissed.'

The lawyer leaned sideways to whisper in his ear, but Renner ignored him and gave Temple a hard stare.

'I want my clothes back and I want a fucking explanation,' he said.

'Before we begin I have to make it clear that you are under caution,' Temple said. 'That means you do not have to say anything unless you wish to do so. However, it may harm your defence if you fail to mention when questioned something that you later rely on in court. Anything you do say may be used in evidence. Do you understand?'

Renner turned to his lawyer and blood vessels in his cheeks flushed, looking ready to erupt.

'You told me this was about being drunk and disorderly,' he said. 'But that's bollocks. What haven't I been told?'

'You're here because we have reason to believe that you've carried out a series of random murders,' Temple said matter-of-factly.

Renner's shoulders went stiff and his jaw dropped. He turned slowly to face Temple again and deep creases appeared in his forehead.

'What are you on about?' he muttered.

Temple ignored the question and said, 'Where were you last night, Mr Renner?'

Renner looked genuinely confused. He blinked hard several times and balled his fists on the table.

'Is this some kind of sick joke?'

'Just answer the question, Mr Renner. Tell me where you were last night before you arrived at The Green Man pub. We know from the landlord that you got there at about nine.'

Renner ran his tongue around his mouth and shook his head.

'I don't believe this. Who am I supposed to have murdered?'

'The question, Mr Renner,' Temple persisted. 'Please answer it and then we can move on.'

Renner swallowed hard and started drumming his fingers nervously on the table.

'I was at home,' he said. 'In my flat minding my own business.'

'Did you leave the flat at any point after our chat at lunchtime?'

'No I didn't. I was upset over what you told me about Cole. I started drinking. When I ran out of booze I went to the pub. I left the pub after it closed and came home. That's when your lot pounced.'

'So can someone verify that you stayed in your flat all afternoon and into the evening?'

''course not. I live by myself and you were the only person who came to the flat yesterday.'

Temple was silent for several seconds as he studied the man before him. Renner's face was now spangled with sweat that had seeped from his pores and was giving off an unpleasant odour.

'I think you should get to the point,' the lawyer said, breaking his silence. 'You should explain to Mr Renner exactly why he's here. It's obviously not because he was drunk in the street.'

Temple nodded. 'Well, let's start with him

explaining to us how he managed to be in two places at the same time.'

'What do you mean?' Renner barked.

'Well, how could you have been in your flat if you were hiding on an embankment on the M4 motorway armed with a rifle?'

Renner's eyes popped out as though on stalks.

'You can't be fucking serious,' he said. 'You're actually accusing me of being the sniper? Jesus, are you insane?'

'We know you were there,' Temple said. 'And we know that you shot down the police helicopter.'

Renner made slits of his eyes and leaned across the table.

'You've got this badly wrong,' he said. 'You're confusing me with Cole. He's the one who has the rifle. I told you that yesterday. Why are you accusing me?'

'Because it was your motorbike that we found at the scene,' Temple said. 'As you know, it was stolen from where you left it, which is why you had to nick a car to get away from there. But the person who stole it dumped it at the side of the road. It's now in our lab undergoing forensic tests.'

Renner sat back and ran a hand through his unruly hair.

'So that's it?' he said. 'You think I'm the

sniper because you found a motorbike?'

'*Your* motorbike, Mr Renner. Records show that you've owned it for the past three years.'

'That's correct,' he said. 'But six months ago I gave it to Cole. I haven't seen it since then.'

'It's still in your name,' Temple pointed out.

'Only because I haven't got around to sorting the paperwork.'

'Can you prove that?'

'Well, you can ask my wife if you like. She'll tell you. She was the one who told me to give him the bike because I hadn't used it in ages.'

Temple and Vaughan exchanged looks. This was something they hadn't expected.

'I swear I'm telling the truth,' Renner said. 'It wasn't me on the M4 last night. I was in my flat before going to the pub. It must have been Cole.'

'So maybe you're both involved,' Temple said. 'A father and son double-act. Two battle-scarred ex-servicemen who've decided to let loose a terrible rage against society.'

'Don't be fucking ridiculous,' Renner said. 'Cole may well have cracked and his default position might be to kill but I'm just a pathetic drunk who's screwed up his life. I don't blame anyone but myself and if you check my army record you'll find that I never actually took anyone's life. And I never wanted to.'

Temple felt the bottom drop out of his stomach. As much as he hated to admit it he was beginning to think that perhaps Renner was telling the truth. There was nothing in his body language to suggest he was lying. And he seemed pretty sure that his embittered wife would back up his claim about the motorbike.

'Do you intend to charge Mr Renner with any offences?' the lawyer said. 'Because if not then I think you should return his clothes and release him. He's answered all your questions and has told you that he was at home when the shootings took place.'

'He's going nowhere for the time being,' Temple said. 'We'll talk to his wife and wait for the results of the forensic tests on his flat and clothes. And meanwhile we also want to know if he has alibis for the times the other motorway attacks took place.'

'I was either at home or walking around the town,' Renner said. 'I've got fuck all else to do since the wife chucked me out and I don't have any money or friends.'

'So the answer to my question is that you don't have alibis for any evening this week,' Temple said. 'That's a pity Mr Renner.'

'Oh, come off it, copper,' Renner said. 'This is total bullshit. You've got the wrong man and you know it.'

Temple decided to suspend the interview. He felt certain that Renner wasn't about to change his story.

'We'll talk again in a while,' Temple said. 'You'll be held in one of the cells until then and you're free to retain the services of Mr Sweeney here or get your own lawyer.'

Renner started to object, but Temple ignored him and hurried out of the room with DS Vaughan in tow. In the corridor he told Vaughan to send someone to speak to Renner's wife and chase up the forensic evidence.

'My gut tells me he's telling the truth, but I want to be sure of it,' he said. 'Meanwhile we need to step up our efforts to find his son. If Cole Renner is the sniper — and it's what I've thought all along — then he's probably planning another attack this evening.'

45

Before convening another team briefing Temple rushed upstairs to Beresford's office to find out what had happened in London. He was anxious to know about the bomb that had gone off in the churchyard where Joseph Roth's memorial service was going to be held.

'Two police officers were injured in the blast,' Beresford said. 'But it could have been much worse.'

The explosive device had been planted in the ground next to Joseph Roth's actual grave on the edge of the small churchyard. It had been timed to go off when the guests were due to gather around the grave for prayers after a short service inside the church. But Vickery had stopped the service from going ahead and the only people in the churchyard at the time were bomb disposal officers with sniffer dogs.

They were still searching for the bomb when it went off and two officers who were standing fifteen yards away were injured, though thankfully not seriously. They were both being treated in hospital for cuts and bruises.

'About twenty people would have been

standing around the grave at that time,' Beresford said. 'It's possible they would all have been killed. Vickery wants to talk to you. He phoned here about ten minutes ago and I told him you were interviewing Renner. How did it go by the way?'

'Badly,' Temple said. 'I'm pretty sure he's not the sniper. He says he gave the motorbike to his son about six months ago.'

Beresford couldn't conceal his disappointment. 'Shit. That's just what I didn't want to hear. You'd better find out from Vickery where he wants to go from here.'

Temple called Vickery on his mobile as he walked back to the incident room. The DCS answered straight away and Temple was relieved to hear his voice.

'It was an ace result,' Vickery said. 'If Hussain hadn't kept the MacDonald's receipt then we would never have known he went to the church. Lord only knows how many people would have been killed.'

It was often the way, Temple reflected. A felon is caught or a plot uncovered because of a seemingly inconsequential detail. Hussain had probably stuffed the receipt into his pocket without thinking. It's what millions of people do every day.

'Does Hussain know about it yet?' Temple asked.

'My boss gave him the news a short time ago and the bastard's gutted. He confirmed it was the target all along. His accomplice tried to divert attention away from it to give him time and opportunity to plant the bomb, which he did two nights ago.'

'Were you there when it went off?'

'I was in the church. The device was buried under about six inches of dirt and put inside a pressure cooker packed with nails. It wasn't very sophisticated but it was loud and effective.'

'So where are you now, sir?'

'On my way back to the Yard. I've called a task-force meeting and you need to update me. With Hussain out of the picture we're down to one prime suspect for the sniper attacks.'

'And it's no longer Martin Renner,' Temple said.

'Why the hell not?'

Temple told him what the situation was and said they urgently needed to circulate a photograph of Cole Renner. This time Vickery was quick to agree.

'I'll get on with it then,' Temple said. 'Meanwhile I suggest we prepare ourselves for another attack this evening. It's the last working day of the week and normally the motorways are extra busy.'

* ★ *

The next few hours passed quickly for Temple. There was a lot to do and a lot to think about.

He got the media department to send out a picture of Cole Renner along with an appeal for information on his whereabouts. The press release made it clear that he was now the number-one suspect in the hunt for the motorway sniper. Temple also agreed to front a press conference later in the day to help get the message out there.

The forensic evidence from Martin Renner's flat failed to turn up anything that would connect him to the shootings. Likewise there were none of his fingerprints on the motorbike, but there were quite a few belonging to his son.

Renner's wife confirmed his story about giving the bike to Cole and she said it had become her son's pride and joy.

Despite the evidence suggesting that Martin Renner was not the sniper, Temple decided to leave him in the cell for as long as the law permitted. At least that way he'd be on hand to answer any questions that came up relating to his son.

The team's reaction to the latest developments was commendable. In spite of their disappointment they got stuck into their tasks with renewed vigour. Temple could tell the pressure was getting to them, though: they were weary through lack of sleep and fearful that another attack was imminent. There were a lot of red eyes and pale faces.

The saturation news coverage of the sniper attacks on the television served only to fuel their anxiety.

There was a constant flow of disturbing images and alarmist narrative. The death toll from all the attacks was repeated every few minutes, along with footage of the scenes on the M27, the M3, the M25 and the M4. Reporters were stressing the point that nobody — except the sniper — knew which motorway would be targeted next. Some even constructed news packages that focused on the difficulty of protecting drivers. They showed miles of motorways bordered by fields and woodlands, embankments that provided cover for a gunman and little-used roads that provided quick and easy escape routes.

'There's very little the police can do,' said a BBC reporter. 'They can't possibly patrol all two thousand miles of motorways at the same time. The sniper can choose a remote location, carry out his attack and be gone long before emergency services reach the scene. On the M4 he made a mistake, but that may not stop him from continuing his killing frenzy.'

No terrorist attack or major crime had ever caused so much alarm across the country and the hunt for the sniper had become the biggest ever undertaken by British police.

DCS Vickery appeared on screen to explain that Yousef Hussain was no longer a suspect in the attacks, but that he was being charged in connection with the memorial-service bomb plot.

The sudden emergence of Cole Renner as the prime suspect came as a shock to many because he was in the army. It didn't take long for the media to find out all there was to know about him. They laid siege to his mother's house and obtained confirmation from the MOD that he was AWOL.

By early afternoon they'd managed to track down several of his army pals, including Ryan Addison, who revealed on camera how he had first raised concerns about Renner with the Military Police.

'He told me he was pissed off with the world and wanted to take it out on someone,' he said. 'After that I spoke to him a couple of times and he said he was living in Southampton.'

Addison went on to describe Renner as a

troubled man and said there were rumours circulating that he had stolen a sniper rifle from the army base at Bulford.

'I've no idea if it's true or not,' he said. 'But what I do know is that security at military armouries is not what it should be. Weapons go missing all the time, including rifles and machine guns.'

Asked if he thought Renner was capable of such extreme acts of violence, he responded by saying that his friend had been trained to kill people and during his training the only emotions he had been encouraged to show were aggression and anger.

'If you programme young men to kill people they don't know and from a distance then maybe you shouldn't be surprised when something like this happens,' he said.

Temple raised his brow at that last remark. It was a nail-in-the-coffin comment that would infuriate Renner if he heard it. And make him realize that Addison was no longer his friend.

Temple decided to give Addison a call. He wanted to remind him to get in touch if he heard from Renner.

Addison was surprised to hear from Temple.

'I've just seen you on television, Mr Addison,' he said. 'It was an impressive interview and if Cole saw it he might be tempted to get in touch.'

'If he does I'll be sure to contact you straight away, Inspector. I have your number on speed-dial.'

'That's good to hear, Mr Addison. But I've also got a question for you.'

'Fire away.'

'Did you know that Cole was in possession of a motorcycle?'

'Of course. It used to belong to his dad.'

'And is it his only means of transport?'

'I think so. He had a car, but I don't know if he kept it after he was given the bike.'

'What make of car?'

Addison had to think about it.

'I'm sure it was a VW. Convertible type. Bright red.'

'Any idea of the registration?'

'Sorry no.'

'Not to worry. But before I let you go can you remember anything else Cole might have said about his current accommodation? I know he mentioned to you that his landlady was pregnant. Well so far we haven't managed to trace her.'

'I'm afraid that's all I recall of the conversation,' Addison said. 'He didn't go into detail and I had no reason to press him at the time.'

'I quite understand. If you do hear from him or remember something that might be important to us just call me. Day or night.'

'I will, Inspector.'

After the conversation with Ryan Addison Temple took part in a conference call that included Vickery, the Home Secretary, a man from the MOD and other members of the task force. He was asked to be specific about the evidence linking Cole Renner to the killings.

'We know from his father that he stole a sniper rifle from the army base,' he said. 'He also told his friend Ryan Addison that he was pissed off with life and wanted to take it out on someone. We've also been told he's suffering from a form of post-traumatic stress disorder, which makes him unpredictable and potentially dangerous. Then the motorbike he was given six months ago was abandoned next to the M4. Finally he disappeared shortly after going AWOL and no one seems to know where he is.'

But before the conference call was over Temple was told about yet another piece of incriminating evidence against Renner.

DC Marsh came into his office with the news that the stolen car driven by the hooded man at the scene of the first sniper attack on the M27 had been found. It had been abandoned next to a deserted farm house just outside Winchester, a few miles from the motorway. Scene of crime officers had processed the vehicle in record time and the only prints found on it belonged to the woman who owned it. But they did find an empty Pepsi can in the footwell of the passenger seat. And on this they found finger and thumb prints belonging to Cole Renner.

It meant they now had solid evidence which placed him at the locations of two of the four sniper attacks.

46

Two o'clock, Friday afternoon and he had a decision to make. Should he or shouldn't he launch a final attack?

Everything had already been planned in meticulous detail and he was ready to go.

The M40 just north of Bicester was the next location; an embankment overlooking the southbound carriageway. He could park his car just one hundred yards away behind a derelict building. He'd even picked out the very bush to use as cover.

It would take him about ninety minutes to get there. It was an easy route from Southampton along the M3, then on to the A34 to Newbury. From there it would be a straight run north past Oxford to the M40.

Before today he'd had every intention of rounding off the week with something really spectacular. He was going to shoot at traffic on both carriageways, but now he wondered if it was worth the risk.

He'd been watching the news and monitoring all the traffic reports, including the live cameras on the internet. And he wasn't convinced the M40 would be anywhere near as busy as it usually was during a normal Friday evening rush hour.

His campaign of terror had been even more successful than he could have hoped. Drivers were too scared to travel on motorways. The cops had been forced to admit that they couldn't possibly guarantee their safety. Thousands of people were apparently leaving work early so they could drive home before it got dark.

And then of course there was the fact that he'd already achieved his goal. The thought of it brought a smile to his face.

There'd been a lot of speculation about why he'd killed all those people at random. Some believed he was a terrorist linked to Al Qaeda. Others that he was a disaffected military man who had lost his marbles. But none of them knew the truth and they never would.

In front of him on the television they cut live to yet another police press conference. It was being fronted by detective Jeff Temple. He tried to reassure the public that the net was closing in on the sniper. He said they now had concrete evidence linking Lance Corporal Cole Renner to the attacks. He urged people to be extra vigilant. He reminded them that there was a £2.5m reward for information that led to an arrest.

But he didn't look very confident. He looked tired. Haggard. Defeated.

Temple took the unprecedented step of urging people not to use the motorways during that evening's rush hour.

'It's just a temporary precaution,' he said. 'We have to assume that the sniper plans to carry out yet another attack. And we want to make it harder for him to do so. But I must stress again that this is a temporary measure.'

The detective's plea helped him to reach a decision. He decided not to launch a fifth attack. Instead of driving up to the M40 he'd pour himself a cold German beer from the fridge and start making preparations for the final phase of his plan.

47

The press conference caused quite a stir. Temple hadn't told anyone that he was going to advise drivers to avoid the motorways. Beresford was the first to voice his concern when they returned to the incident room.

'Why the fuck did you say that?' he demanded to know. 'It's not what we agreed and it's like an admission of defeat.'

'Hopefully it will save lives,' Temple said. 'There's nothing else we can say or do to minimize the threat to drivers. So it's our only option. If enough people heed the warning the sniper might be persuaded not to bother.'

'Well, I'm not sure the powers-that-be will agree with you.'

Temple shrugged. 'That's the least of my worries.'

Beresford was right, of course. Vickery was on the phone within minutes balling him out.

'You should have checked with me first,' Vickery said. 'I would have told you it's a fucking crazy idea. It'll cause mass chaos and misery on every other road.'

'So how else do we stop another bunch of

people from being murdered tonight?' Temple said.

'We find the bastard responsible. That's how. We don't make the situation much worse. Drivers are shunning the motorways anyway. They don't need encouragement from us.'

'I made the point that it's only a temporary precaution,' Temple said. 'So there's no reason to get worked up about it.'

'So what happens on Monday when people return to work and we still haven't caught the sniper?' Vickery said. 'Do we tell them it's OK to start using the motorways again? Or do we advise them against it, in which case the chaos will continue and in all fucking likelihood the country will be brought to a standstill?'

'I suggest we worry about that when the time comes,' Temple said, keeping his voice calm. 'For now, let's concentrate on finding Cole Renner.'

Vickery took a deep breath and then softened his tone to ask Temple for an update. He then said he would stay in London that evening so he could respond if there was another motorway attack anywhere in the country. He would also coordinate the efforts of the task force outside the Southampton area.

The rest of the afternoon was manic. Police in uniform poured onto the streets of Southampton with copies of Cole Renner's photograph. From the incident room calls were made to estate agents and private landlords in and around the city.

Temple gave interviews to the local TV and radio stations and interrogated Martin Renner once again in the presence of the duty solicitor. He was hoping he'd reveal something new about his son and when he didn't Temple felt obliged to tell him he was no longer a suspect.

Renner did not kick up a fuss or demand an apology. Instead he asked for a cigarette and a lift home.

'You might want to go and stay somewhere else for a while,' Temple said. 'Your address is known to the media and I doubt they'll leave you alone.'

'Well, I'm happy to talk to them,' Renner said. 'So long as they pay me up front.'

Temple gave him a look of utter contempt and then stormed out of the interview room before saying something he might regret. He went to his office to sift through mounds of paperwork and answer calls. His TV was showing a rolling news channel and his computer was tuned to the AA Traffic site.

He stood at his window as dusk descended

on Southampton. His features were taut; he could feel the tension zinging round his body. This was when the great Friday rush hour usually got under way. But according to the reports that were coming in, the country's motorways were running smoothly and there was no congestion on any of them.

Sky News had reporters stationed on the M25, the M1, the M40 and the M5. They all had the same story to tell — that there was about a sixty per cent reduction in the amount of traffic on the carriageways.

The four sniper attacks had all taken place between five and six. But Temple did not breathe a sigh of relief until his watch said 7 p.m. That was when DCS Vickery called to tell him that although most motorways were virtually deserted it was chaos everywhere else.

'Every town and village close to a motorway is completely gridlocked,' he said. 'Major and minor roads are at a standstill and it'll take commuters forever to get home.'

'But at least nobody's been shot,' Temple said.

* * *

So the big news of the night was that the sniper did not strike again. It prompted a rush of speculation. There were those who said it was probably because he was too scared after his close shave with the police on the M4. Others reckoned it was because there was far less traffic on the roads.

Temple's name came up during the various TV discussions and interviews. It was generally accepted that his televised warning had convinced many motorists that it wasn't worth the risk. But it also provoked an angry reaction from people who were caught up in the traffic chaos. They described what he'd said as an over-reaction.

On the plus side no one had died. The working week had ended without another awful bloodbath. And it gave the task force teams a much needed breathing space.

In the incident room the relief was palpable. A couple of detectives patted Temple on the back and said they were glad he'd said what he had on air. They told him to ignore the criticism. He held the last briefing of the day at eight when the night shift took over. He said it was important that those officers who had been working throughout the day should go home and get some sleep.

The good thing about the creation of the task force was that he didn't have to worry about running out of people. Reinforcements had been joining the team from other forces throughout the day and there were plenty of detectives on duty overnight.

'My phone will stay on,' he said as he brought the meeting to a close. 'If we get a lead on Cole Renner I want to know about it straight away.'

He didn't actually leave the building for another two hours and when he called in at the hospital Angel was fast asleep. He didn't wake her. Instead he sat next to her bed for a while because he felt an overwhelming urge to be close to her. So much had happened over the past four days and for much of the time he'd pushed her to the back of his mind. She was not only seriously injured, but also desperately worried about her future. And he hadn't been very supportive. But he promised himself that when this case was over he would take time off to look after her. There was no doubt in his mind that she was going to face a long, uphill struggle, especially if there were long-term symptoms associated with her head injury.

Angel was still too young to have her hopes and ambitions crushed. She'd be devastated if she was no longer fit enough mentally and physically to pursue a career path with the Force.

He was dog-tired by the time he got home,

but his mind refused to relax. And when he finally went to bed at midnight he struggled to get to sleep. When he closed his eyes he thought about Cole Renner and he wondered what had prompted him to embark on his savage rampage?

He also wondered what he would feel like when he finally confronted the bastard. Would he be able to hold himself back or would he try to tear him apart? Renner had killed thirty people and seriously injured dozens more. No punishment could possibly fit his crimes.

As far as Temple was concerned he deserved to suffer from now until eternity for what he had done.

48

The breakthrough came the next morning, Saturday, when a woman named Megan Trent arrived at the central police station in Southampton.

Temple was behind his desk going through the notes left by the night shift detectives when he got a call from the front desk. The duty inspector said that the woman had information on Cole Renner and that she was insisting on speaking to him. She was actually the fourth person to turn up that morning in response to the various appeals. Hundreds more had phoned the task force hotline in the hope of claiming a share of the multi-million pound reward. Most were deliberate time-wasters or people who genuinely believed they had spotted Britain's most wanted man.

For that reason Temple's reaction on being told about Megan Trent was less than enthusiastic.

Until the duty inspector mentioned that she was a local landlady.

And that she was pregnant.

That's when his pulse kicked up a gear and

he jumped to his feet.

'Get someone to bring her straight up to my office,' he said.

Three minutes later Megan Trent was escorted into his office. She was in her early thirties and about three months pregnant. She had a sharp equine nose and blond hair that was wispy and unwashed. Her face was square and chubby and without makeup. She was wearing black leggings and a dark blue anorak. On her feet she wore a pair of snow white Adidas trainers. The word chav came to mind and it struck him that she didn't look like a typical landlady.

Temple got up from behind his desk and introduced himself.

'Please sit down, Mrs Trent,' he said.

'It's Miss,' she said. 'But just call me Megan. Everyone does.' Her voice was hard-edged and with the hint of a Hampshire accent.

'May I take your coat?'

She placed her large fake leather handbag on his desk and let him help her off with her coat. Beneath it she had on a tight fitting yellow T-shirt that clung to her bloated body like an extra layer of skin.

'Can I get you a drink?' he asked. 'Tea? Coffee?'

She shook her head. 'No thanks. If I do I'll

need to wee. I'd rather just tell you why I'm here.'

Temple sat back down and rested his elbows on the desk.

'I gather it's about Cole Renner,' he said.

'That's right,' she said. 'I know where he is.'

Temple felt his chest contract.

'Really? Where?'

She swallowed hard and took a deep breath. 'He's in my house. He's my tenant. I've been renting the upstairs flat to him for the past couple of months.'

Temple stared into her wide green eyes and leaned further across the desk towards her.

'Are you absolutely sure it's him?' he said.

She nodded. 'I'm bloody positive. It's the name he's been using. And I saw his picture this morning.'

'So why didn't you phone us?'

'I came into town early to do some shopping. Parked opposite the station and went into Tesco. That's when I saw the newspapers and his picture on the front pages. I got a shock I can tell you. Almost gave birth there and then. I walked straight over here because I knew it'd be quicker than phoning.'

'So you didn't see his photo last night on the news?'

310

She shook her head. 'I don't watch the news much, especially not on Fridays. There's too much else on the telly.'

'So where was he when you left home?'

'He was in bed. I heard him because he snores loud enough to wake the dead.'

'Does he always sleep in late?'

'Most mornings he does,' she said. 'I'm pretty sure he doesn't have a job.'

'So what else can you tell me about him,' Temple said.

She shrugged. 'Not much. He keeps to himself. Most days he goes out in the afternoon and doesn't come back until the evening. Then he goes straight upstairs and I don't usually hear a peep from him. He keeps his door locked when he's not there. The flat is self-contained and has its own bathroom and kitchenette.'

'Does he have his own transport?'

'He has a motorbike that he usually leaves out front on the drive, but it wasn't there this morning for some reason. I thought at first it was because he wasn't home. Then I heard him snoring.'

'You did the right thing coming here,' he said.

'If I'd known sooner, I would have told you,' she said. 'I feel so bad about that. To think that he's been living under my roof all this time and I didn't realize he was a murdering scumbag.'

'It's not your fault, Megan. You weren't to know.'

'It still rankles, though. I don't want people to blame me for not sussing him sooner.'

Temple got up and walked around his desk to place a hand on her shoulder.

'No one will do that,' he said. 'Now just sit quietly for a moment and try to relax. I need to go and talk to my colleagues about this. And I need your address.'

'It's twenty-seven, Purbeck Road. That's in Southampton.'

'Great. I'll be back in a few minutes.'

He stepped out of his office and closed the door behind him, then dashed through to the incident room.

He quickly called for silence and told the team what Megan Trent had said.

'Bloody hell,' DS Vaughan bellowed, jumping out of his seat. 'Is she sure about that?'

Temple nodded. 'She has no doubt it's him and don't forget he told Ryan Addison his landlady was pregnant. She says Renner was in bed when she left the house earlier. With any luck he still is. So I want an armed unit ready to move in ten minutes. I'll let Beresford and Vickery know.'

Temple went back into his office and asked Megan Trent if there was anyone else in the house with Renner. She said there wasn't. She said she lived alone downstairs and explained that her former boyfriend had left her several months ago.

Temple then went to his computer and brought up Google Earth.

'I'd like you to show me your house on this,' he said.

Temple typed her address into the search box and within seconds he was zooming in on Purbeck Road. He turned the screen towards her.

'That's my house,' she said, pointing.

It was a 60s-style terraced house in a nondescript street. Temple adjusted the mouse and used the street-view mode to study the property from all angles. It had two floors, a short driveway and a small front garden. The fenced-in rear garden had a square lawn and small crazy-paved patio. It backed onto another garden.

'This image is probably quite old,' Temple said. 'Has it changed much?'

'No. It looks exactly like that now. More's the pity. It needs renovating, but I can't afford to do it.'

'Are the houses either side occupied?'

'The one on the right is. A couple with a

teenage son. The one on the left is empty because the owner is very old and quite ill. He's been in hospital for months.'

It was all the information Temple needed.

'Now listen to me, Megan,' he said. 'We intend to go to your house right away. I want your permission to make a forced entry if we have to. Is that all right?'

She clamped her lips together and nodded.

'Good,' Temple said. 'And I want you to wait here. I'll get someone to take care of you.'

He stood up and moved towards the door, adrenaline flooding through his veins.

'Can I ask you a question?' she said.

He stopped, turned.

'Sure. What is it?'

Her eyes narrowed slightly. 'It's the reward money. Will I get it if you manage to arrest him?'

'I don't see why not,' he said. 'But there's usually a long drawn-out process so be prepared to wait it out. And keep your fingers crossed in the meantime.'

She gave a little smile. 'I will.'

49

Before descending on Purbeck Road in force Temple sent an unmarked police car to recce Megan Trent's house. The officers parked across the road and reported back that there was no sign of life and the curtains were drawn across the upstairs windows.

The head of the Tactical Firearms Unit was told to assume that Cole Renner was inside and that he was armed with a sniper rifle. Therefore extreme caution was called for.

Three armed response vehicles moved into the immediate area along with dozens of officers in protective vests and military style helmets with visors lowered. They carried semi-automatic weapons and Taser guns.

Temple knew that this was going to be a delicate and dangerous operation. It was a residential street and it wouldn't be possible to evacuate the residents without raising the alarm. But he also knew that they had to move in quickly. They couldn't afford to hang about. The longer they left it the riskier it became.

Megan Trent had given him her door key and he discussed with the team the possibility of simply going up to the house, unlocking the front door, and rushing in. It was a risky manoeuvre, though.

They also considered calling on the house phone. Temple had got the number from Megan who told him the phone was downstairs in the kitchen. If Renner answered then they could try to talk him into giving himself up. But if he was still asleep then they didn't want to wake him. Key to success with most police raids was the element of surprise; the aim was to swoop suddenly and forcefully and to catch the suspects unaware, and preferably while they were half asleep and disoriented.

The problem was they had no idea if he was in bed or up and dressed. Or if he was even in the house. In the end they decided to storm the property from both sides and give Renner as little time as possible to react. They'd go in with stun grenades and tear gas.

First step was to gain entry to the house directly behind Megan's property. This was achieved easily enough, although the family living there were understandably alarmed when they were asked to open their home to a bunch of helmeted storm troopers.

Once the officers were in place and ready to charge the back of the house, the head of the Tactical Firearms Unit gave the command for Purbeck Road to be sealed off at both ends. Then his officers hurried along the pavement towards the house.

Temple stood back behind the cordon. He'd donned a ballistic vest and was clutching a radio. His heart was pumping as he watched the operation get underway. He had a view of the front of the house as the officers closed in.

But just as the assault team reached the driveway to number 27 an explosion of breaking glass stopped them in their tracks.

Temple watched, horrified, as one of the ground floor windows crashed outwards and the officer who was leading the raid was blown off his feet.

★ ★ ★

'Pull back, pull back, pull back.'

The team leader's frantic words blared out of every radio.

Even as he issued his order, another shot was fired, this time through a window at the back of the house. All hell suddenly broke loose. The wounded officer was dragged back along the pavement by two of his colleagues, leaving a trail of blood in his wake. At the same time the street cordons were moved back and everyone shifted position so they

317

were no longer in the line of fire.

Much to Temple's relief word quickly came through that the second shot had not hit anyone. The bullet had been fired into the lawn. But one officer down was one too many. It was a disaster that showed they had under-estimated their quarry. Cole Renner had obviously spotted them closing in. Maybe he had even been waiting for them to appear, having seen himself on the news.

And now he was determined to make a last stand. He was armed and lethal and had nothing to lose but his life.

The gunshots had alerted the other residents in the street to the fact that something was happening. People opened their front doors and appeared at their windows. It prompted a senior officer to issue a warning through a megaphone for them to stay indoors and away from windows.

An uneasy quiet descended on the street, broken only by the passing of a low-flying aircraft overhead.

Temple felt sick at the thought of a long drawn out standoff. They would have to try to evacuate the other homes now and that wasn't going to be easy. The whole situation had spiralled out of control. It had become even more dangerous and unpredictable.

'It's a fucking mess,' Beresford said as he

arrived on the scene. 'What the hell are we . . . '

But he didn't get to finish the sentence because just then another shot rang out.

★ ★ ★

This time Renner did not fire through a window. The shot was confined to the inside of the house. It immediately gave rise to speculation that Renner had taken his own life. It was a common enough scenario. An armed felon is cornered and sees no way out other than suicide. But, of course, they couldn't be sure. Maybe he had fired the shot to make them think that's what had happened, so that he could get them to break cover and take down more police.

Temple grabbed the megaphone and moved along the pavement towards the house at a half-crouch. He made sure he remained screened by garden hedges and when he was close enough he put the megaphone to his mouth and spoke into it in a flat voice devoid of intonation. 'Come out of the house, Mr Renner. There's no escape. Disarm yourself and open the door.'

There was no response.

Temple took out his mobile and called Megan Trent's home number. He let it ring for a full thirty seconds, but there was no answer. He retreated back along the pavement and spoke to Beresford and the head of the Tactical Firearms Unit. They decided to fire tear gas shells into the house through the windows. Then follow through with a frontal assault.

The signal was given a few minutes later. Guns popped and windows caved in. Smoke started to fill the inside of the house.

There was a lot of shouting and screaming as cops in masks charged forward. The front door was smashed in with a battering ram and men poured into the house.

It took them five minutes to announce that there was no longer a threat. But it was another ten minutes before Temple was able to enter the house.

50

Cole Renner was in the living room slumped on a leather sofa. There was no mistaking him even though his head was virtually severed from his shoulders.

His right hand still clutched the rifle he'd used to shoot himself in the throat. It was lying next to him on the sofa and Temple saw immediately that it was the same model as the one the sniper had been using.

Dark-coloured blood had exploded out of the gaping wound along with shreds of bone and dark gristle. His eyes stared ahead, glazed and expressionless. His mouth hung open, tongue lolling out. The blood was everywhere: on his face, his clothes, the wall, the sofa, the carpet. He was wearing a white T-shirt, black jeans and a pair of casual brown shoes. There was stubble on his chin and it looked as though he hadn't shaved in ages.

Temple stood in the small, grim room taking in the scene, his eyes smarting from what remained of the tear gas. The firearms officers had ascertained that there were no other persons in the house. And a quick search had determined that there were no explosive devices waiting to go off.

The room smelled strongly of blood and cordite. In one corner a large flat-screen television was switched on and showing BBC rolling news. They were still reporting on the sniper attack on the M4 and no doubt Renner would have seen the photograph of himself and realized the game was up.

Temple's mind was a whirlwind of emotions. He was glad it was all over and that Lance Corporal Cole Renner no longer posed a threat to the public. But at the same time it was a shame he was dead as now they wouldn't be able to question him and might never know why he'd done it.

The house was gradually filling up with SOCOs. Temple and Beresford decided to explore before the forensic work got under way in earnest. They went into the downstairs kitchen which was small and drab, with fading lino on the floor and a back door to the overgrown garden. The downstairs bedroom, where Megan Trent presumably slept, was clean and tidy and the bed had been made. The fitted wardrobe was crammed with women's clothes.

There was a landing at the top of the stairs. The loft hatch in the ceiling was open and an aluminium ladder had been lowered. A police officer was up there checking it out.

'It's a shared loft space with the house next door,' he said when he appeared through the opening and saw Temple and Beresford looking up at him. 'But it's virtually empty and there's nothing up here but a few boxes of junk.'

'Leave them be,' Temple said. 'Forensics will need to go through them.'

To the left of the landing was a bathroom and to the right a door that gave access to the studio flat that Renner had been renting. The flat was pretty basic and consisted of a tiny living room with a built-in kitchenette and a bedroom. In the bedroom they found a treasure trove of evidence linking Renner to the sniper attacks.

A rucksack similar to the one being carried by the man in the CCTV footage was hanging off the back of a chair. Inside was a box of .338 cartridges and a can of red spray paint. In one of the bedside drawers they discovered a fold-away map of Britain's motorway network and the locations of the four sniper attacks were marked with red felt-tip pen. There was also a fifth mark around a spot on the M40 near Bicester.

'There are no more after that,' Temple said. 'I wonder why he decided to stop there.'

Beresford shrugged. 'Maybe he just hadn't got around to selecting any more targets.'

In the free-standing wardrobe they came across an anorak with a hood, a few shirts and three pairs of shoes. Under the bed was a battered suitcase filled with documents and photograph albums and a range of personal belongings such as old watches and books. But there wasn't much else in the flat. No laptop computer, no diary, no journal containing an explanation of his motives.

In that respect it was a disappointing outcome. But Temple wasn't going to let that spoil the fact that they had finally brought Cole Renner's reign of terror to an end.

* * *

Crowds quickly gathered at either end of Purbeck Road. A police officer with a video camera was recording the scene while another was taking photographs. This was now routine on major incidents.

Other officers started calling at every house in the street to reassure frightened residents and explain to them what was going on.

Dr Frank Matherson, the pathologist, arrived to examine the body and formally pronounce Renner dead.

'He probably pulled the trigger with his thumb,' he told Temple. 'It's an awkward way to kill yourself but usually does the trick.'

324

He said he would carry out a post-mortem first thing the following morning, but did not expect to come up with any surprises.

Before long the area was packed with newspaper reporters and television camera crews. DCS Vickery turned up late morning and made a beeline for Temple who was standing outside the house briefing a couple of his detectives.

'So I missed all the fun,' Vickery said with a broad grin before he went on to congratulate Temple on bringing the case to an end.

'It could have gone better,' Temple said. 'Renner's dead and an officer was shot.'

'Well, I've just been told the officer's condition is not serious,' Vickery said. 'He suffered a shoulder wound. A couple of inches to the right and it would have been a different story. As for Renner, well I never expected him to give himself up anyway.'

Temple gave Vickery an account of how it had all come about.

'Megan Trent is at the station,' he said. 'We need to get a formal statement from her and explain that she needs to find alternative accommodation for a while.'

'I suppose she's in line for the reward then,' Vickery said. 'Last I heard it had reached just over two and a half million.'

'She's already asked me about that.'

Vickery shrugged. 'Who can blame her? I for one won't begrudge her a penny of it. Christ only knows how many more people would have been killed if Renner had survived beyond today.'

51

Temple went back to the station at noon, leaving Vickery and Beresford to stage an impromptu press conference in Purbeck Road. He was happy to shun the limelight in favour of getting his team together so that he could bring them up to date and thank them for all the work they'd put in.

The mood in the incident room was buoyant. Someone had even cracked open a bottle of champagne. Temple accepted a glass and answered questions from those detectives who hadn't been to the scene. He was told that DC Marsh had gone earlier to break the news of Renner's death to his mother and father. The mother had taken it very badly apparently, but Renner senior had given the impression that he intended to cash in on his son's notoriety.

Temple then called the hospital to check if Angel had heard the news. She had, of course, along with virtually everyone else in the country by that time.

'I'm proud of you,' she told him.

'I'll be in as soon as I can,' he said.

'Well, there's no need to hurry. I'm actually

feeling a bit better. And I've had a long chat with the doctor. He's confident that I will eventually be able to go back to work.'

'Of course you will. There's never been any doubt in my mind.'

He told her he'd visit the hospital later and went to find Megan Trent, who'd spent the morning in one of the hospitality rooms. He told her what had happened and explained that for the foreseeable future her house would be a crime scene and she wouldn't be able to live there. He expected her to be upset, but she wasn't.

'I'm glad the bastard is dead,' she said. 'I only wish I could have been there to see it.'

'I'll arrange for some of your belongings to be brought to you,' Temple said. 'Do you have any friends or relatives you can stay with?'

She shook her head. 'I don't have any family. I was an only child. My dad's dead and I lost touch with my mum years ago.'

'What about friends?'

'Most of my pals are living in flats the size of cardboard boxes. None of them can put me up.'

'In that case we'll sort out accommodation at a local hotel for you,' Temple said. 'We'll want you to stay in Southampton in the short term.'

'That's fine with me,' she said.

'Are you sure there isn't someone we can call? Someone who could come and stay with you.'

'I'm sure. I'll be fine. I'm used to being by myself.'

'I'm afraid you can expect a lot of attention from the media,' he said. 'Your name is already out there as the owner of the house. And it won't take them long to find out that it was your information that led us to the motorway sniper and so you're entitled to the reward.'

She stared at him, wide-eyed. 'Is it really over two million pounds?'

He smiled. 'Two and half million at the last count.'

She shook her head. 'I don't believe it. It's so much money'

'Not in this context,' he said. 'Thanks to you, Cole Renner won't be killing any more people on our motorways.'

He left her then and got a junior detective named Royce to get a formal statement from her.

'Get her a room at one of the better hotels,' he said. 'I think she deserves it.'

★ ★ ★

Temple divided the rest of the afternoon between paperwork, meetings and liaising with forensics. At least there was no need to prepare for a major trial. In that respect Renner's death was a good result.

It would have taken weeks to get the evidence together to ensure that the bastard went down for life. The task now was to make sure they hadn't missed anything and to get the answers to some of the big questions — like why a young squaddie in the British army had suddenly turned into a homicidal maniac.

The team retreated to the pub at six after Vickery and Beresford announced that they were buying. Temple agreed to go along for a quick one before visiting the hospital.

He found it strange to be back in the pub where this nightmare week had started. It was still uncomfortably fresh in his mind — the news that there had been a bad crash on the M27 and then the call from Beresford telling him to go to the scene.

'Cheer up, Jeff,' Vickery said as he sidled up to him at the bar. 'It's over. Your life can get back to normal.'

Temple held up his pint. 'I'll drink to that.'

'And just so you know the task force will be officially dismantled tomorrow,' Vickery said.

'It'll be up to you guys to sort things out down here.'

'What about you?'

'They want me to oversee the Hussain case. There's a hell of a lot of work to be done on it.'

'Makes sense,' Temple said. Then he held out his hand for Vickery to shake. 'Until the next time then.'

Vickery grinned. 'Until the next time.'

Temple left the pub half an hour later and went straight to the hospital. Angel was excited to see him and she wanted to know everything that had happened during the day. He settled into the chair and told her. It wasn't until he'd finished that she shared *her* good news with him.

'I had more tests this afternoon,' she said. 'And guess what? The clot's shrunk slightly. The thinners appear to be working.'

Temple beamed a smile. 'That's terrific news.'

'I know. And the doctor reckons that at this rate it could be gone completely in a few weeks.'

Temple could hardly believe it. It felt as though a ten-ton weight had been lifted from his shoulders. It was the perfect end to a horrible week and that night when Temple got home he treated himself to a large whisky before going to bed. He slept like a log for the first time since Monday.

But that was only because he had no inkling of what was going to happen the next day.

52

Temple woke up early. By 7 a.m. he was shaved and showered and on his second cup of coffee.

Outside it was a bright Sunday morning. The sun had made its first appearance of the week and the sky was pristine blue. The weather perfectly reflected the mood of the nation.

The death of the motorway sniper was getting the full treatment on TV and in the newspapers. There was joy and relief that the nightmare was finally over. People living in Purbeck Road were interviewed and they described how the police had descended on their street. Megan Trent was frequently mentioned, but no one had yet spoken to her. Her neighbours described her as a quiet woman who kept to herself and none of them knew much about her.

Beresford popped up on every television channel along with Hampshire's Chief Constable. They announced that ballistics experts had confirmed that the rifle Renner had used to kill himself was the same one used in the sniper attacks. And that he had stolen it from an army base in Wiltshire. They also revealed that shells and motorway maps had been found in his bedroom. And they mentioned for the first time that Renner's motorbike had turned up at the scene of the last attack on the M4.

Some serious questions were also being asked, though. An MP had demanded an investigation into security at military armouries. He wanted to know how Renner had managed to steal a high-velocity rifle so easily and how often such things happened. Two newspapers focused on the problem of disaffected and battle-scarred soldiers. They pointed out that Cole Renner was not the first soldier to go on a deadly rampage and that ex-servicemen formed the largest group in Britain's prisons. The vast majority had been convicted of violent crimes.

Temple knew that Renner would be written about and analysed for years to come. He had earned himself the dubious distinction of being one of the country's most notorious mass-murderers.

After a cereal breakfast, Temple set out for the office. He spent a couple of hours answering emails and pulling together his report. Then at lunchtime he went to Purbeck Road to check on the progress being made by the SOCOs.

People were still gathered behind the police cordons at either end of the street and the media were very much in evidence.

The technicians continued to pore over every inch of the house. In Renner's bedroom they'd found a writing pad containing scribbled notes about each of the attack locations. There were references to bridges, escape routes and the distances from motorway embankments to places he could leave his car or motorbike.

'There's something I want to show you,' said John Samuels, the officer in charge of the crime scene. He was a surly, muscular guy with jug-handle ears. He gestured for Temple to follow him out onto the upstairs landing.

'Take a look at that,' he said, pointing to a tiny dark stain on the grey carpet about half the size of a 5p coin. 'We spotted it this morning. It's blood and it matches Renner's. There's another one on the stairs that's barely visible to the naked eye and another on the loft ladder. What I can't figure out is how they got there. We know that Renner wouldn't have been able to move after he shot himself. And the spray from the impact was confined to the living room.'

'Is it fresh blood?' Temple asked.

Samuels nodded. 'No older than yesterday.'

'So maybe he cut himself shaving and the

blood dripped from his chin,' Temple said.

'I put that to Matherson. He says there are no cuts on Renner's face or body.'

'That's strange,' Temple said. 'What about a nosebleed or something?'

'Maybe, but it seems unlikely.'

'So can you explain it?'

Samuels shrugged. 'Well, it could be that someone was standing close to him when he shot himself. Whoever it was would have got blood on their clothes from the spray. Then some of the blood could have dripped onto the floor when that person went upstairs.'

'But Renner was alone in the house at the time,' Temple said. 'Or at least that's what we assumed. And the front and back doors were locked so there was no way out.'

'That's not strictly true,' Samuels said.

Temple wrinkled his brow. 'What do you mean?'

'You've probably been told already that this property shares loft space with the house next door. The one to the left. There's no partition wall in between. It's not uncommon in terraced houses built in the sixties and seventies.'

'I think one of your people mentioned it yesterday when he was looking around up there. So what are you saying? That someone could have climbed into the loft and then got into the neighbouring house?'

'It's entirely possible. It wouldn't have occurred to me if not for the blood. It made me think about the various ways it could have got there.'

'Did you find any blood in the loft?'

'None at all.'

'What about the neighbour's loft?'

'I went through myself,' Samuels said. 'That house is empty. The old guy who lives there is in hospital, apparently. Anyway, there are no blood stains, but I tested his loft hatch and I was able to lift it straight out of the ceiling.'

'So the loft could have provided a means of escape if there was someone in the house with Renner when he took his life?' Temple said. 'Someone who didn't want us to know he or she was here.'

'That's right. It's just something for you to think about. There's no evidence to support that idea except for the little mystery of the blood.'

The blood specks were an intriguing development and Temple did not know what to make of them. After all, Renner had been alone in the house when Megan Trent left to go shopping only a short time earlier. Was it conceivable that he had let someone in soon after? And could that person have been there when the raid began?

Temple felt a flare of unease. He didn't like it. They would need to come up with an explanation for the blood. He did not want to be faced with any unanswered questions.

He was still mulling this over ten minutes later when Dr Matherson called him on his mobile. The pathologist said he was in the process of performing the post-mortem on Renner and something unusual had cropped up.

'Can you drop by?' Matherson asked, his tone ominous. 'I'd rather not talk about it over the phone.'

As Temple drove to the mortuary, his heart started pounding like a great caged animal. He was concerned about the specks of blood. So concerned that he phoned DS Vaughan.

'I want you to liaise with Samuels,' he said. 'See if you can figure it out between you. We need to find out how it got there.'

When he arrived at the mortuary he could feel his nerves start to rattle. He hated the place and had to stiffen his spine and take a deep breath before going inside.

After scrubbing up he donned a sterile suit and was shown into the autopsy room by one of Matherson's assistants.

Renner's naked body was face up on the dissecting table beneath an unforgiving white light. His chest had been opened and some of his organs had already been removed and put into trays.

Temple usually shied away from attending PMs. Years of working on murder cases had not desensitized him to the horrors of watching a body being filleted. He turned up only when he thought it was really necessary or when he was asked to.

'You'll not be surprised that the cause of death was a gunshot wound to the throat,' Matherson said as he peered into Renner's chest cavity. 'The shell did massive damage to his arteries and shattered the back of his skull. He would have died instantly.'

'Is that why I'm here?' Temple said, cocking his brow. 'So you can tell me that?'

Matherson stepped back from the table, put down his scalpel and removed his long surgical gloves. Then he walked over to another table and picked up a sheet of paper.

'I took some routine blood and urine samples when he came in yesterday,' Matherson said. 'The lab did a rush job on several of them and this is the first toxicology report. It's shown up something that I didn't expect.'

'What's that?'

'Flunitrazepam.'

'Pardon me?'

339

'It's more commonly known as Rohypnol.'

Temple felt his forehead contract.

'You mean the so called date-rape drug?' he said.

Matherson nodded. 'The very same. I'm sure you're familiar with it.'

'Of course. We've had a few cases down here where young women had their drinks spiked with it and then got raped.'

'Then you know it's a prescription-only sedative that's about ten times stronger than Valium. A dose will knock someone out in minutes and a person can remain uncon-scious for up to twelve hours. When taken with alcohol it leads to disorientation and loss of memory.'

'Why would Renner have it in his system?'

'Well, it's usually prescribed to people with chronic insomnia, but it's meant to be used in small doses on a strictly short-term basis and not to be taken with alcohol. Renner here has got high levels of the drug in his system. And it seems he washed it down with a significant quantity of booze. It's obvious from the state of his liver that he's a heavy drinker.'

Temple was puzzled. Rohypnol was a notorious drug that was first labelled the 'date-rape' drug in the nineties when sex attackers started using it because of its high potency. All they had to do was drop a pill in a girl's drink and wait for it to take effect before having their way with her. Afterwards the victim remembered nothing.

'I'm confused as to why Renner would have self-administered this drug,' Matherson said. 'Normally it's only given to hospital patients because it causes muscle relaxation, headaches, dizziness and slow psychomotor responses. These symptoms last for quite a while.'

'I see what you mean,' Temple said. 'It would have made it difficult — if not impossible — for him to carry out the attacks.'

'Precisely my point.'

'But for all we know he might have decided to pop a pill or two yesterday — knowing he wasn't about to launch another attack today. Maybe he just wanted to make sure he had a good night's sleep.'

'Or maybe someone else popped the pill into his food or drink,' Matherson said. 'It's certainly worth looking into. I'm also surprised that this man is in such piss-poor condition for someone his age. He's malnour-ished and severely underweight. It's as though he suffered a sudden deterioration in his health over recent weeks.'

'Could he have been ill?'

'I won't know that for sure until I've

completed the post-mortem and had all the toxicology reports back.'

'So what else is unusual about him?' Temple asked.

Matherson shrugged. 'Nothing really. He's perfectly normal in most other respects. An average Joe. Height five foot nine. Shoe size eight. Own hair and teeth. Plus he's — '

'Just a sec,' Temple interrupted him. 'What did you say about his shoe size?'

'That it's an eight. On the small side I suppose for someone of his stature.'

'So you've measured his feet?'

'Didn't have to. I undressed the corpse when it got here. Saw his shoes. In fact they're still here with the rest of his clothes. Someone from the lab was meant to pick them up last night. I had to remind them this morning.'

Temple's heart started to gallop. He whipped out his phone and called the incident room. He asked for DS Vaughan and when Vaughan came on, he said, 'I need you to check something out on the evidence log.'

'I'm listening,' Vaughan said.

'SOCOs collected a couple of shoeprints from the scene of the first attack on the M27. They produced a plaster cast of one of them. Look it up on your computer and check the details.'

While Temple waited he asked Matherson to fetch the bag containing Renner's clothes and shoes so that he could drop them off at the lab.

When Vaughan came back on the line, he said, 'You're right, guv. I've got the photo of the cast up on the screen. It includes all the measurements.'

'So what size shoe left the imprint?' Temple asked.

'A size ten,' Vaughan said.

53

Temple knew he had no choice but to think the unthinkable. What he had learned in the last hour cast doubt on all the assumptions that had been made.

First there were the specks of blood on the stairs and landing in Megan Trent's house. Samuels had been right to bring it to his attention and raise the question as to how it had got there. Was it really possible that someone else had been in the house when Renner was shot?

Then there was the Rohypnol found in Renner's system. It simply didn't make sense that Renner would dose himself up with a drug that would turn him into a zombie and give him bouts of amnesia. To have carried out four attacks over four evenings would have required him to be sharp and alert. He'd have had to get to the locations, set himself up on the embankments, then fire the rifle with pin-point accuracy. Surely that wouldn't have been possible with booze and Rohypnol sloshing around inside him.

Finally there was the evidence of the shoe prints. He remembered when they were pointed out to him on the embankment above the M27. Right next to where the spent shell casings were found. Three clear impressions — two in the grass and one in a patch of damp earth. Left there by a man's size ten shoes. But Cole Renner wore size eight shoes. So unless he'd put on a pair that were two sizes too big it could not have been him on the embankment. And if that were the case, then who the hell was it?

He posed the question to the team back at the incident room after briefing them on what he had learned. They all stared at him in stunned disbelief, including Beresford who immediately expressed concern about how it would look when it was made public.

'Maybe he had an accomplice all along,' DS Vaughan said. 'They could have been working as a pair — while one of them shot at cars, the other could have kept a lookout.'

Temple shook his head. 'That doesn't tally with what we saw on the CCTV footage from the industrial estate. One man drove to the M27 in a stolen car and walked towards the motorway with a rucksack on his back. There was no one with him.'

'Then perhaps Cole Renner didn't carry out the attacks,' DC Marsh said. 'What if his accomplice did? A man who wears size ten shoes.'

'That doesn't really explain Renner's fingerprints on the drinks can in the stolen car or the fact that his motorbike turned up next to the M4.'

'The idea of an accomplice does lend weight to the theory that someone was with him when he killed himself,' Vaughan said. 'And that person could have escaped from the house through the loft into the neighbouring property. He would have been able to walk out later in all the commotion without being noticed.'

'Well, if we think there was someone else in the house then we can't rule out the possibility that Renner did not take his own life,' Temple said. 'Perhaps he was murdered by someone who wanted it to look like suicide. It'd explain the blood on the stairs and landing.'

'But not the Rohypnol in his body,' Vaughan said. 'That's the bit I can't get my head around. It doesn't make any sense.'

'None of it makes sense to me,' Temple said. 'And that's why we need to do a full review of all the evidence and talk again to everyone we've interviewed. We'll start with Renner senior. Bring him in for questioning and see if he knows anything about Rohypnol. And check his shoe size while you're at it.'

'What about Megan Trent?' DC Marsh asked. 'She might be able to shed some light on things. If Renner was heavily into drugs and booze she'd probably know about it.'

Temple turned to DC Royce, the detective who had taken her formal statement. He asked him if she'd mentioned drink and drugs.

'She mentioned nothing about that,' he said. 'She said Renner spent most of his time locked in his room and had no visitors while he was there. And she's adamant that when she left the house yesterday he was the only person inside.'

'So what do we know about her?' Temple said. 'Have you run a background check?'

'I did,' Royce said. 'She's three months pregnant with her first child. She's aged thirty-two and she's a bit brassy if you know what I mean. She has form for shoplifting and benefit fraud. She's also known to social services. She was the victim of serious domestic abuse three years ago: a violent husband who badly beat her up. He's in prison and she's divorced from him.'

'So who's the father of her baby?' Temple said.

'A boyfriend who dumped her a few months ago. She's now single.'

'How long has she been renting out the flat?'

'Four years,' Royce said. 'Her husband was a builder and he converted it into a self-contained flat because they were struggling to pay the mortgage. She says she's still struggling because she's out of work.'

'I think I'd better have another word with her,' Temple said. 'Did you put her up in a local hotel?'

'The Grand Harbour, guv,' Royce said. 'You told me to pick one of the better ones.'

Temple spent the next half hour asking for ideas and assigning tasks. Royce was told to go back to Purbeck Road.

'Get SOCOs to check out the house next door,' he said. 'See if they can find any evidence to back up the theory that someone dropped in there via the loft.'

He told DS Vaughan to go back over all the evidence and send a team to bring Renner's father in for further questioning.

'And round up all the photographs and video footage taken in Purbeck Road immediately after we went in,' Temple said. 'We might get lucky and spot someone who shouldn't have been there.'

54

Temple arranged for Megan Trent to be brought back to the station. He explained that they were hoping she could help them clarify some issues that had cropped up.

She was still wearing her black leggings and yellow T-shirt and she looked pale and anxious.

He decided to have an informal chat with her in his office rather than subject her to a formal interview in one of the rooms downstairs.

'How's the hotel?' he asked, when she was seated across the desk from him.

A hesitant smile. 'It's nice. Not something I'm used to.'

'Well, try to make the most of your time there. It's on us.'

'I'd rather be in my own home,' she said.

Temple nodded. 'I can understand that. Hopefully you'll be able to return in a few days. We'll finish our work there and clean the place up for you.'

'Thanks.'

Temple shuffled some papers on his desk and said, 'There are some questions I need to ask as a result of our investigation.'

She raised an eyebrow. 'What sort of questions?'

'Well, we now believe there was someone in your house with Renner when he shot himself. Have you any idea who it could have been?'

'I don't understand,' she said. 'I was told he was by himself.'

'He was when we entered the house,' Temple said. 'But we've come across evidence that indicates there was someone with him just minutes before. We believe whoever it was climbed into the loft space and gained access to the neighbouring property.'

Megan's body seemed to stiffen and she shifted her weight on the chair.

After a couple of beats, she said, 'How is that possible?'

'There's no partition wall between your loft and the one next door on the left,' Temple said. 'Did you not know that?'

She gave a small shake of the head. 'I've never been up there.'

He had no reason to doubt her. In all the years he'd been married to Erin she never once ventured into the loft, partly because she was terrified of the spiders that lived up there.

'You said Renner was in his flat when you came into town,' Temple said.

'That's right. I heard him snoring.'

'And can you be absolutely sure that there was nobody in the flat with him? Maybe a woman.'

She thought about it for a second and shrugged. 'I suppose it's possible, but I think I would have known. To my knowledge he never brought anyone back.'

Temple pursed his lips as if he was about to whistle.

'What about Renner himself?' he said. 'We found drugs in his body and in his flat. They would have turned him into a virtual zombie for a lot of the time.'

Megan bit on her bottom lip and swallowed. 'He often looked drowsy when I saw him and I put it down to booze because I knew he was a heavy drinker. But to be honest I didn't see much of him.'

'So on the few occasions you spoke to him he never mentioned that he was taking a drug known as Rohypnol?'

A frown tightened her forehead. 'Are you talking about the date-rape drug?'

'I am.'

'Then no he didn't. But why the hell would he take that?'

'That's what we're trying to find out, Megan. And we will. It's just a matter of time.'

Her eyes left his face and looked down at her hands which were curled one into the other in her lap. She appeared uncomfortable suddenly, beads of perspiration glistening above her top lip.

Temple leaned forward across his desk, keeping his face blandly genial. 'Are you sure you're telling me everything, Megan? It's just that I find it strange that Cole Renner was living under your roof as your tenant and yet you know so very little about him.'

She lifted her head, met his gaze. 'I don't see what's strange about it. Like I told you before, he kept to himself. Sometimes I wouldn't see him for days and when I did he was never keen to stop and chat. It was like he was shy or had too much on his mind.'

She held his gaze for a moment and he saw tears welling up in her eyes.

'Are you all right?' he asked her.

'Of course I'm not all right,' she said sharply, wiping at her eyes with a finger. 'I feel awful. A man was shot dead in my house and I've had to move out. Now you're accusing me of withholding information even though I was the one who tipped you off about him.'

'I'm not accusing you of anything, Megan.'

'Well, it sounds like it to me. I've told you

all I know. I can't help it if it's not what you want to hear.'

'Look at it from our viewpoint, Megan,' he said. 'Cole Renner was a tenant in your house while he was carrying out a series of attacks on motorways. After each attack he went back to his flat. So it's hard for us to believe that he didn't make some kind of impression or have contact with anyone else. And then on the day he died we were led to believe he was alone in the house, but now it turns out that he probably wasn't. So it's a mystery we need to solve. And for obvious reasons you're best placed to help us.'

'That's what I've been trying to do,' she said.

'And I appreciate it, Megan. I really do. So if I've upset you then I'm sorry.'

She took a tissue from her bag and blew her nose. Then she said, 'Can I go now?'

'In just a moment,' Temple said. 'I've only got a couple more questions and I'll keep them short. The first is about the keys to your house. Can you tell me who has them apart from you and Renner?'

'Nobody.'

'What about your ex-boyfriend? He lived with you, didn't he?'

'Not permanently. He had his own place and when he buggered off I got the key back.'

Temple picked up his pen.

'I think I'd better talk to him anyway. What's his address?'

'I don't know. When he was with me he was renting a flat in Winchester, but I never went there. He told me he was moving to London.'

'What about a phone number?'

'I don't have one. He changed his phone so I couldn't claim money off him for the baby.'

'What about his old number?'

'I deleted it.'

Temple supressed his mounting irritation and asked what her boyfriend's name was.

'Michael Corley,' Megan said after a moment's hesitation. 'He's a labourer.'

'Do you know if he has a criminal record?'

'I don't think so, but it wouldn't surprise me if he had.'

Temple paused for a beat and said, 'The officer who took your statement told me about your ex-husband. I gather he's still in prison.'

She nodded. 'He is for now. But he's due out in four months. I expect he'll come back here looking for trouble.'

'So why don't you move away?'

'I don't see why I should,' she said. 'And even if I wanted to I don't have the money.'

'You will have when the reward comes through.'

'I'm trying not to build my hopes up. Knowing my luck it won't happen.'

'There shouldn't be a problem,' he said. 'The money was offered up in good faith and no one else has come forward to claim it.'

'I've been thinking that I might not get it because I have form,' she said. 'I'm sure you know about my previous convictions.'

Temple grinned. 'Of course I do. But they won't be taken into account. I can't see any reason why you won't get the money.'

★ ★ ★

Temple arranged for Megan to get a lift back to the hotel. Then he went to the incident room and asked DS Vaughan to try to track down her ex-boyfriend.

'All she's given me is his name,' he said. 'It's Michael Corley and he's a labourer. Maybe he's living in London. I'd like to speak to him.'

'Any particular reason, guv?'

Temple shrugged. 'I've got this feeling in my blood that Megan Trent isn't being entirely open with us. She might be holding something back.'

'Such as?'

'I'm not sure. Maybe she had her suspicions about Renner and is now reluctant to say so for fear it'll jeopardize the reward money.'

'And what do you think you'll get from her ex?'

Temple shrugged again. 'I don't know, but he might provide us with some useful background information.'

Temple knew he was clutching at straws, but he also knew he didn't have much choice. Every lead, however tenuous, needed to be followed through.

He spent the next couple of hours interviewing Martin Renner again. The guy had been brought to the station under protest because he'd been dragged away from an interview with a newspaper reporter who was paying him a five figure sum.

Renner senior offered up nothing new and Temple was convinced he had nothing to do with the shootings. The man seemed genuinely shocked to be told that his son might not have been the sniper after all.

'What the fuck are you talking about?' he said. 'Who the bloody hell else could it be?'

Temple couldn't tell him because he had no idea.

55

'You shouldn't have come here, Megan. It was too risky.'

'But you said I could.'

'That was before Temple hauled you in for fuck's sake. How the hell do you know you weren't followed?'

He stamped across the room to the window and looked outside for the umpteenth time. The flat overlooked the road at the front. Beyond it was a small, untidy park. There was a man walking his dog in the park and cars were parked bumper to bumper along the road. But there was nothing unusual going on. No sign of any cops.

'I'm sure I wasn't followed,' Megan said. 'I went back to the hotel first.'

He turned to face her, his features rigid.

'This is not good,' he said, his voice hoarse. 'Are you sure you haven't fucked up? Did you say something to make the police suspicious?'

She shook her head vigorously. 'I swear I didn't. I said exactly what you told me to say.'

'Then how do they know that Renner wasn't alone in the house?'

'He said they had evidence.'

'What kind of evidence?'

'He didn't say.'

As he paced the room he reeled from what Megan had told him. It was a devastating blow and it had come as a complete shock. It didn't make sense. He was so careful. After shooting Renner he had slipped upstairs and into the loft, then into the neighbouring property. Half an hour later he walked out on to the street and away from the scene. There were no mistakes. The set-up was perfect. The sniper took his own life because he was cornered. Case closed.

So what had the police discovered to make them think that it wasn't so straightforward?

'What do you think we should do?' Megan asked him.

He knew what they should be doing right now — and that was celebrating their success with a bottle of champagne. The £2.5 million reward money should be in the bag. It was supposed to herald a new beginning for both of them. No more money worries. No more struggling and taking shit.

But now there was a risk that it might all fall apart. Temple was bound to carry on probing. He already knew about the Rohypnol and the escape route through the loft space. It would only be a matter of time before he found out that Michael Corley didn't exist, that Megan had made up the name in a moment of panic.

The detective would then discover the truth about her boyfriend. The neighbours would be bound to recall the name of the man who was a frequent visitor to the house over many months. And then the game would be up.

'Shall I make us a drink?' Megan said through trembling lips. 'I could do with one.'

He rounded on her, his eyes blazing.

'Will you shut the fuck up?' he yelled. 'I need to think this through. This is not how it's meant to be and I've got a really bad feeling about it.'

Tears welled up in her eyes and she started to cry. He'd never seen her cry before and it made him even angrier. He had a sudden urge to slap her, but he resisted it. Instead he slumped down on the sofa and buried his face in his hands.

He couldn't believe that this was where they were after all that had happened.

★   ★   ★

He'd met her ten months ago when he'd been in Southampton for a reunion with some old army pals. The venue had been a pub in the old town and Megan had been serving behind the bar. They'd got chatting and at the end of the evening he'd asked her out.

At the time he'd been at a low ebb in his life: sick of feeling that he was an outcast, with no place in society. And he'd been taking medicine for depression.

She understood him and she was sympathetic because she too was struggling to contain the flames of anger and resentment.

They were both down on their luck. Both skint. Both traumatized by past events. And both resigned to the fact that they would never get any help or support from anyone.

Their relationship quickly blossomed and they were soon talking about moving in together and maybe getting married. When she fell pregnant they'd both been delighted.

And that was when Cole Renner turned up.

He was on the run with nowhere to live. They said he could stay in the flat which was empty at the time. Soon after moving in he got drunk and told them about the rifle he'd stolen from the army base.

'I'm going to kill myself with it,' he'd announced. 'But not before I make my mark on this fucked up world.'

He was an emotional cripple, his mind twisted out of shape by post-traumatic stress disorder; a disaster waiting to happen.

'I plan to target a motorway,' he told them both. 'Drivers are sitting ducks. I found that out in Afghanistan. I lost count of the number of rag-head truck drivers I shot out there. This time I'll just keep on shooting until there's only one shell left in the magazine. And that shell will be for me.'

He was serious. They saw that. At first they urged him to dump the rifle and seek counselling. They said it was an insane idea. But then he told them he got the idea from a news story on the internet. It had been about an army vet in the States who shot and killed two motorists on a highway. It caused such alarm that a huge reward was immediately offered.

'The only reward I want is to be remembered,' he said. 'I want everyone to regret what's been done to me.'

The next day he told them he'd come to his senses and couldn't go through with it. He begged them to forget that he'd even mentioned it.

But they couldn't forget. A seed had been planted in their minds and they couldn't stop thinking about it. They were intrigued by the possibility of how easy it would be. And by the prospect of a huge reward.

They were spurred on by the fact that they shared the same values and harboured the same resentments. Neither of them believed in God or the concept of a Judgement Day. And they both knew instinctively that they'd be able to live with what they were planning to do. After all, in a world where life is cheap, killing is no longer such a big deal. It's just a means to an end.

The secret is to remain detached, he told her. Never establish an emotional connection with your victims. Where possible kill only strangers. And preferably from a distance. It was stuff he'd learned in the army.

She understood and accepted what he said. Partly because she was a woman who lacked compassion. Partly too because she'd always regarded herself as a victim — and blamed everyone else for the fact that her life had been so shitty.

And so a plan began to take shape: a plan that would entail targeting more than one motorway in order to generate a big reward. And with the money they were going to secure a better life for themselves and for their unborn child.

They talked about how they would spend it and where they would live. First it was France and then Spain. And when the reward pot grew beyond their wildest expectations they began contemplating somewhere more exotic.

56

After interviewing Martin Renner, Temple was summoned to the Chief Super's office to take part in a conference call. The three other participants were Vickery, Hampshire's Chief Constable and a bod from the Home Office.

They'd been briefed by Beresford and they wanted Temple to update them and provide all the details.

They listened in stunned silence as he outlined the facts about the bloodstains on the stairs, the Rohypnol in Renner's system and the problem with the shoe print found at the scene of the attack on the M27.

'If you put it all together then you have to conclude that Cole Renner might not have been the sniper,' he said. 'And he might not have committed suicide.'

It was hard for them to accept that everything was suddenly up in the air. There were all kinds of implications. They had already announced that the motorway sniper was dead and that the task force was being dismantled. To backtrack now would be a major embarrassment.

But even worse would be having to reveal

that the sniper was probably still out there and perhaps planning another series of attacks on motorways.

'With hindsight we should have played it down until after all the forensic evidence had been analyzed and the post-mortem completed,' Temple said. 'Instead we were too anxious to allay public fears. We accepted the situation at face value because the evidence that presented itself seemed irrefutable. Renner had been cornered. Then he shot a police officer before shooting himself. He used the rifle that was used in the attack and his flat was crammed with incriminating evidence. So it was the obvious conclusion to draw.'

'Then maybe he was set up,' Vickery said.

'That's certainly a possibility,' Temple said. 'The drugs could have been used to control him. For all we know he might not have been aware of what was going on.'

'What about the landlady?' Vickery said. 'Surely she must know something.'

Temple told them about his conversation with Megan Trent.

'I intend to talk to her again,' he said. 'Meanwhile we're running some checks on her.'

The conference call concluded after several decisions had been taken. The Home Office guy said he would brief his boss and the Prime Minister. Temple said he would return to Southampton straight away. And the Chief Constable said he would talk to the press department about the best way to handle the fall-out.

They also agreed not to go public with the latest developments until they had to.

Temple returned to the incident room in a state of high anxiety. He felt responsible for what was happening. It was a right fucking mess and he was struggling to make sense of it. He decided to retreat to his office and start reviewing the evidence again. What had they missed? Who hadn't they talked to? Could he really rely on the forensic evidence that had been presented to him?

DC Marsh collared him as he was grabbing a coffee from the machine. Her face was flushed and she was clearly excited.

'I've found something, guv,' she said. 'You need to come and see it.'

He followed her across the room to her work station. She'd been reviewing the video from two police cameras that had recorded the scene in Purbeck Road after the raid.

'You asked me to look out for any familiar faces or for anything unusual,' she said. 'Well, take a look at this.'

There was an image on her screen showing

the front of Megan Trent's house. Marsh tapped her computer keyboard and rolled the footage.

'This sequence was recorded about half an hour after the shooting,' she said. 'As you can see there's a lot going on.'

Indeed there was. The area in front of the house was packed with uniforms. Temple got a glimpse of himself as he emerged from the house shortly after looking at Renner's blood-soaked body.

'Now check this out,' Marsh said as she touched her finger against the screen. 'The house to the left is supposed to be empty. But look — there's a man coming out of the front door.'

Temple felt his heart leap as the guy closed the door behind him and strode onto the pavement where not a single officer paid him any attention.

Then he turned left and walked along the street away from all the commotion.

'Do you recognize him?' Marsh said.

Temple nodded. 'Too bloody right I do.'

57

He was still pacing the room trying to decide what to do. Every couple of minutes he looked out of the window. The evening was drawing in and it was dark. He was relieved to see that the street was quiet: no sign of uniforms or squad cars.

Megan had stopped crying at least. She'd poured herself a beer and was sitting on the sofa drinking it whilst watching television. On the news they'd mentioned her name several times. They were making her sound like the hero of the day because she'd tipped off the police about Renner. And a police spokesman had said she was in line to receive the huge reward.

It bolstered her confidence and made her think that they could still get away with it.

'Maybe we should just hold our nerve,' she said to him. 'I don't see how they can prove we were involved.'

He could see that she didn't appreciate the gravity of the situation. It was like she was in denial, blinded by the thought of all that money, but he was fully aware that things had changed dramatically and it made him feel nauseous and dizzy.

The police had discovered things they weren't meant to and their suspicions had been aroused. He could no longer predict what would happen next. Which meant he couldn't be certain that Megan would eventually collect the reward money. Despite what they were saying on the TV.

He knew the police would persist and they might eventually piece together the whole frigging jigsaw. They'd be bound to concentrate on Megan because Renner lived and died in her house.

From what Megan said about her chat with Temple it was clear the detective had doubts about her story. He'd be checking and double checking everything she'd told him. He'd find out she'd lied about her boyfriend. And then he'd try to apply enough pressure to make her confess.

And if she did confess she'd tell him about the plan they'd hatched together which entailed convincing everyone that Renner was the sniper. This included leaving an empty drinks can in the stolen car he drove to the M27 and riding Renner's motorbike to the M4 so it'd be caught on CCTV.

And then she'd tell Temple how they'd kept Renner in a drug-induced state until they were ready to fake his suicide. All so that the police would believe he acted alone and cease their investigation.

It had all gone so fucking well too. Like a perfectly choreographed stage play. After Megan had been to see Temple his reaction had been predictable. He'd ordered his officers to descend on the house. Then the raid had played out exactly how he'd hoped it would. Everything came together so smoothly. Or so it had seemed.

'What is it?' she asked him. 'Why are you looking at me like that?'

'Because you need to wise up, Megan. Everything has changed. I think maybe we should cut and run.'

Her eyes widened. 'Are you really serious?'

'Deadly.'

'But what about the money? You killed thirty people so that you could get your hands on it.'

'Don't you think I know that? But we won't be able to spend a penny of it if we're banged up in prison for the rest of our lives.'

He didn't have a back-up plan because he didn't think he'd need it. He assumed the police would simply accept the evidence in front of their own eyes and that would be it. With hindsight it had been a big mistake.

'Do you really think they're on to us?' Megan said.

He looked at her. Her face was as white as

a sheet and he could see that it had finally dawned on her that they wouldn't be sailing off into the sunset with over two million quid in the bank.

'We have no choice but to assume they are,' he said.

He went to the fridge and took out a beer. His hands were shaking and he could feel the adrenaline gushing through his veins.

He sipped at the beer as he walked over to the window. He peered out, hoping and expecting to see that the view hadn't changed.

But it had.

Several police vehicles were blocking the road out front and men in dark uniforms were piling out of them.

58

Temple recognized the five-storey block of flats in Portsmouth as soon as he pulled up outside it in his car. He'd driven past it only a few days ago on his way to meet Ryan Addison in a local café.

Addison was wearing the same clothes then that he had on when he was caught on the police video emerging from the house next door to Megan's.

Temple had been shocked to see him. After all, the former squaddie was the very person who had first raised concerns with the military police about Renner's state of mind. And he'd also told Temple that Renner's landlady was pregnant.

There was only one conclusion Temple could draw from this: Addison had wanted to stitch Renner up and he had gone to elaborate lengths to do so. Temple was now convinced that Addison was the sniper and had wanted to pin the blame on his army pal. Addison must have shot Renner and got blood on his clothes in the process and then left a trail of it on the carpet as he scrambled up into the loft.

371

But a couple of things still mystified Temple: motive for one. Why on earth would Addison kill so many people in cold blood? He hadn't come across as a dangerous psychopath; quite the opposite in fact, but then who could ever tell what goes through the mind of any battle-scarred soldier?

And then there was Megan Trent. Was there a link between her and Addison? Surely there had to be. It would explain why she seemed to be holding something back.

★   ★   ★

Addison's flat was on the second floor facing the front. Seconds after watching the video on DC Marsh's PC, Temple had contacted Portsmouth police and asked them to put it under surveillance.

A few minutes later they confirmed that there was a light on in the flat and that someone had been seen looking out of a window.

So the armed response team had been warned to expect resistance as they stormed the building.

Temple followed them inside and up the stairs. It was a grim place, with muck on the floor and graffiti on every wall. But he hadn't expected it to be any different. This was cheap accommodation in an insalubrious part of town.

The raid was carried out with slick efficiency. Armed officers rushed up the stairs and moved silently along the landing before breaking down the door to flat number seven.

They rushed in, yelling at the tops of their voices, their guns at the ready.

But much to everyone's surprise and disappointment the tiny flat was empty. There were only a couple of rooms so it took mere seconds to search it. Portsmouth police had been watching the building from the front and rear. They were confident that no one had left it since the person was spotted at the window.

'We need to check upstairs,' Temple said.

Two of the team were way ahead of him and were already bolting up the stairs. There were three more flights and Temple was out of breath by the time he reached the top landing.

'All clear,' one of the officers shouted.

But a second later the same officer drew Temple's attention to a door just to the right of the lift. The wood next to the handle was splintered and it looked as though it had been forced open.

'It must lead to the roof,' the officer said.

Temple fell in behind the officers and

mounted the concrete stairs two at a time. They had to pass through another unlocked door to gain access to the flat roof. It was dark up there and Temple felt the crisp air enter his lungs.

All three of them stood for a moment getting their bearings. Traffic howled below them. Above them stars filled the sky. About ten yards away stood a small brick structure that probably housed the power supply to the building. It was the only object that provided any cover.

'We're police,' one of the officers shouted into the night. 'We're armed and we strongly advise you to show yourself.'

There was an immediate response and it was totally unexpected. Two figures appeared suddenly from behind the structure. Temple recognized both of them.

Ryan Addison and Megan Trent.

Addison was holding Megan in front of him with one hand around her neck. The other held a large kitchen knife and it was pointed at her throat.

59

'If you come any closer, I'll kill her,' Addison said in a cold, calm voice.

Temple moved forward cautiously and raised his arms.

'Take it easy, Ryan,' he said. 'The building is surrounded and you're going nowhere. Just let her go.'

'Fuck you, Temple. I mean what I said.'

'I'm sure you do,' Temple said. 'You've already murdered thirty innocent people so I don't suppose you'll hesitate to kill one more.'

Megan let out a moan as Addison applied pressure on her throat. Her eyes were bulging from their sockets and tears were streaking down her cheeks.

'So let's talk about it,' Temple said. 'Tell me why you did it. Get it off your chest. I'm curious to know.'

Addison grinned. 'I'd have thought that was bloody obvious,' he said. 'We did it for the money. The reward. Why else?'

Temple shook his head despairingly and his hands balled into fists.

Jesus, he thought. Thirty people had been

killed so that this evil bastard could benefit financially.

There was a time when Temple would have been shocked that an individual would commit a series of murders purely for gain. But not anymore. For a great many people life held little or no value. Such people were not hindered by a conscience. Their minds were filled with dark matter that allowed them to rationalize any action, no matter how heinous or immoral.

Temple had no doubt that Addison would have no problem living with what he had done.

'So you calculated that the more people you killed over the course of a single week the higher the reward would be,' Temple said.

'It was a good plan,' Addison said. 'And it would have given us a better life. But you had to go and fuck it up.'

'You were never going to get away with it,' Temple said.

'How did you know it wasn't Renner?'

'You made a few mistakes,' Temple said. 'You left a footprint on the embankment above the M27. Your feet are bigger than his. You left bloodstains on the carpet in Megan's house after you shot him. And you should have made sure you weren't being filmed when you let yourself out of the house next door.'

Addison muttered a few curses and shook his head. At the same time he lost concentration and loosened his grip momentarily on Megan's throat. She seized the opportunity to struggle free.

He tried to hold on to her, but she threw herself forward and fell onto her face.

In the same instant one of the officers let off a shot and the bullet pummelled into Addison's right shoulder. The knife clattered to the floor and he was sent staggering backwards.

'Hold your fire,' Temple screamed out.

Addison managed to stay upright, clutching his shoulder, and as Megan scrambled to her feet he yelled out to her.

'I'm really sorry, babe. It wasn't meant to end like this. Please take care of our child.'

Then Addison turned around and stumbled unsteadily away from them. His intention was obvious. He was going to throw himself off the building and deny justice to his victims.

Temple reacted before either of the officers. He rushed forward, determined not to let the bastard take the easy way out.

Addison's wound had sapped his strength and was slowing him down. He almost tripped over his own feet as he lurched drunkenly across the roof.

Temple was still trying to catch up when

Addison got to the edge of the roof and stopped briefly to raise his arms in a diving motion.

It gave Temple the fraction of a second he needed to reach the man before he plunged over the top.

But as he lunged forward and grabbed Addison around the waist he almost sent them both over. Addison tried to wrench himself free by twisting his body around. Temple was thrown off balance and his right shoe scraped over the lip of the roof. For a moment he thought they were going to topple into oblivion.

But then he felt a hand grab his left arm just below the elbow and pull him back.

'I've got you.'

It was one of the officers and he had a firm grip on him. The other officer managed to seize Addison by the hair and drag him away from the edge.

It took a moment for Temple to regain his equilibrium. Then he inhaled deeply and yelled at Addison, who was on his back, his face scrunched up in pain.

'Now you can bloody well answer for what you did, you no-good piece of shit.'

60

Addison spent the rest of the night in hospital under armed guard. The bullet had caused extensive damage to his shoulder and he'd lost a lot of blood. But the wound was not life-threatening.

While they waited for him to recover enough to be interviewed Temple talked to Megan Trent who was in a real state and couldn't stop crying.

But after she told him the whole story he had absolutely no sympathy for her. As far as he was concerned she was as culpable as her boyfriend.

He took great pleasure in formally charging her with being an accessory to murder and he told her he would do all he could to make sure she spent the rest of her life in prison.

Addison later confirmed everything that Megan Trent had said and he went on to describe in detail how he'd carried out the attacks.

He showed absolutely no remorse and talked about his many victims as though they were members of an opposing army.

Temple charged him with five counts of premeditated murder and warned him that more charges were to follow.

Epilogue

Angel was discharged from hospital five days later. She was still in pain from the injuries to her lung and ribs and had been told to get plenty of rest.

Thankfully she'd had no more seizures. The blood clot in her head had got a little smaller, but she was going to have to continue on the medicine for many more weeks.

She was upbeat despite living with the threat of further complications suddenly developing. She was determined to return to work eventually.

Temple was still trying to come to terms with the fact that he had almost lost her. The thought of it gave him palpitations, but fate had been kind to him for once. Angel had survived and would recover fully in time. So he knew he had a lot to be grateful for.

Yousef Hussain and his accomplices had been charged with various offences under the Terrorism Act and DCS Vickery was heading up the case against them. He was also involved in making arrangements to reschedule the memorial service for police officer Joseph Roth.

The sniper attacks still dominated the news agenda. And not just in the UK. It continued to be a major, ongoing story around the world.

At the same time there was a growing realization that someone else might eventually do what Ryan Addison had done. After all, he had managed to cause mayhem across the country with very little effort.

The government was called upon to take action to make the motorway network safer. In response the Prime Minister had decided to set up an enquiry.

But everyone knew it was a waste of time. A ghastly precedent had been set. It meant that in future anyone travelling on Britain's motorways would always be vulnerable to attack from a psycho with a gun.